The killer picked up his rucksack, nodded at the still-stunned group and walked away, up the overgrown path towards the houses.

The rest smoked fags, slowly calming down.

'Fuck's sake,' said one.

'I wouldn't trust that cunt as far as I could throw him,' said another, nodding after the killer.

'What the fuck did Luke do, anyway?' said the third, still staring at the limp body.

'Fuck knows,' said the kid. 'He did enough anyways. Snitch?'

'Fuck's sake. He'd never snitch. Never. This is cuntin civil war. There'll be wigs on the Green before this is played out.'

'Come on boys. Into the river with him. I'm gaggin for a pint of cider.'

'He's still pumpin.'

'Leave him a minute, so.'

So they smoked more cigarettes, watched the blood ooze. The twitching heart finally stalled completely. Two lifted the upper body - an arm and an armpit each - and the other took the feet. The ruined corpse slipped into the water and sank quickly, towards the deepest current. The machete followed, glinting. A flood was up.

PURE MAD
A NOVEL

The Author's Cut
By Gary J Byrnes

Print and ebook versions available from all good online retailers.

www.GaryJByrnes.com

@garyjbyrnes

PURE MAD

The Author's Cut

For Bernadette

Gary J Byrnes
July '21.

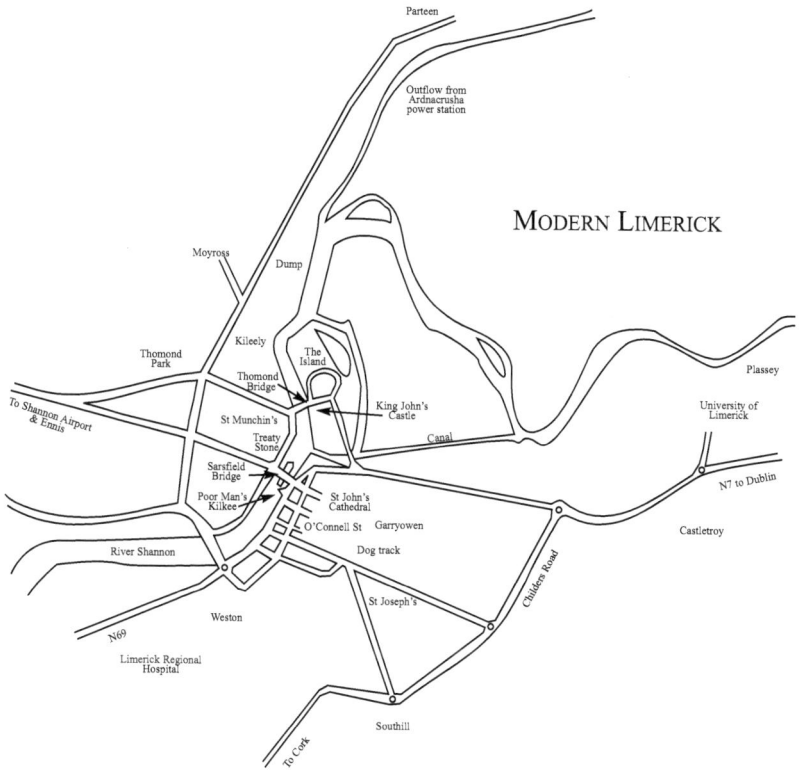

MODERN LIMERICK

Parteen

Outflow from
Ardnacrusha
power station

Moyross

Dump

Kileely

Thomond
Park

The
Island

Plassey

Thomond
Bridge

King John's
Castle

St Munchin's

University of
Limerick

To Shannon Airport
& Ennis

Treaty
Stone

Canal

N7 to Dublin

Sarsfield
Bridge

Poor Man's
Kilkee

St John's
Cathedral

Castletroy

O'Connell St

Garryowen

Childers Road

River Shannon

Dog track

N69

St Joseph's

Weston

Limerick Regional
Hospital

To Cork

Southill

And so to Limerick City, in the Year of Our Lord
2005.

FOR GLOSSARY OF LIMERICK SLANG, SEE
APPENDIX 1

PURE MAD - The Author's Cut

PROLOGUE

From a high window, just beyond my reach, seven o'clock sunshine fills the little room, makes the thick white walls glow. Magical and calming.

'Pure mad? I dispute that. I'm just a bit frazzled is all.'

'Prove it.'

'Okay.'

'Tell me.'

'Everything?'

She nods. 'Start typing, please.'

'Careful what you wish for.'

'The first line is so important,' she chirps.

I hit the letter P. 'Here we go.' Then it flows.

'Just get it down, spill it out. It's therapeutic. Everybody loves a good story.'

CHAPTER 1. HEADWRECK

For about three seconds I'd been ready to jump into the black vastness of the Shannon, end it all. Three random seconds.

'You're a waste of space, Charlie. Other than that, you're all right, man. You're all right.'

I said this to my shimmering reflection.

Funny how a few miniscule biochemical spasms in my brain make me consider killing myself. First time ever and I almost did it. Bizarre shit.

'Tool.'

Damn coming down.

My head hurts, standing there by the dirty water, dead-buzzing, jaded, watching, waiting. The bottle of Volvic helps, but chemical intervention calls. I go back to the car. Open the boot and root around in my gadget bag. In amongst the receipts, torn fag boxes, camera bits and assorted junk, I find two Solpadeine. Soluble codeine - heroin's sister - heaven in an OTC tablet. Into the bottle. Down the hatch. Plop, fizz, gone.

That's life: plop, fizz, gone. When the sperm meets the egg, the fizzing starts, grabbing molecules, using DNA blueprints to make a human. I think I actually get it: I'm a chemistry set. With sentience. The chemical reaction is my body and brain, the resulting energy my soul. Me. This becomes clear as the city goes about its yawning business around me, its collar up and its head down.

So my lineage started with a virus or a bacterium in a primordial sea. Four billion years of evolution later and this is the best DNA can do? Fizzing me? Fuck's sake.

Soon to be gone.

But at least awareness is a beginning. A glimpse of some sort of understanding. Is life just the illusion of greatness? The transient byproduct of biochemistry, the rearrangement of molecules, media-driven consumption and self-propelled ego.

My system craves nicotine, so the cosmic chemical clarity fades, replaced by a fumbling search through my clothes and vehicle.

I nervously readjust to the slow, grey world after a four day weekend of slow death. Christ, it's all so slow, even the water is thick and heavy. My hands shake as I light a smoke.

The codeine molecules are shifted through my system, quickly suppressing the pain signals from my crucified brain. Thank fuck for the Periodic Table. I smoke.

Nothing doing across the river, so I root around again and find the tiny wrap of coke dregs I'd stashed in a film canister. Nobody about so up it goes, through a manky fiver.

My teeth go numb from the dental anaesthetic - Novocain - the dealers use to cut the cocaine. I sense my pupils dilating with a quiet clank and my brain welcoming the Class A narcotic, maybe twenty-five percent proof, with open receptors. Nice to see you, it says, betraying me yet again. Check the time. 9.52 AM. Due now. Everything sharper. Better. But the coke's all gone.

Double-check the SLR, my trusty old Canon EOS1 with a 300 zoom. Focus in on the little park behind the museum. There's a mean crow - grey black, lumpy beak - on a fence, across two hundred metres of high water. I take a picture of it. No drugs left. Damn you crow. Maybe it senses me. It flaps away to its friends, busy with last night's stinking burger and kebab debris over in Arthur's Quay park. Collective noun for crows? Murder. They'd eat shit. Focus is good and sharp.

Then in she comes, with big paper bags from expensive boutiques. Shakes fading, heart beating in my damn ears now. She waits in the shadows of a gazebo, half-hidden by a pillar. She lights a cigarette, stares out at the water. Nervous now it's going down.

There he is, walking quickly through the trees. Thinks he's real clever. Line up the shot. I'm yawning now, but wide, wide awake. He glances around, smiles, joins her in the half-light. I adjust exposure, check light levels. She says something to him. He shrugs and smiles. Click. The kiss. Click.

He pulls her against him. She doesn't resist and kisses him full on the lips, her tongue reaching deep inside his mouth. There's nobody else in the park, too early even for winos, and they won't be seen. This is a sexual liaison which needs to be kept between just two. They hide well. She puts a condom on. Laughs.

Yes, he's coming. There, her hand rubbing furiously. His expression, classic. And, with my Canon, I take quality snaps of their adultery. Someone was going to pay dearly for this ride. They always did when I witnessed.

There must be a few molecules left in the wrap?

Now, his hand up her skirt, her silent moans and her head thrown back in mute ecstasy. Nothing I can hear anyway. She's nice, even from this range. Dark - near black - hair in a bob, tanned, good smile. She was like a 1950s Italian movie star. Sophia Loren maybe.

I can almost smell the sex. I want to. Fuck it. So I mull over the worth of it all, the illicit fuck. Me taking pictures of it, a professional voyeur. My life in general. Everything.

I slowly respond to the visual stimulation, the knowledge of the act, the swishing cocktail in my veins. Don't blame me, don't judge: it's autonomic.

Look at them. Like dogs. Thirty-six. I glance about, stick in a fresh film in two seconds flat. Welcome to your life, Charlie Doyle. Sad, really.

Jesus, is she looking at me?

Christ, I need to score.

CHAPTER 2. SLICE

Skin. Fat. Muscle. Vein. Bone. Artery. Cartilage. Spinal cord. Windpipe. Blood.

Each parted at the right time, making way for the machete blade. There was no resistance, barely a sound. Just a wet whisper. The head remained in place for a long second. Then it fell off to the side, tumbled, came to rest - face up - on thick grass.

The brain inside, numbed by enough forcibly-injected heroin to calm a bull, felt nothing. But for four long seconds, it was alive on the grass.

The killer kicked the kneeling body forward, but not quickly enough to avoid all the blood jetting from the dead man's jugulars.

'Fuckin gowl,' he said, wiping the blood from his cheek with a sleeve.

The others stayed back, not a peep.

'Who's fuckin takin this?' asked the killer, holding the deadly weapon between thumb and forefinger.

'I've to get rid of it,' said a young kid, his face white, like a ghost in a baseball cap.

'Alright kid.'

The killer dropped the machete at the boy's feet, grabbed the head by its hair. He took a black plastic binliner from his pocket, shook it open, dropped the head into it. The bundle went into a rucksack. Then he took a cloth from his pocket and wiped his face dry, removed his latex gloves and tossed these and the cloth beside the blade.

The killer picked up his rucksack, nodded at the still-stunned group and walked away, up the overgrown path towards the houses.

The rest smoked fags, slowly calming down.

'Fuck's sake,' said one.

'I wouldn't trust that cunt as far as I could throw him,' said another, nodding after the killer.

'What the fuck did Luke do, anyway?' said the third, still staring at the limp body.

'Fuck knows,' said the kid. 'He did enough anyways. Snitch?'

'Fuck's sake. He'd never snitch. Never. This is cuntin civil war. There'll be wigs on the Green before this is played out.'

'Come on boys. Into the river with him. I'm gaggin for a pint of cider.'

'He's still pumpin.'

'Leave him a minute, so.'

So they smoked more cigarettes, watched the blood ooze. The twitching heart finally stalled completely. Two lifted the upper body - an arm and an armpit each - and the other took the feet. The ruined corpse slipped into the water and sank quickly, towards the deepest current. The machete followed, glinting. A flood was up.

The gloves and rags were put on the pool of blood and a pint of petrol and a match saw to them.

A dripping black cormorant - fishing relentlessly all afternoon - broke the surface nearby

with a prize catch, a late salmon smoult. The fish
wriggling in her beak, the proud bird's bottle green
eye looked to shore. But her audience had vanished,
leaving just a pall of dirty smoke.

CHAPTER 3. DEAD WATER

And just a couple of weeks before, didn't they have the craic away in the swamp?

'Gissum bullets. Gawan illuh?' said Mickey from Limerick.

The range assistant just a college kid working a summer job. Getting more nervous by the second. Only schmuck on today. *What did the guy say? Sounded like he wants bullets. Jesus H. What's going on?*

Mickey was agitated, taking tiny steps away from the water's edge, reflexively pointing his assault rifle at a disinterested reptile.

'Gawan, tis like he's scoffin at me.'

'I can't let you shoot the wildlife, sir,' stammered the manager. 'State law. Would you maybe like to get started? With the targets?'

Mickey took a final drag, then flicked his cigarette butt at the alligator. It didn't stir. The gang followed their sweating host across the empty parking area, past the big rusting sign that said ED'S TARGET RANGE, FLORIDA'S FAVOURITE FOR GUN FUN. Ed's was gouged out of the swamp, out of the endless patchwork of saw grass and stagnant water, everything flooded by the first heavy rains of summer. The crazy crew hired the place exclusively for the day. Five grand, plus ammo. Ed said they'd be gone by noon. The sun and the mosquitoes would win out. Then you get home early, do what you gotta do, okay? Figuring he'd been dumped in the shit by Ed, the kid offered them some cold beers, maybe it would calm them down.

'I'm goin to need a good few beers,' said Greg, the guy who was looking after the bills. 'I'm sweatin like a black.'

That the man who served him was African American didn't matter to Greg. Never even registered. He drank the bottle of Miller in one slug. There was another bottle in his hand three seconds later. Luke was driving their rented Ford Galaxy, so drank Coke. He smiled, hoping Greg would get shitfaced so he could maybe drop the hand on Jean at some stage. She sat across the rickety table from him, sipped a beer, gave him the eye when Greg wasn't looking. Mad bitch. Birds shrieked suddenly from nearby reeds.

'So,' said Mickey, 'how many have you fed to the crocodile?'

'Alligator. No sir, that kind of stuff only happens on TV.'

'We've the river back home,' said Luke, now armed. 'That'll get rid of antin. C'mon. Let's riddle these cardboard cunts!'

Mickey, Luke and Jean took it all really seriously, practicing with assorted handguns, rifles and shotguns. Greg and the other two had the odd go, but mostly just drank and smoked and talked about Disney World until their throats were hoarse. The great mountain of sand behind the targets took a pounding. After a break for lunch of fried chicken with biscuits and corncobs - from Chicken Ranch just off the turnpike - they shot some more, kill rates improving. They took photos with a disposable camera.

Greg O'Doherty took a break, sat on a folding chair by the water. Drank a beer, his eighth. The manager joined him.

'Sir?'

'Yep?'

'Your wife's a really good shot.'

'She's great, isn't she? Fuckin lethal.'

'Really hot sir. She'd be a good cover girl for that magazine, *Guns & Ammo*. If you don't mind me saying.'

Greg considered threatening the guy for leching after his wife. He could never take that shit. At all. But it was too fuckin hot, so he just said 'Yeah'.

Unaware of his close escape, the guy went further, saying 'This isn't just a bit of holiday fun, is it?'

Automatic fire crackled from the range, scarcely a pause between salvoes. The birds were long gone. The alligator had disappeared, but she lurked a couple of inches beneath the oily surface. Just in case.

'The AKs, they're so fuckin loud we can't have any kind of decent practice back home. Ye Yanks have the right setup. I love this. Now we're up to speed, the gun fear is gone. That first burst. Critical.'

The manager froze, harsh reality at last slapping him across his face. He instantly dismissed the idea of calling the cops. Six armed lunatics and him, middle of the Everglades? No, focus on survival.

'If your friend wants to shoot something, I can maybe arrange it.'

'Good lad,' said Greg.

Greg gave him five hundred dollars.

Then the guy, Danny was his name, took Mickey and Luke out in the airboat, let them shoot a couple of small gators. Mickey turned the gun on him, but only as a joke. *Fuckin lighten up, kid.* That night, after a few beers in his cockroach hotel, and not shaking so much, Danny called Ed. He told Ed where he could stick his job, spent the rest of the summer renting lounge chairs to fat girls on Fort Lauderdale beach, across the highway from the Westin where the steaks were good.

CHAPTER 4. CLEVER LUKE

He was up early and out of the house by six. She snored on. Christ, he hated her most of all when she was asleep.

He drove out the N7 in silence. No sign of tails, but he went the long way anyway. Then he met the boys in a rough field past the waterworks. At the end of a long boreen down to the fog-shrouded river. They were in a desolate mill ruin. Standing around. Smoking. Nervous.

'Where are they?' asked Luke.

One of the boys, Mick, nodded towards a crooked doorway, a dark room beyond. Luke took latex gloves from his jacket pocket and put them on. They all watched *CSI*, even *CSI Miami* and *New York*. Mick, who also wore gloves, also was well-tanned, handed him an automatic pistol, a Beretta nine mill. Luke cocked the pistol, had no fear of it.

Two men sat in the dewy dark, shivering. They wore damp shirts and had plastic shopping bags over their bruised heads, loosely. Their hands were cable-tied. They were slumped against the cold wall, jerking to life when Luke appeared.

'I've a message for ye from my brother,' he said. 'We're takin over Garryowen, right?'

Then he shot them both twice. In their faces. Before they could even start to beg for their lives.

He threw the gun into the river, where it would stay for a hundred years. A fat black bird flew low over the water, heading downstream to feed. It veered to avoid the Beretta.

Luke gave his gloves to the lads for burning and left the scene pronto.

Straight to the gym, made it by seven. Town dead quiet. A coffee and a smoke, a few exercises. The place busy enough, a couple of nice birds on the treadmills. A bit of banter with them, keeping his options wide open. They were nurses, just off the night shift. Unwinding. Nice arses, pounding away on the rubber.

But Luke was very wound up. So into the sauna, hours to kill, time to think. Two oldish guys in there, business types, tiny towels. Fucking dead if they tried anything.

'Morning,' said Luke, smiling, always conscious of the alibi and the forensics. Every second, unless he was pissed.

He sat in the empty corner, pine slats scorching, and closed his eyes. All he could think about was Jean. She was like no other woman he'd ever done. As well as the danger, which heightened every sensation, she was just so deadly. The smell of her, her skin, her hair. Man.

Doing the dirt with your brother's wife was about as low as you could go. Fuck it, no. No it's not. There's a dozen things worse than that and he'd done most of them. Just as long as Greg didn't find out. That would be major shit. Major. Greg would have to die. No two ways about it. Nothing else would cover his arse. Nothing.

Fuck it. Just don't get caught.

As far as the missus knew, he was in the gym from seven to eleven every single Wednesday and the odd Friday. Had to keep the old sex machine in shape. God, there's nothing so good in life as a good shag. Fucking nothing. He'd fly out, get screwed, get back for a shower to wash away the forensics. Beautiful. And it always worked. He'd had ten affairs in two years. But Jean was different. Unusual. Special care. Keep some distance. Avoid anyplace obvious. Today might be only a handjob, but fuck it. It would do.

Luke could wait no more. He knew she'd be waiting. He left the sauna, showered quickly. He dressed, threw on his long trenchcoat and left the gym by a quiet side entrance. Alibi covered. Forensics covered. He had a grin on his face, delighted with himself and his cleverness. Beautiful, Luke. You're a fuckin beaut.

CHAPTER 5. OLD

They finished. They kissed. He took off the condom, tied a knot in it, put it in his coat pocket. Classy.

With a wide smile, she left, heading back to her MasterCard grazing. He waited a short while, gazing into the river. Then, his face still flushed, hands in pockets and a cigarette at his blood-filled lips, he left too. Fine. I had photos of French kisses, a sticky handjob, a fingerfuck and that unmistakable look between a couple that says: I like to fuck you.

Dress it up in pink ribbons with roses, any old shit, it all boils down to fucking. Primal instincts delivered again. Job done.

Unloaded the film and labelled the two rolls. I looked at the river again. Stared. It was black as oil and just as dirty. Bubblyscum gathered in the quiet places, rubbish eased by, breaking the reflection of the mean sky.

I drove in across Sarsfield Bridge. Into town, towards Dave's. Time to get the pics developed. Deliver to the mystery client straight away. Get paid. Bling.

Parked. Across William Street to Dave's shop. The sign said: DAVE'S PHOTOGRAPHY, THE FUTURE IS DIGITAL. Dave was busy with a customer, a suit, trying to flog him a pricey digital camera. His highly desirable assistant, Fiona, stood at the counter. She smiled my way.

'Hi Fiona. You're looking dangerously sexy for a Wednesday.'

'Oh yeah?'

'Yeah. How's the new dad?'

'Dave wants to keep the session goin at lunch. You comin?'

'It's been, what, five days already? But yeah.'

She came from the wrong side of the wrong side of town, but I could live with that. Her eyes were fixed on mine and I detected a slight increase in her breathing. She seemed interested. Or I was just delusional. I couldn't really tell anymore.

Jesus, I could see her on the cover of *FHM* magazine, she was that hot. Dave did those pictures - 'glamour' - on the side, actually had a *Loaded* cover once, long time ago now. I stared hard at Fiona's chest, copped myself, examined my fingernails instead. She made me feel old.

I haven't been laid in three months. Nearly a hundred days, but I'm not counting. Dave lost the sale, came over.

'How's your brain?'

'I genuinely can't believe I got a job done this morning. I'm that sideways. Have ye decided on a name yet?'

'I'm tied between Peter and Paul.'

He had the dreamy, sozzled look of a first-time father, worrying over which Munster rugby player to name his son after. Funny. Wait till he has to start changing nappies.

I gave him the two rolls of thirty-six. He had a pro black and white processing system, last one in town. I still used black and white because it gave me the most consistent results and I fucked up less on it. Plus, grainy mono photos always looked more private detective, more credible.

'Under an hour to contacts. That okay?'

'Great. This could be the handiest little job ever.'

As if.

CHAPTER 6. REVELATION

To the pub, which had mirrors, loud eighties music and a fair crowd. I ordered two vodka tonics, conscious of my breath that early in the day. It was barely noon. Explained my cashflow situation to Dave. He shrugged it off and handed me a fifty to keep me going. Tried to squeeze some dirt, like *Was he shagging Fiona or what?* No joy, he only wanted to talk about his son and Wasn't that the best wetting the baby's head ever?

An age later, Fiona came. She carried a large, brown envelope, which she handed to me. Our fingers touched for a not-negligible half a second.

'Drink, Fiona?'

'I can't. The shop.'

'You may as well lock up for lunch now, love,' said Dave. 'We'll eat here, okay?'

'For a change,' she said.

I opened the envelope and looked at the two contact sheets. The pictures were good, damned good. Excellent shot of her with his dick in her hand. No doubt about what was going on there. No fucking doubt whatsoever. Good job. I smiled. One shot looked like she was making eye contact with the camera. Coincidence.

'Let's see,' said Dave.

He was always eager to see my work, particularly if it involved people screwing.

I gave him the sheets of tiny pictures, all laid out for easy viewing and the selection of the half dozen or so that my client would accept as indisputable proof of his wife's infidelity.

'Well, well. This morning? Jesus, so that's how the other half lives. Exhibit A, your honour. Note the cock in the hand.'

Relieved by the quality of the shots, I stepped outside and called the client.

'I've got them. The castle? Okay, the castle courtyard, four o'clock. Fine. On the dot,' was my side of the conversation.

Returning to Dave, I found that Fiona had taken her seat. Dave hadn't gotten her a drink, so I jumped in.

'Bacardi and coke, Fiona?'

She smiled and nodded. Dave looked a bit pale, so I got us two more vodkas. In for a penny.

'Alright Dave?' I asked.

'Yeah,' he mumbled, sheepish.

'C'mon man. Spit it out.'

He glanced at Fiona.

'Tell me what's wrong. We've no secrets here, do we Fiona?'

'I think I recognise the guy. Do you know him?'

I looked closely at the little pictures. He looked vaguely familiar, as do most people when you live in a pocket-sized city. I shrugged.

Dave took a little fold-out magnifier from his arse pocket and held it to the contact sheet.

'Yep. It's him. No doubt.'

'Who?'

'One of the O'Dohertys. I don't know which one. Look.'

O'Doherty? My heart stopped for a second. Fiona nodded. I held my breath and looked at the man's grainy face through the magnifier. It was an O'Doherty, one of the gang. The gang. For sure. How did I miss it? Too busy looking at the woman, I guessed. Imagine a young Jane Fonda with a black bob.

CHAPTER 7. GOOD COP, BAD COP

Detective Pat O'Connor was in good form as he drove alone to Karpov's spread. Since he'd transferred back home from a two-year stint in Tallaght and Blanchardstown - Dublin's Wild West - things had been looking up. The Dublin cops used to slag him, saying *Well Pat, isn't this a nice rest from Stab City anyways?* and he'd say *Give me Limerick any day.* So he did his job well, worked on his connections, got promoted back to home.

He got the best of assignments now, like tagging along with Russell Crowe the time he came to town to pay homage to the memory of Richard Harris.

Pat was a clever cop, a very good shot, a natural. And confident. His public persona: clean-cut stand-up guy. Any Limerick-visiting VIP that needed armed protection got to meet Pat. Bill Clinton, even. Now there was a man that Pat bragged about meeting. He had this charisma. Pat framed a photo of himself and Bill having a pint in Ballybunion. He hung it on his living room wall, in his house out in Castletroy. He also admired JFK and James Bond. The Fleming Bond.

But inside Pat was something much grimmer, hiding from the cameras in the darkest cul-de-sacs of his practical, busy mind. As his brain ticked through his tasks at hand - it always did, even while he slept - he worked on the details of his biggest operation yet. People would die, maybe three or four. Maybe a woman. Maybe. He shouldn't have to get his hands dirty, but you never know. Anyhow, he was making it all happen. Karpov was ready to fork out a few million for the job. He didn't know how much. Just that he stood to take well over a million. A million fucking euro! Just hide it well and early retirement was a certainty. Contacts could fix everything. Every damned thing.

He smiled at his prospects. To pass the time, he stuck registration numbers of cars ahead of him - out the Ennis road - into the car's Pulse computer database. It was slow as fuck, a piece of shit, but sometimes hit paydirt. Nothing today. He banged the machine with the heel of his palm as it stalled again.

He arrived at Karpov's place. High wall, heavy gates, cameras, the lot. A sign said to approach the intercom and gave all the usual warnings.

His job today was official. He would check the guns that Karpov's bodyguards were legally allowed to carry.

He buzzed and a deep Russian voice boomed back at him, like *The Wizard of Oz* or something. It sounded like *Welcome, come on in*. Or it could've been Russian. The gates clicked, then opened quickly. Pat got back into the car and drove in slowly. A man sat on a deckchair, walkie-talkie in his hand, just inside the gate. He smiled and waved.

Pat parked on the wide sweep of pebbles outside the house, beside a burgundy Rolls Royce, a fat jeep and a couple of seven series black BMWs. Place was huge. *Brideshead Revisited.* One time. But the Russians have taken over now. It's all about the money.

A strong-looking, familiar man bounded down the steps. Tanned, dripping with white gold and dressed in a shining silk shirt, grey pants and deck shoes, he exuded wealth. Simply, relaxed billionaire at home. He grabbed Pat in a fierce bearhug, a faint smell of drink off his breath.

'Pat, Pat. So good to see you.'

'You too, Mikhail. You been working out?'

'I like you. You are my main man, you know that?'

Pat flushed. He couldn't help it. This was a good thing to hear from the world's twelfth richest man. Twelfth and rising. Christ. This was it. Never a better chance. And he'd only been introduced a week before.

'I'm only following orders, Mikhail. You know that. The fact that you're sound as a pound only helps. You don't have to butter me up at all.'

He said Sound as a pound, laughed again and led Pat in for a drink. It was champagne, the good stuff, and caviar - Chekhov's favourite food, said Karpov - on funny little crackers. Pat didn't like caviar much, but he ate it anyway, pretending that he loved it and was reared on it.

Karpov talked a mile a minute. Pat couldn't really keep up, though he was considered by many to be razor sharp. He touched on the meteoric oil prices, Iraq, Irish politics, personal friend Bill Clinton, George W Bush: *The W makes him, don't you think, Pat?*, al-Qaeda, the price of vodka. This guy was unreal. Pat was dizzy, like a kid meeting a movie star.

The subject changed to Pat's business. Just when Karpov wanted it to. He called to a man, dressed in a kind of butler outfit - white jacket, white gloves - who stood in the hall outside the lounge. They conversed in Russian, master and servant. The man nodded formally and glided away. Pat always felt uneasy when within a foreign language conversation. You just never knew what the fuckers could be saying about you. So he made a mental note to take some language lessons, learn some Russian.

'Come, Pat. To the garden.'

Karpov held an arm outstretched, pointing to the back garden. Pat followed him through the vast conservatory.

The garden lay below a wide veranda, all cast-iron furniture, lion statues and flowers in pots. Must be an acre of manicured lawn.

Karpov led Pat across the lawn and through a gap in the bushes. A rough path brought them to a long clearing. Two men waited, standing to attention, army-style. They wore black fatigues. Fortyish, impassive faces, crewcut hair, fit. One had a snake tattoo on his forearm, probably a unit logo. They watched Pat from out of the corners of their eyes. Didn't miss anything.

Karpov spoke Russian and the men relaxed. He turned to Pat.

'These are my personal bodyguards. They travel with me at all times. They are the only members of my staff to carry guns.'

'Background?'

'Russian special forces. They both fought in Afghanistan and Chechnya. Very bitter wars, but very good experience, yes? I would trust them with my life.'

Pat nodded, knowing that these guys had killed, no empathy.

'Any sign of post-traumatic stress?'

'In what way?'

'I don't know. Rages? Alcoholism? Depression?'

'Nothing.'

'And the weapons?'

Karpov gave an order and one of the men turned to a suitcase-sized metal case on the grass beside them. He unlocked and opened the case. Inside were four Glock pistols with silencers, four stun grenades, two nightvision goggles and two commando daggers. The pistol magazines held bullets. Pat found a folded A4 sheet in his inside pocket. He went through the motions of comparing serial numbers on the weapons against his Excel printout on Garda letterhead. The list of authorised weapons checked out, except for the silencers and stun grenades. So he signed and dated the sheet.

'All done,' said Pat, smiling.

Karpov nodded and gave an order in Russian. His men got the Glocks and proceeded to load and cock them. For the briefest instant, Pat considered reaching for his revolver, a standard issue Smith & Wesson snubnose thirty-eight.

'Time for their practice,' said Karpov. 'Three times a day they must shoot.'

Over lunch, Pat told Karpov about his plan. How it was in motion. How it would all work out fine, leading to Greg O'Doherty's funeral and Karpov dominance in the mid-west.

Pat said There were only two potentially loose cannon. The IRA, who better stay out. And Charlie Doyle, who better play his part and not mess things up. Or he would die, the fucking loser.

CHAPTER 8. TOTAL DISCRETION

I stared at the pictures. I thought through my options, chancing to say that the processor went on fire or I slept it out.

'How did you get the job?' asked Dave.

My head was reeling as the reality sank in. I had in my possession proof that a member of one of Limerick's most notorious crime families was doing the dirt. This was the kind of information that got people killed. And the client. Who's the client?

'I got a call last week, from my ad in the phone book, I supposed.'

CHARLES A. DOYLE
PRIVATE INVESTIGATIONS
CASES INVOLVING INFIDELITY
HANDLED WITH TOTAL DISCRETION

'The guy told me where and when to take the pictures. He said he thought his wife was fucking around. Offered two grand cash for fast photos. I'm meeting him later. He did sound a bit rough, but who doesn't these days? *Fuck.*'

'I guess he made you an offer you couldn't refuse, ha?'

I ordered more drinks.

'Shouldn't you be keeping your wits about you for meeting this guy?'

Was he insinuating that my client would try to bump me off to keep his secret safe? Was he a criminal, one of the O'Doherty circle of friends? Does he already know that his wife is being shagged by a member of the most feared crime empire Limerick has ever known?

'Where you meeting him?'

'King John's Castle. Four.'

'Just don't go up the towers. It's easy to slip and fall, you know.'

'You're fucking hilarious Dave, you know that?'

'That's what people keep telling me, bud. I'm wasted in this damn town.'

'Yeah man. Try Vegas.'

Fiona offered to head back early to print up the shots I wanted. Without emotion, I selected the best half-dozen, marked them and off she went. Dave said he'd be over to collect the prints in a while. Then he turned to me, looking serious.

'You need some back-up, dude? I'll come with you, if you want.'

It was sinking in. At last.

'If I'm to die today, there's sweet fuck all that you or I or anyone can do about it.'

'The cops, maybe? Pat? You know he's gagging to put the O'Dohertys out of business. They're pure mad, those fuckers.'

'I know, I know. But if I involve the cops, then I'm dead for sure. No, I'll play it by ear for now.'

'You sure you don't smell Pat in this?'

'Why?'

He shrugged and we dropped it. Pat was a mate.

We clinked glasses and Dave got in another round. If I was to die, then I was damn sure going to enjoy my last few hours.

'Pints tonight, yeah?'

'Yeah.'

'Now, while I make excuses to my lovely wife, can you try and organise some Charlie, Charlie?'

'Yes, I hear there's snow forecast.'

'Good. I hope to have a hot young thing to keep me warm well into the night. You're my excuse, okay?'

'What's new?'

Dave went back to the shop to ring his wife, see how the baby was doing, no pub noises in the background. I called my dealer and he said I could call to his place any time. There was always a steady supply of Colombia's finest. Limerick, you are a lady. I was starting to feel good. A few drinks and the prospect of some coke and a shag will do any man the world of good, even with the vague threat of sudden, untimely death hanging over his head.

Dave got back and handed me an envelope. I checked the photos, making sure that nobody in the pub could see over my shoulder. Printed up as ten by eights, the images were startling. Pure sex jumped from the photos. And yes, he was clearly an O'Doherty. I recognised the face from the newspaper coverage of an aborted murder case.

This guy had been up for the brutal slaying of a young street dealer from a different gang. Though it had happened in town in broad daylight, no witness was insane enough to take the stand. He got off scotfree.

Luke O'Doherty. He was trouble. Disgusted with myself for not smelling a rat sooner, I shoved the pictures back inside the envelope and held on tight. It wasn't leaving my hand until delivered to the client. Whoever the hell he was. More drink.

So the time came for me to go to my possible doom. Dave finished his drink, wished me luck, went back to the shop half-cut.

Assuming I wouldn't be dead, we'd arranged to meet at my place at six.

I strolled off down the street towards the river, thinking *Janey Mac! Why me?*

CHAPTER 9. THE ISLAND

Just fourteen, Robert Dunne rode like the wind, clipclopping along a quiet Long Pavement Road. He held on tight to the package, bagged and wrapped up in his horse blanket, holding the rope reins with his left hand. By the feel of it, there were two handguns inside. Revolvers. And what felt like a machete. About two foot of a one.

They were from a secret stash, one he never heard about before. Mr O'Doherty had been specific when he rang the night before. Go to Parteen. Early. Get a package from behind a wall near the bridge. Deliver it the back way. No problem.

And nobody else was to know about it. On pain of death. Par for the course, but stressed this time more than normal.

With the pieball doing ninety and the job half done, Robert began to relax. Mistake. He didn't spot the squad car until the cops were beside him, slowing down as they approached. He galloped on, trying to look nonchalant, but taking care not to ignore the cops. He and his kind wouldn't. The cops were the Ying to the gangs' Yang. Each side needed the other, to affirm existence.

They passed smoothly by and he turned his head. They swung a u-turn, lights flashing, siren like a banshee.

In a second, he calculated that across the old dump was his best chance. A twist of the rope and heels dug in and the horse responded, clearing the concrete fence at the side of the road with ease.

Across the tricky stream, the weedy plain and into the foothills of the vast piles of old rubbish they went, tearing up clods of newspapers, plastic bags and nappies through the thin layer of topsoil. He felt like John Wayne. Robert breathed through his mouth and spoke words of encouragement to Betty.

He stole a glance back towards the road and saw the police car pulled in at the dump entrance. They weren't coming on foot. His ears didn't pick up the distinctive low thudding of the pork chopper, so he allowed himself a smile.

At the crest of the waste mountain, Robert stopped the horse. The tinker camp squatted to his left, all smoulder and junk. In front, past the squad car, the railway tracks led to the Moyross sprawl, endless acres of corner territories and horseland. The cops turned back around and continued on their way, towards Parteen. Robert knew he was in the clear. The cops must've figured he was on the mitch from school, that's all. Luke and Greg told him he was still clean and to keep it that way: worth more. Just another loose kid. Chasing him across the dump wasn't worth the hassle. For no good reason anyway.

'Lazy old fools,' he said, and 'Good girl,' continuing down to the river and across the ghostly railway bridge to the Island. No sentry saw him. All in bed, signing on later, all I'm off to work, love and Sure, amint I an artist; I draw the dole.

The sun broke through and his - of course - brilliant white horse shone for a moment, flashing behind the rusty girders. The hills behind slept in a gloomy blue haze. Robert opened the bundle and held the deadly blade to the sky. His horse galloped across the open spaces between the heavy sleepers. One false step would mean disaster. So he smiled and roared, urging his horse on. The Shannon rushed by below. It was more like a scene from *Excalibur* than *True Grit*. He stopped when he reached the Island, resting the horse and smoking a little rock of crack cocaine, thinking to relax his heart, but actually making it beat one hundred and thirty times every minute for a full seven minutes.

Along by the busy river, passed the spot where I had taken the bastard pictures. My spine ached.

Crossed Thomond Bridge - popular spot for fishing, photos, suicide - the castle looming. I realised, with a nasty taste in my mouth, that I was on the Island.

This was the oldest part of the city, an island on the Shannon that offered some protection from the marauding Vikings and psychos who regularly sailed up the estuary in the olden days. When the British took over, they put their garrison on the island and the castle built by King John eight hundred years ago still stands.

Now the Island belonged to the O'Dohertys. They ran their massive drug business from safe houses in the middle of a huge housing estate, right behind the castle. The corporation-built housing scheme could be entered by just one road. The Island was a place of random murder, casual prostitution, endemic drug abuse, organised depravity. Funny really, that it was also the focal point of Limerick's tourist industry. You couldn't make it up.

It would make sense to meet me in the castle if it was an O'Doherty that had hired me. It would be suicidal for their rivals to meet me on O'Doherty turf. But why would an O'Doherty need me? Was it Luke testing me? Some stupid game? It was common knowledge that the police had set up night vision cameras on one of the castle's lofty turrets, as it gave a good view of the road into the Island. The cops would be unlikely to be there during the day and even more unlikely to be looking back over their shoulders into the courtyard. Clever.

As I walked with deliberate casualness towards the entrance, I noticed two tough-looking guys sitting in a spang-new black Ford Mondeo. They looked at me, but I couldn't make them. Dublin plates, so possibly cops. Or O'Doherty goons. Or common or garden drug dealers. Or just people. Or serious tourists, Russians maybe. Sweet paranoia, no harm. They weren't looking at me and they didn't seem to be play-acting.

I paid my entrance fee, bitched like a child about how expensive it was and said it was no wonder there were no Americans about. The woman at the counter just smiled and asked me to enjoy my visit.

I passed through the foyer and the crappy tinwhistles and teatowels of the gift shop. Down the steel staircase into the wide open courtyard. I'd never been in the castle before, like how many Londoners have been to Madame Tussaud's? But I was actually mildly impressed, life being full of surprises.

The cobbled ground stretched down towards the river, with the rooms and towers to the right and the museumy bit and tat shop behind me, in the modern entrance annex. Standing alone in the middle of the large yard by a smoky fire was a big, unpleasant-looking guy, wearing a heavy, black leather coat. He was chubby, bald and unshaven. Normally I love stereotypes. He made eye contact with me. My man.

I strolled over, trying to look relaxed. It wasn't easy, especially after I tripped on a cobblestone and nearly fell on my semi-drunken ass. I made it to him. He kept his hands deep in his pockets, so no pleasantries required.

'Got um?'

'You mean the pictures? Yeah, here.'

I handed him the envelope, which was now fairly grubby from my nervous hands. He opened it and pulled out the pictures, looking around to make sure nobody was watching us. He had ACAB inked across his knuckles. All cops are bastards. I suppose, if you're a gangster. His beady eyes nearly popped.

'The fuckin slut bitch. I knew it. Whore! I fuckin knew it.'

I was used to seeing the reactions of people who've just received proof that their spouse was doing the dirt on them. It was never easy, so I adopted the professional approach of not caring, not getting involved on any level. This guy was little different. I stayed dead quiet and looked at the ground. He pulled his mobile from a pocket and sent a fast text.

'Okay, that's that' he said finally, his pockmarked face red with controlled rage. 'Here's your cash. Good job, kid.'

He took a fat envelope from his jacket pocket and handed it to me. I didn't feel it would be a good idea to check it.

'It's all there. On the nail.'

Like the fucker read my mind. Okay mister, so are you going to bump me off?

'As long as this doesn't get out, there'll be no trouble from me. Understand? You were recommended to me, to be trusted.'

'Recommended by whom?'

'Has anyone else seen these? Did you do um up yourself?' he asked, changing the subject forcefully.

I slurred something, then pulled myself together.

'Yes. No. I mean nobody's seen them and I did do them myself.'

I was starting to lose it. He grabbed me roughly by my chin and stared into my bleary eyes. He was a strong fucker.

'Good. Now, wipe my number out of your phone and make like you never even heard of me. If I need you again, I'll ring you.'

He turned to walk away while I was going through my mobile's phonebook looking for the entry labelled NEWCLIENT2. All fingers. But I had to find out who he was and called to his wide, receding back.

'Who are you? So I can forget you properly.'

That was probably the dumbest thing I'd said all year, but he replied anyway.

'I'm Greg O'Doherty and these pictures are of my wife and my cuntin brother. My ex-brother. You never met me, aright?'

What I'd give for a brother, even a bollicks of a one. Growing up an only child was no fun at all.

'Right, thanks,' but he was gone, clanging up the steel staircase.

I was not in good shape. I went into one of the towers, quickly checked the cash, which was fine, and thought about climbing up for the view. But my dreadful stomach and fearful vertigo said Bad idea. I needed to escape.

Outside on the street, the two goons had gone, so I deduced they were O'Doherty's muscle. Greg O'Doherty, normally described in the media as The Godfather of Limerick. Jesus, Mary and Joseph.

I flagged down a perfectly-timed taxi, glancing around Castle Street uneasily, tumbled in and patted the leather seat in thanks. For I would not stumble around the Island alone with fifty cents in my pocket, let alone two grand.

CHAPTER 10. HEAVEN

The taxi hurtled back to town by Bridge Street past the city courthouse - gangs, armed cops, kids, media all hanging about - then up O'Connell Street. Turned right towards the new bridge, took me to my dealer's place, in one of the new dockside apartment complexes. Steamboat Quay (and he a steamer!), just around the corner from my own house. I was delighted with myself. Appreciated my easy life for a few choice seconds.

Brian's pad was fairly swanky, with deadly views of the river. I stood on his rooftop balcony and smoked a fag while he fixed some vodka tonics, complete with umbrellas, ice and lime. Quality.

'I could do with going on the rip tonight, I'll tell you.'

'Well, this should help.'

He handed me a small Ziploc bag, full almost to the top with white powder. Two grams, maybe? There was a logo printed in white on the bag, one I hadn't seen. It was a snow-capped mountain, with the word HEAVEN under it. Sweet as a fucking nut.

'Mind if I do a line?' I said, eager. Too eager.

'I'll join you. Let me get the stuff.'

Good-looking, into intelligent chat, always sorted. If I was gay, Brian would be my type.

So I leaned against the balcony railing, watching the river in its quiet progress to the sea. A number of excited people had gathered by the quayside just upriver from my position, towards Poor Man's Kilkee. They were pointing at something trapped in the eddies downstream from the wall of stone that jutted into the river. A police launch arrived on the scene, flashing blue. I got Brian's binoculars, normally used for watching people undressing across the river and up in the Clarion hotel. Much better.

He laid out four lines on a vanity mirror and we took two each. The hit rushed forward and assaulted us, resistance futile.

I was filled with energy, clarity, vitality. Fake, chemical, but tangible and lovely all the same. With supreme confidence, I took my drink to the balcony, master of all I surveyed. I gushed like a demented idiot about how great life was, half-watching the drama on the river below, babbling. There was a bit of a shimmer to my vision, amplified by the binoculars. But things were sharper, edges cleaner. I felt fucking fantastic. The crash would come, I knew that.

But I didn't care. As long as I had cash, there would always be more. The stereo pumped out a Verve CD, *Bittersweet Symphony* at full tilt. *Try to make ends meet, you're a slave to money, then you die.* Fuck. But the drugs do work. Now. For me. So I sang.

'Hang on, action,' said Brian, his wide eyes drawn to the river.

More of a commotion on the water. Cries, a diver, dayglo jackets. The Coast Guard Sikorsky, all red and white, swooped up the estuary and hovered near us, its rotors forcing spray from the river in kaleidoscopic patterns that lured me down. Then a body was pulled from the water, on to the launch's deck. It was headless. A no-brainer, I knew in my aching gut that it was O'Doherty's cheating brother. Luke.

'Rather you than me, sunshine,' I said.

Then I raised my glass and said *Clink*.

She sat on the bed, propped up on four pillows so she could see out the narrow sash window. The bottom panes of glass were frosted, so she couldn't see the others walking around in their endless circles or sometimes going crazy in the big field below. So she looked at the sky. Today, the clouds were like snakes in a blue sea. Any meaning eluded her. She'd once heard of snakes called water moccasins and thought *What a lovely name for a snake*. What peace she enjoyed.

At the time it happened, she wasn't in control. But she understood now. Christ, they'd all drive you mad in the general ward. But this was nicer, with a nice nurse to look after you and a bit of peace and quiet. And the food was better, too. She'd have to stay here. Just keep cutting the wrists. Sure, it didn't even hurt and look at this for a fine time. She genuinely felt better.

Time evaporated.

But some things stayed with her, like feeling sorry for her poor husband, who had to get the two doctors to sign for her to come in and get herself straightened out. After what he'd put her through, serves him right. Slashing her wrists probably gave him a fright, too. Still, she worried about him and how he was getting along without her. Sure, he couldn't even boil an egg.

And, most of all, she fretted over her poor boys. She didn't know what would become of them. She imagined so many fearful events, tragedies, manias. And her tarot rarely lied. It must end like this for all of us, she concluded. Lonely, confused, frightened. When the thoughts came on too strong, she asked the nurse for more medication. Then she'd stop worrying. Instead, she'd look at the clouds.

CHAPTER 11. BETRAYED

Deirdre Doyle often listened to Leonard Cohen. Charlie would give out to her, saying *Any chance of some happy music?* But she didn't want his druggy reggae or trance on in the house. Anyway, Cohen was a poet.

The days had dragged by while he set up his private detective business. She wasn't happy about him chucking in his steady security job and taking out a fat credit union loan on a whim. Her main problems: he obtained his detection expertise from Elmore Leonard novels and a mail order course. Plus, he spent all his working days and nights looking for adultery. Finally, he could get killed if he took on the wrong client.

Actually, the last problem wasn't such a biggie.

So she listened to the CD to the end, packed the essentials, drove the kids out to her mother, went to meet her lover. Charlie wouldn't get home until the middle of the night, out of his head, full of shit about how he was finally going to make a killing. But no more audience.

Driving to see her lover - at his sprawling modernist pile past Killaloe - gave her a unique thrill, an electric buzz through her nervous system. Why do women cheat? Because the simple act of having sex with someone on the sly was enough to give a buzz just like the first time, the very first orgasm. There was never any real risk of getting caught so the thrill just came from knowing that she was screwing behind Charlie's back. And he, with all his detective bullshit, didn't have a clue. She smiled. Anyway, it was his big mistake, screwing Sara. Snotty bitch. He still thought she didn't know.

And he didn't even have a clue about her revenge fuck with his so-called best friend. The dope. But, all over now.

CHAPTER 12. WIRED

I sent Dave a text to let him know we were sorted and that I was still alive. His reply said Body in rvr! Ur mate? I told him Yeah. He was due at my place at six, so I scooted back to mine. Put a slab of those tiny French beers from Tesco on the floor beside me. Drank eight watching *Richard and Judy*. Couldn't sit though, kept walking around, doing pointless shit, like dusting picture frames and arranging magazines on the coffee table so all the corners were squared off. I was wired for sound.

Then Dave came, pounding on the door like he was the fuzz or something. I changed the TV channel.

'Listen, latest news is two more fuckin' bodies have turned up. No IDs yet, but there's talk of connections to the O'Dohertys.'

'Fuck me. What in the name of Jesus is going on? In. Quick.'

I locked the door, checked it, then checked the back door and low windows. Secure. My head began to spin, which I feared was becoming its normal rest state. I sat down heavily on the couch. Dave joined me, started on the beer.

'Like I say, there's talk that the O'Dohertys did it,' he said.

'Talk?'

'Yeah, in the pub.'

'You went back?'

'Why the fuck not? They're dropping like flies around here. Why not enjoy what time we have?'

He had a point.

'I honestly thought the body they fished out earlier was you, Charlie, I really did!'

'No worries, man. O'Doherty was grand, he just threatened me lightly and paid up. Who are these new two?'

'No clue yet, might come out later. So where's the coke, dude? Let's get cracking man. Carpe diem and all that.'

'Here's the coke, there's the mirror. Now can you look after yourself while I have a shower?'

The shower radio crackled as a breathless reporter on a dodgy mobile filled the presenter in on the latest killings. The cops were saying, off the record, that the two were heavies from O'Doherty's rival gang, the Brownes. They'd been found a few miles outside town. Both shot twice in the face. There was a big forensics operation going on and it looked like there wouldn't be any positive IDs until morning. No major doubts about how they died though. The radio batteries died.

'Gowl of a thing!,' I roared.

I shaved badly with my near-blunt blade, ripped that little web under my right ear for good measure. I stood in the weak shower, blood flowing generously from my cut and down my body. I just stared at it, hoping it wasn't some kind of freakish symbolism.

Out of the shower and the cut still bled. I found an old container of talcum powder and put a lump on the cut. It soaked up the flow and, after a little more was applied, the blood clotted. I dressed quickly, loose jeans, clean shoes and a stripy shirt.

A small photo was wedged into the top corner of the bedroom mirror frame. It was of me and my family, back in the days when I had one. I looked bored, she looked pissed off. The kids looked happy enough, but how were they to know? Now it's all dysfunction. Officially. A choke in my throat turned out to be a lump of coke. Down to Dave. He was really eager now.

'Listen, we're going disco dancing tonight.'

'What's wrong with a club?'

'And the shots are half price 'til midnight,' he said, knowing exactly how to push my buttons.

'That's sorted then. Let's go.'

'Doesn't kick off until ten. We might as well chill here for a while?'

'Nah. I feel like pastures new. Let's go.'

'Where?'

'Let's just follow our noses.'

We finished our drinks and found bars. The Old Quarter, The Cornmarket, Smyths, The Icon, Nancy's. After some bleary, condensed hours talking gibberish to disinterested strangers, we decided to make our way up to the Royal George and the disco.

This decision would unleash two new chains of events. One of violence, fear and confusion. One of outright horror.

CHAPTER 13. WHAT SHE FOUND MOST STRANGE

Human depravity no longer held any surprises for her. She'd seen too much. So she swapped Nigeria's urban chaos, scorching grassland and steaming rain forest for concrete streets, corner shops, new cars.

Her trip began with a regular job that went wrong one day. She'd met the guy - a sweating German, about sixty, backpack - at Lagos Airport. She held up a name sign as the passengers from the Lufthansa flight came through arrivals. He was in shock, like the other first-timers, smiled gratefully when she caught his eye. It was her job to put him at ease. She took his arm and led him straight through the gangs of pickpockets and muggers in the airport building. She said nothing, even when a young boy tripped the man and he fell heavily. She helped him up and pulled him faster.

Outside, the air was thick with heat, smoke and mosquitoes. She took him past the line of taxis to an unmarked car. The driver smiled a mouthful of golden teeth, the man beside him fidgeted with a machine gun. The German froze.

'Show him your ID,' she said.

The man with the gun handed his police ID to the driver, who held it open for the German to see.

'Okay,' he said and got into the car.

'Without protection, we wouldn't make it into the city,' she explained as the car lurched into traffic and sped away from the roaring jets and screaming travellers.

On the bumpy highway, she advised the German to keep his head down to avoid the searching eyes of the gunmen who drive up and down the airport road.

'I need to stop, please,' he said. 'I need a drink or I will have a heart attack.'

His English was good. He seemed intelligent. So why had he fallen for this?

'We can't stop now,' she said, rubbing his shoulder. 'When we get to Lagos, then we will stop for a drink before we complete the contract. You have the deposit?'

'Yes, yes. Okay.' A smile. 'Thank you.'

Before they left the highway, a car ahead of them was attacked by robbers. They shot the driver dead and, when the car crashed off the road, they attacked the passengers, taking everything, leaving them bleeding in the bush.

Night fell quickly.

She sighed with relief when they reached the suburbs. There was a drinking shack where they could take a private room. Let him have his drink, she thought. Poor fool.

They stopped in a dark laneway so he could get into the bar without being seen, attracting attention. The driver and the cop waited in the car.

He wanted whiskey so she ordered a clean bottle and two glasses and took him through a filthy passageway to a tiny room with a tea chest table and a tattered couch. On the wall, pictures of topless women, some white, some black. On the floor, spilt drink and bloodstains. Local music - unknowable chanting against a backbeat of jungle drums and synthesisers - blared from a wired speaker. He gulped a drink. And another. He paced the room, holding onto his rucksack, fearing he would be robbed at any minute.

Not yet, she thought.

She was tired, poured herself a drink.

Suddenly he was on her, forcing her neck back with his forearm while his right hand explored her new panties. Strong for an old guy. She tried to scream, couldn't. His whiskey breath was all over her as he whispered to her in German. 'Meine Schönheit.' She managed to reach her handbag, groped for her nail file.

She found it and swung it hard into his neck. He stopped his assault, stood up. He tried to speak, but all that came from his mouth were bubbles of spit and a trickle of blood. He fell backwards heavily, hit his head on the ground, spasmed.

She got to her feet and quickly explored his rucksack. A bundle of euros in an envelope. She knew she would be blamed for this trouble, that she would sacrifice her life to appease the German consul. So she took the money and ran, ran through cholera-ridden alleys to the ID maker.

Getting to the promised land was arduous. But she was now a UN-registered potential genocide victim. With nobody to protect her, she'd be in line for having her genitals mutilated or her limbs chopped off for muti rituals or just for the hell of it by children with AKs. She had her proof: family death certs, photos, a genuine passport and official stamps, so she was shown a sort of tolerance on her journey through officialdom. That made it bearable and she appreciated that. Others, millions more across Africa and Asia, had no luck at all. But all her money was spent.

The bureaucrats in Ireland still struggled to show human emotion, their brows creased by the endless floods of poor and dispossessed. So many hopefuls amazed at Ireland's economic excesses, minimum wage opportunity and actual welfare system. It's all relative, the Irish would say. Still, she got on with it.

What she found most strange: Gangs of women drunk and falling around the streets at night. None but the very old and very crazy in church on Sundays. White men desperate for her body. Police not interested in anyone unless they had committed murder. Nobody able to speak French.

Her payday came in a white envelope marked Department of Justice, Euality and Law Reform. Inside, a work permit conditional on her joining a list for a council house in Limerick. She'd never heard of Limerick, knowing only Dublin's north inner city and a seedy State-financed hostel. Multi-ethnic. Packed with Eastern Europeans, too coarse for her, with their constant come-ons and bootleg vodka. She survived on a paltry hand-out, vouchers. So she walked down a threatening, addict-infested

O'Connell Street, under the gleaming Spike and sat on the Liffey boardwalk with the junkies and winos and Spanish students and thought about it.

She went back to the hostel and started packing.

So she wound up in Knockalisheen, just outside Limerick. Her new home used to be a 1940s army barracks. Now it was home to immigrants from twenty-seven different countries. Etoile lived in a corrugated iron-clad billet, a dozen tiny partitioned rooms down each wall. The military Zen was gone, replaced by a barrage of photos, art and smells from all over the planet, every bedspace a desperate statement of identity.

She made certain to become friends with a powerful woman, Precious, a woman who worked muti magic. Precious took an interest in Etoile, began to teach her the many secrets of her ancient gift.

One evening, Etoile helped Precious perform an abortion on a woman from Sudan. It was Friday, so all the guards - private security, alcoholics to a man - were drinking in their Portacabin and playing cards, forty-five. They went to the woman's room. Then Precious gave her a herbal drink which contained an abortificant, RU-486.

'Relax, child,' she said.

Precious and Etoile went outside and smoked cigarettes.

'She is lucky,' said Precious. 'She is from Darfur. She has been given asylum and doesn't need the baby now. Do you like it here, child?'

'I want to stay. The air is so fresh against my skin. Yes, I like it.'

'There are fortunes to be made. Trust me. I will teach you my ways. You will be my apprentice.'

Precious saw something of herself in Etoile, but she also saw an insecurity, a kind of fear.

They returned to the patient after two hours. Precious gave her another drug, this time a prostaglandin to help dilate her cervix. Then she used a vacuum aspirator to suck out the embryo. Though abortion was illegal in Ireland, she got the drugs and the tools and the clients easily enough.

Etoile flinched as the little glass jar filled with globs of flesh and clotted blood. The job done, Precious rubbed the woman's forehead and gave her a morphine injection. The husband paid Precious five hundred euros in fifties and stayed with his wife.

Precious washed her gear, then packed it into a small black leather bag. The jar of wasted life she gazed at.

'How will you dispose of it?' asked Etoile.

'You have much to learn child,' laughed Precious. 'This is worth many times more than the operation itself. Almost pure stem cells! The highest bidder will get this.'

She placed the jar inside a fold in her robe and went to her room to prepare potions.

So Etoile found a job in a supermarket and got to see how a developed Western economy functioned.

Then she applied for a better job, doing massage therapy for a fake doctor who offered holistic healing to bored women with lots of money. He liked her, thought she had an exotic air about her, felt his clients would enjoy having her around, felt her bottom at the end of the interview. She took the groping, then took the job.

The system caught up with her in the form of an inspector from the Department. He was waiting when she came out from town on the special bus, one evening after work. The manager met the bus and took Etoile to an interview room in the administration block. The man looked like a cop, showed a nondescript ID. He quizzed her at length about her allegedly dead family. Showed her a document supposedly signed by her father - a Nigerian national, not Senegalese at all - just weeks before. She kept her story up and cried with fear and confusion. She wasn't sure if he bought it. He said he'd have to make enquiries, that he'd be back soon and that she could keep working, but not to leave Limerick. And to sign a book in Henry Street Garda Station every week. She said Yes of course.

But inside she screamed, raged.

CHAPTER 14. WELL HELLO

Approaching the club where the disco had just kicked off, I realised that I was officially out of it. Two ugly bouncers lurked by the open doors, watching me closely. There didn't seem to be anybody else going in.

I feared a deserted disco, club being too fancy a description for the place. But no, the place was mobbed. *YMCA* played, floor-shakingly loud. We paid, a tenner each, my treat. We stuck our coats in the cloakroom.

'Three fucking quid to hang up a coat? They've some cheek,' muttered Dave.

'Chill, man. I'm just hoping it's not gay night.'

I gazed at a delicious African-looking woman who stood by the bar. She'd been watching me. The gap on her!

She smiled back. Bingo. Closer so.

'My name's Charlie. What are you drinking?'

'Whatever.'

My kind of woman. I shouted and shouted and shouted and eventually got three vodka Red Bulls. I felt a boogie coming on. It started at my feet, then my chin got going. I looked at her and drank in the sight. She wore a skin tight red dress. She had a figure to go to hell for and she knew it.

'You here alone?' I asked.

'I'm with a couple of friends. Thanks for the drink.'

'No probs. Boyfriends or girlfriends?'

'Girlfriends. My husband's at home minding the kids.'

Okay so.

'Doesn't he mind you being here?'

'Do I look like I care what he thinks?'

'No. It's rapid here tonight, isn't it?'

'Rapid.'

My radar switched on. As did a tingle in my groin. If I played my cards right, I could be on. I took her by the elbow and led her towards a quieter corner, where we could talk, not shout. I had enough of that lark in my marriage.

'Where you from?'

'Garryowen.'

'No, originally. You weren't born in Garryowen, were you?'

'I'm from Senegal, Dakar.'

'Is that where the Paris-Dakar rally ends up?'

'Very good. You impress me.'

'And isn't it where Patrick Vieira's from?'

'Qui? Who?'

'Plays for Arsenal. Football.'

'Ah, oui.' She pronounced it way.

'I used to live near Highbury. Big fan.'

'Formidable.'

Her French accent was gorgeous, arousing.

'How did you manage to get in? Is Senegal so bad?'

'Economically, is not too bad, I suppose. But my family suffered religious persecution. That's how I got a visa for Ireland. My father was butchered. And my mother. And my sisters.'

'Christ.'

'Yes. We're Catholic. We were. Just two percent of the population. The rest are Muslims, with a few indigenous religions thrown in, witch doctors, muti, all that craziness.'

'Did your husband come here with you?'

'No. I met him here,' she smiled. 'He's an Irishman, just like you.'

'Fuck me. This is getting just a little too complicated.'

'Let's dance.'

She led me by the hand to the crowded dance floor. The slow set.

'So what's your name?'

'Etoile. It means star.'

'Star? Nice. Apt.'

'How charming you are, Charlie.'

If she was trying to sweet talk me, she was succeeding. As well as the flattery, her hands caressed my arse and her big, juicy breasts crushed my chest. I'd never had sex with a black woman before, never even kissed one. My brain said Be careful, but my crotch said Do your bit for race relations, son.

She lifted her head, and its smell of lilies and sandalwood, from my shoulder and brought her lips closer to mine. This was it. Her lips were big and soft, yes, but she didn't kiss or taste any different from any other women. I was slightly disappointed. Only slightly. We snogged the whole way through George Michael's Careless Whisper, eighties love songs never having gone out of fashion in Limerick. My heart was beating too fast. My dick was too hard. Fucking coke, no blood left for my brain. I needed to sit down before I fainted.

We found a soft seat and she sat on my lap, her arms around my neck. We talked for a while. Her friends came round. Not as hot, unfortunately. But that didn't bother Dave, who'd hooked up with an amazing babe from someplace well east of Limerick. Funny how all these people wound up in Europe's last outpost.

I was dizzy, beginning to hallucinate, throbbing nausea at the pit of my stomach.

Dave disappeared again and I asked Etoile if she'd like to come back to my place for a while. She said 'Yes, but I have to get home by four.'

No problem.

CHAPTER 15. GHOST TOWN

We got our coats back and headed out into a humid, still night. Town was dead. Sometimes that's good, sometimes that's bad. That night it was bad. We walked through empty streets, her heels clicking, my mouth laughing. I felt good, holding her hand, imagining the sex, until we turned a corner and saw the three teenage knackers walking towards us.

They were eating chips out of brown paper bags, the stink of vinegar drifting, burning my tender sinuses.

Each had a shaven head, wore the knacker uniform: hoodies, sports gear, Nike logos. Eyes of sharks, predatory and emotionless. Out of it on something serious. Big fucking trouble, in other words. My muscles tensed, adrenaline flooding my alcohol-sodden bloodstream. My fists were clenched before they even registered me. I held Etoile's hand tightly.

Suddenly, contact.

'Look at the nigger lover, lads!' one cried, 'Do you like niggers, shom?'

I said nothing. She looked at me, scared. We kept walking.

'Stupid gowl. Look at you, shom! What's wrong with Irish birds?'

'Fuckin gowl,' chirped the last.

I thought they'd just take the piss and pass by. They didn't seem much older than thirteen or fourteen, but those little fuckers are often the most dangerous. They can kill or rape and only get a couple of measly years in a home. And the fuckers know it, as do the gangsters who use them to transport drugs and guns.

They got closer, staring into our faces, ready for their feeding frenzy. Etoile tightened her grip on my hand. They stopped, blocking our way.

'I hear they like it up the arse, shom.'

'You'll have a brown langer tonight, you gowl. One way or the other.'

'I bet she's a cheap whore an all, the dirty fuckin monkey.'

This last comment was too much for me. First rule of streetfighting: Get In First. My heart was crashing through my chest, every muscle ready. Cocaine literally makes you feel invincible. I let go of Etoile's hand.

'Finished?' I asked.

Dead eyes looked back, especially on the biggest one, in the Man U tracksuit. Wasn't used to getting lip back. Slow bewilderment. He reached a hand inside his jacket. My cue.

I flicked my cigarette into the middle-sized one's face and loafed the big one first, right between his vacant eyes. A satisfying crack and he fell to the ground in a crumpled heap, his knife clattering. The others were stunned, which gave me time enough to kick the little one hard in the balls before he had a chance to react. Number three lashed out at me with his fist, but he only caught me a glancing blow off the side of my head. I felt nothing, turned to face him.

I saw surprise in his baby face - this wasn't how it normally went - and he backed off, just a fraction. I lunged for him and managed to grab him by his shellsuit, gave him a headbutt just as squarely as I'd done his buddy. He was a little shorter than me, so my skull's arc ended on the bridge of his nose, which made a wet crunch and then bled heavily.

He was on the ground then, while the guy with the sore balls just stood there, clutched his crotch, a look of pained confusion on him. There were tears in his eyes, just a fucking child. Anger welled up inside me. I hadn't been in a fight in years. I'd always used my mouth to avoid aggro, but now I was relishing the fight, close to losing it completely.

'Now, ye little cunts. Are ye finished?'

Silence. Good for them. I was ready to kick them to death. I really, really wanted to. Etoile held my arm, pulling me away.

'I'll take that as a yes.'

She was unscathed, and she took my hand. The knackers shouted after us - You're fucking dead, you gowl - but I wasn't listening. The main cop shop was up ahead and I didn't want to risk a public order charge. Not tonight, no fucking way. Etoile kept telling me how brave I was and how much of a gentleman I was. That helped, but a heavy, throbbing pain began to boil up in my forehead, while the nausea in my stomach was overtaken by a sense of dark foreboding. I thanked God they'd only one knife on them.

CHAPTER 16. NEARLY NEVER WON ANYTHING

So we got back to my place. My head wasn't bad. Some bruising and a little blood. It would be shit in the morning, but there was no need to interrupt the planned romance with a late night trip to casualty in the pain-wracked hellhole that is Limerick Regional Hospital. I fixed some screwdrivers and offered her a line of coke. She'd never taken it before, so I coaxed her into trying a little line. She snorted it and coughed and sneezed for about ten whole minutes. We laughed. I had no such trouble and the drug helped to ease the throbbing in my forehead, to forestall the agony that would surely come. I fished out my favourite Bob Marley CD, *Babylon By Bus*, and stuck it on.

'Not all black people are obsessed with Bob Marley, you know.'

'Sorry, I just thought - '

'Like you said yourself, colour is only skin deep.'

'So what do you like?'

'Got any Bowie or U2?'

'U2? You what? Only every album they've ever done. Hang on. Are you fond of sand dunes and salty air?'

'Of course.'

'Then it'll have to be Groove Armada, won't it?'

We kissed for an age on the couch, happy mood music, just a little lamp lit. I wanted to make love to her right there, but she'd only let me fondle her remarkable breasts. This Catholic thing seemed genuine. 'Too soon,' she said. 'Too soon.'

We talked and she seemed to get me. After three, I called her a cab. She kissed me for a long time while the cab waited outside. I gave the driver a tenner. Before they drove off, she opened her window and kissed me again.

'See you next week at the disco?'

'For sure! Good night!' Something jumped in my brain. 'Hey! What age are you, by the way?'

She looked me straight in the eye and smiled. 'Nineteen.'

And she was gone.

Half my age. For fuck's sake.

There was no way out. She'd tried to force the door open with her feet, her back arched against the back wall. No good. It was pitch dark, but the surfaces smelt and felt like wood. She figured she was in a wardrobe or something.

She could have been in there a day or just a few hours. She had nothing to which she could relate time. The prick'd taken her watch, her rings, her necklace. When he grabbed her off the street and into his van, this was the last thing she expected. She knew him to see him, knew he was a hard man in Moyross, knew he was a fucking nutter.

'Let me go, you prick,' she screamed at him.

He slapped her hard in the face and warned her to shut up. He pushed her face into the passenger seat as he drove. She knew that nobody outside could see her. She was in deep shit.

He drove to a house out the road, a quiet place with not a sinner around. He took her by the hair and dragged her into the house. Up the stairs and into a bedroom. She was afraid he was going to rape her. It was what she feared most.

'Be quiet and be good and you'll be alright,' he said.

His face was impassive, showed no emotion. Then he put a rag over her mouth. It smelt of chemicals, went right through her mind and she blacked out.

When she woke up, she was in the wardrobe. She was thankful that she hadn't been raped and expected the police or her mother to open the door any minute.

'Thanks mam,' she'd say. 'I promise I'll be a good girl from now on. For always. I love you mam.'

She practiced this over and over, whispering to herself, not knowing that she had much more to fear.

CHAPTER 17. BLACK LABRADOR

The rest of the night passed slowly, with sleep a distant, formless desire.

My ticker was still going ninety and the pain in my head was back more than ever. I spent the night pacing the house, turning things on and off. Then the sky woke up, so I closed the curtains and made tea.

I smoked cigarettes with early morning Sky News on low. I almost choked when LIMERICK GANGLAND SLAUGHTER scrolled across the screen. Volume, quick.

'Police in Limerick in the Irish Republic are investigating three brutal murders which have shocked a city that has seen more than its fair share of violence in recent years. Yesterday afternoon, the decapitated body of a man was pulled from the River Shannon,' said the talking head.

Cue footage of the scene I'd witnessed from Brian's balcony.

'The man was identified as a member of one of the city's top drug gangs. The rest of his body hasn't yet been found. Later that day, a grisly scene unfolded just outside the city, when the bodies of two men were found in a derelict mill, by a woman walking her dog.'

Cue footage of police tape across an open gateway into an old ruin. Nightfall. Powerful floodlights on metal tripods and forensics guys in white plastic overalls milling about.

'Police have not yet formally identified the two men, who had been shot in the head, but local sources believe that they were members of a rival gang. It is now feared that a tit-for-tat war has broken out between the gangs, the prize being control of Limerick's drugs market.'

They skipped on to the next item, which was yet another suicide bombing in a Baghdad restaurant, so I turned the volume back down low.

'Now Limerick tops the Iraq war.'

I often spoke aloud to myself. It was part of the adjustment from family to single life. My heart, which had become relatively relaxed, was now pumping full blast again. My hands shook as I made another joint. The penny dropped, rattling my brain as it bounced off every tangled neuron. O'Doherty was using his brother's death to start a turf war. If he planned it right, the Brownes would be confused and scared shitless and the cops would stand back and let him get on with it.

Why so keen to kill? Limerick has more than its share of big colleges. That's over fifteen thousand students who like nothing better than a couple of Es a week and hash every night. Add in the demand for speed coming up to exam times, plus the indigenous drug-using population - coke is their preferred buzz - and you've got a massive market. It's been said many times that drug dealing is just capitalism taken to its logical conclusion. And so it is.

So O'Doherty used me. But why? I'm the only one who can connect him with his brother's murder and upset his plan. So why? What does this fucker have in store yet?

Bollocks. What a fucking dupe. My addled brain couldn't comprehend which cog in the machine I was supposed to be, besides the spare prick who was taken for a ride.

I had a terrible feeling in the pit of my groaning stomach, a feeling of dread and impending fucking doom. Good morning.

TV recycled the Limerick story every hour, but they had nothing new to add, so I switched on the radio in the kitchen. The local stations were full of it, nationals too.

The dog was a black Labrador, name of Dora.

I caught sight of my face in a small round mirror on the fridge. I looked like shit. My forehead was a massive purple and red bruise. It would have been obvious to a nun that I'd headbutted someone. Fuck. And the pain. Plus, there was this tedious ache. Deep inside, right of my bellybutton. Liver or kidneys or something. Fuck again. I fished in the drawers for some Solpadeine. Eureka! I took the last four. They fizzed gently in a glass of tap water and the pain in my head began to ease within minutes of drinking the foul concoction. If I had to vote for the best invention in human history, headache tablets would be right up there with the Pill. And vodka. And cocaine. All chemicals.

I washed my face with a wet cloth. I made a mental note to go into town later, find something for my bruise. Holistic, pharmaceutical, anything. For now, a bag of frozen peas ought to help. The freezer was bare, save for some frozen pancakes, assorted bread ends and half a bag of corn-on-the-cobs. So I held a Green Giant against my tender skull, worried about winding up in a freezer myself.

CHAPTER 18. HARD DOUGHNUTS

So Dave arrived, carrying a bag of doughnuts.

'They're from yesterday. What happened your head? You look like the fucking elephant man.'

'I was bringing that bird back, whole other story, I'll tell you, and three little knackers called her a nigger whore. There, on Henry Street.'

'Little fuckers. And you nutted them?'

'Two. One I gave an unmerciful kick in the balls, ruptured him.'

We laughed at my exploits.

'Who were they?' asked Dave, some concern on his face for the first time. 'You know you'll see them again, yeah? This fucking kip of a town is too small for you not to. Did you recognise any of them?'

'To be honest, no. All I saw was the skinhead haircuts and the Nike suits. They were just standard knackers.'

'Fuck. We'll have to ask around. They should be easy enough to spot for a few days, anyway.'

'Would they have gone to a hospital?'

'Who'd know that? Sara?'

'Yeah. If they went to the Regional, she'd have names and addresses. I'll call her. Coffee?'

'Cool.'

We went to the kitchen, which faced north and was always the coldest and darkest room in the house. Not pleasant. Maybe it helped to mess up my life in that house, my days always beginning with dark cereal and frigid coffee.

There was a week's worth of dirty dishes and spoiled food, every work surface hidden.

'So, you reckon O'Doherty's behind everything?' I asked, clearing a space in the chaos.

'No doubt. He is the puppet master, your Svengali.'

'Or Geppetto. Am I Pinocchio? Am I next?'

'I don't know. I don't know why he'd bother using you for the pictures. He could have just killed him anyway.'

Dave pondered, rubbing his chin in an exaggerated way.

'Fuck this for a game of soldiers,' I said.

'Maybe for his family? Whatever about framing the Brownes for it, he knows the truth'll come out at some stage. The pictures are his insurance for the family,' said Dave, making sense.

'But how can the truth come out if I'm the only one who knows? Did he kill him himself?'

'Fucking weird.'

'Hang on a sec. In the castle, as soon as he saw the pics, he sent a text, like he was giving the execution order.'

'Well, there was no fucking around anyway. The body was found just a bit after you met O'Doherty. It must have been dumped at the far end of the Island and floated downstream towards Brian's when you got there. The timing's right.'

'So O'Doherty's heavies, or some contracted fuckers, killed him, cut off his head, then fucked him in the river. Nothing to connect O'Doherty. No forensics, nothing. And I'm his alibi.'

'Clever.'

'You don't get to rule Limerick's biggest gang without being a special breed of fucker. This guy's something else. I'm in deep fucking trouble, Dave. Deep shit.'

'Up Shit's Creek.'

I drank some coffee quietly. The day was off to a horrific start and it was only just gone nine. I thought again of Sara, rang her. It was a calculated gamble.

I hadn't called her in a couple of weeks. We used to be shag buddies, meeting every so often for a late night or early morning bit of sex, depending on her shifts. The chemical spark between us – once unstoppable – had died quickly. She was a doctor: nice car, access to drugs, fabulous arse and a definite mad streak. But too serious, too analytical, too controlling to put up with me forever. And she cost me my marriage. Okay, she was the straw that broke the camel's back, so.

'Hi babe, how you doing?'

'Long time no hear. Got yourself a new girlfriend?'

'No, not really. What can I say?'

'Say you're sorry.'

'Sorry.'

'That's better.'

'Okay,' I said.

'And?'

'And I was wondering if you were working last night?'

'No, I'm only after starting. Why?'

'I'm just trying to track down a couple of young fellahs. They were in a fight in town around two or three this morning. Two head injuries. They might have gone out to ye for dressings or whatever.'

'Age?'

'Early teens. Standard knacker types.'

'You were in a fight with them weren't you?'

'Yeah.'

She was quiet for a few long seconds.

'Well I'm not sure if I want to give you the information you need to go after them.'

'I'm not going to, I promise.'

The thought hadn't really occurred to me. What would I do? Call to their houses in Moyross or Southill or Weston and threaten them? What a damned mess.

'I just want to know where they're from, self-preservation, that's all.'

'Okay. I'll look it up on the system. Call you in a while. Later.'

I turned to Dave, who'd been listening in.

'If we can find them, it might be better to scare them off,' he suggested.

I looked at him, an eyebrow raised.

'Go on.'

'You know what it's like. You will meet them again some time. If they recognise you, they'll stick a knife in you. It's not good news, but it's reality.'

'It bites.'

We sat down for a while, smoking joints, watching the news. I began to melt into the couch. Then my phone rang. The display flashed Sara.

'What's the story?'

'I suppose it's a case of do you want the good news first or the bad news?'

CHAPTER 19. REALLY BAD NEWS

Sara sounded just a tad anxious. And she was used to dealing with stress. So, not good.

'Good news, please. Good news always gets priority.'

'Good news is that none of them was seriously injured. We got one with a broken nose and one with, wait for it, a ruptured testicle.'

'Shit. Who are they?'

'Well, that's the bad news. They're from Moyross. One's called Jimmy O'Rourke and the other's Sam Flynn, of *the* Flynns.'

'Flynn, from Moyross,' I repeated, so Dave could hear. The colour dropped from his face and he mouthed a silent Fuuuck.

'Yeah. He's the one with the busted ball. He's, let's say, upset. Broken nose was allowed home, but ball boy is still in. I checked. He's got a few blokes in with him now.'

'Blokes?' My blood froze.

'Yep. Real heavy-looking. Three of them. And their language is worse than yours,' she laughed. 'Do the names mean anything to you?'

'One, yeah. The Flynns in Moyross are part of a Provo splinter cell. Hardcore, well-armed nasties.'

'IRA?' she whispered.

'Not exactly. Maybe Real IRA. It's just a handy cover for their dealing and thievery. Helps scare the competition away.'

'Well you better be careful. Sounds like they're coming after you. Have you called the police?'

'No. I don't think I want to. Not yet, anyway. Can you go back and try and overhear anything?'

'I'll see.'

'Be careful. Oh, Sara?'

'Yeah?'

'Any idea how long he'll be kept in?'

'Could be a couple of days. I'll try and find out.'

'You're an angel.'

Dave was still quiet. He shook his head, as if trying to dismiss what he'd just heard. But it wouldn't go away.

'This is deep, deep shit, bwana.'

'I know, man. I know.'

My hands began trembling and I made my way to the stash box for my drugs. My crutches. I imagined I heard the squealing tyres of a stolen car as it crashed through my front door. I looked through a narrow gap in the curtains to see three huge seagulls ripping open my rubbish bags, which hadn't been collected. Again. The birds looked at me derisively and continued their work. They had my number, the bastards. I cursed them and went back to Dave in the kitchen.

'Maybe you could call O'Doherty?'

'For what?'

'To put some pressure on the Flynns, as a favour to you.'

'Why would he want to do me a favour?'

'You're his alibi. You're worth more to him alive than dead.'

'Thanks, Dave.'

'I'm sorry. I didn't mean it like that. I'm just trying to think of a way out.'

He had a point.

'You're right. It might be my best bet, now that you mention it.'

'Do the Flynns work on their own?'

'As far as I know, yeah. I'm not sure where they get their drugs from. I'll have to find out.'

'Who'd know?'

'A copper. I'll call Pat.'

'Won't he finger you for the ball-breaking?'

'Probably. I don't think he'd care.'

'Give him a ring.'

I called Pat, who was at work and couldn't talk. He sent me a text twenty minutes later, saying he'd meet me after work for a pint. He'd confirm later. I replied *Cool*.

'Okay. We should know more about the Flynns by tonight.'

'Should you stay here or head to my place?'

'With your wife and heir there? Nah.'

'What am I supposed to do for you so?'

'You know what you could do? Make me another set of O'Doherty's dirty pictures. As an insurance policy.'

'Okay. Where did you put the negatives?

'They should still be in my jacket. Hang on.'

Got my jacket and rummaged in its many pockets, found the negatives, thanked the stars that they hadn't been lifted by the cloakroom jockeys at the disco.

He held the negs up to the light, what light there was.

'You know what, Charlie?'

'What?'

'These could be worth a fortune to the papers. A mint. Maybe ten grand.'

'Are you insane?'

'Think about it. If we could do it so there was no connection to you, who'd know? It would frame O'Doherty for the murder of his brother as the jealous husband and we'd get the cash. Or you'd get the cash, they're your pics.'

'O'Doherty would kill me in a second.'

'If he could get hold of you, maybe.'

'You mean leave town?'

'Why not? You hate it here anyway.'

'No, Dave. Just get the set of pics for me. Please.'

I said I'd call him around noon. I double-locked the front door after him and looked out through the crack in the curtains. Black clouds tumbled in from the south and spat gobs of tepid rain at my window. Spat at me.

My phone rang. It was Sara, reporting that Flynn's testicle was fucked and would have to come out. He'd be in for a week either way.

Worse, she overheard him talking to his brothers. There were two older Flynns and they did most of the business. They were old-fashioned nutcases. Sara heard them talk of getting the boys out and catching whoever did the ball breaking. But they didn't seem to know my name, which was good news. They spent lots of time on their phones, which meant that the bush telegraph was crackling with questions about an incident on Henry Street in the early hours. Maybe I had a breathing space. Maybe I was clear. I thanked Sara and asked her to keep tabs as much as she could.

I drank more coffee, then decided to risk a trip to the health food shop and the chemist. My forehead bruising was getting blacker and I didn't want to be recognised as Flynn's attacker for very long. I wore a Yankees baseball cap, pulled right down at the front. It really worked, totally hiding the damage. My confidence returned.

Dave's suggestion that I get out of town played on my mind. Maybe he had a point: I realised that I didn't really like what Ireland had become. What it had made me. What it could yet do to me.

CHAPTER 20. SEX WORK

The brothel in Limerick was a disappointment. During the day, with all the lights on and no distractions, the filth and stink disillusioned her further. The Romanian cleaners did their best but the place was beyond redemption. Used to be a cheap hotel. Nothing like the gleaming, purpose-built clubs back home where she'd learnt the business and caught Karpov's eye.

A late spring in Moscow and, over a frigid glass of Dom Perignon, he was delighted to learn of her degree in business and her desire to manage. He immediately offered her a position.

'Believe me, Leila, if I'd known you before, you would have won Miss Russia. Third was the best you could have done without connections.'

'You know me now,' she laughed.

Weeks later, Leila found herself in Limerick, a place she'd never even heard of.

She was made manager of Pussy Galore, of which Karpov owned half. Indirectly, of course. He would soon own it all and he had great plans for the Irish market, so Leila's role had superb growth potential. He insisted that she dance also.

'You are so beautiful, it would be bad business to keep your divine body covered up.'

She didn't mind. She also didn't mind having sex with him when he needed it. To Leila, sex was simply a biological function, like eating or going to the toilet.

So she was generally happy. She'd just have to put up with the customers, which was easy for her. They were all the same, the Irish, the Chinese, the Arabs, the Russians, the blacks. All were easy to read, easy to manipulate, easy to exploit. Some thought they were cleverer, in control. They were simply deluded. Their wealth was sucked from them over time, by a highly professional operation, run according to the mantras of the Harvard Business School.

Karpov promised that he was grooming her to run his operations in Ireland, everything. So she learned about human-trafficking, the drugs trade, weapons and the smuggling secrets that made everything possible. Taught by the master.

'The front is what's most important,' he told her repeatedly. 'That's our cover, our visible means of support. All else comes from that.'

'You have so much money already,' she teased. 'Why risk it all?'

'Risk? There is no risk. We have friends at the highest levels of government, society and police. They all want money and I can give them that. Sex and thrills also. The local criminals are illiterates, mere thugs. They are but a slight distraction, one that will soon be erased.'

'How?'

'All in good time, Leila. Remember, there is one advantage I have over all the players.'

'Your good looks? Your charm? Your sophistication?'

'I'm smarter,' he laughed. 'Now let's go over your Excel projections.'

CHAPTER 21. LUCKY?

The nearest bookies was just around the block, under Sarsfield Bridge. I whistled in and chose a few bets after a leisurely read of the form. There were one or two names I'd been watching out for. That was a good omen. I put a hundred each on the noses of five horses. I would stand to win about four grand if they all came in. I checked my slips, took a slow look around the roomful of wily delinquents and split.

I picked up some stuff in a chemist's, then shot into Tesco, weaving past the small army of security men that kept the barbarians from the gate.

My eye was caught by a TV monitor. It was still Limerick on the news. The face had changed, but the story was the same. They named Luke O'Doherty and showed a grainy old photo of him, with a bushy head of sandy hair and a thick moustache. He was good-looking, in his way.

'Where's your head, Luke?' I muttered.

I strolled home with the shopping bags cutting into my fingers and was at my door in five minutes.

I cleaned the house. It took two hours and I was shagged by the end of it, despite having drunk a few cans. Sara rang. On her way. I checked the bed and positioned two condoms under my pillow in case I got lucky. Kept the third in my pocket.

I lit some candles and answered Sara's knock just before five. She looked good and gushed with sympathy after a look at my forehead. I was ordered to lay on the couch and was fussed over for a good ten minutes as she cleaned and dressed the wound. She washed her hands and disposed of the medical waste. I now had a big dressing stuck to my forehead. I looked like the victim, no more the aggressor.

'Don't worry. You can take it off in two days. It's just to protect the bruising while it heals. I put some cream on to help. You still look okay.'

'Promise?'

'I'll prove it,' she said, sitting down beside me then.

She kissed me slowly and firmly. Her hands squeezed my hips and her legs shifted.

'Would you like a drink?' I asked, changing the subject, uncomfortable.

'I thought I was getting something else.'

'I just feel - '

'Feel what, Charlie?'

'I feel guilty. I know it's stupid. This house, the past, whatever.'

'You're right. It's the past. Why don't you sell up and get a nice new apartment or something? Is it really permanent with Deirdre?'

'I'd say so. I'm just empty, no feelings for her. I'd have to give her half, even though she's with her rich mammy and daddy.'

'You'd have enough. A small mortgage on top of your share and you'd be fixed.'

'You could be telling the truth.'

'You know I am.'

She kissed me again and gently pulled me closer to her. She undressed us both. I put a condom on.

My guilt grew heavier as I lay on her for long minutes. The baggage. She writhed, but nothing happened.

'You're hurting my hips, love.'

'Sorry, must be the stress and all.'

Our love was a zero. All gone.

I pushed myself off her and she pulled her legs up. We sat on the couch together and switched on TV. We watched the news with glasses of Beaujolais and ordered in a pizza.

Drinking more wine we caught a movie on TV, *Barbarella* with Jane Fonda. Then we went to bed and she fell asleep straight away. My forehead ached like a bitch and I was pissed off, felt useless, decrepit. I drifted into an uneasy sleep, all my contradictions jostling for attention as I wondered exactly who was out to get me.

A tiny white cottage. By the beach. A dog. Hammocks. Me with a little fishing boat on the sand. Fixing nets, painting the boat. Small work, but deeply satisfying. There's someone in the house, a woman - dark hair, tanned skin - and she's waving out at me. She looks happy.

The smell of the sea and the screeching of gulls. Looking out to sea to sense the swell. Come go with me. Do I hear kids laughing, or is that the birds?

This doesn't fit, complains my brain.

CHAPTER 22. THE VALUE OF LIFE

Precious had learned her skills in South Africa, under her grandmother's guidance. It amazed her that, given how science had come to dominate the world - even eclipsing religion in the developed north - muti continued to grow in popularity. But she wasn't complaining, for it had made her the richest woman in the shanty. She was respected.

She'd been travelling for seven years, had worked her way up to Zimbabwe, across to Nigeria, Ivory Coast, Senegal and on to Europe. Europe was easily the most profitable leg of her long business trip. There were many migrants who had done comparatively well in England, yet still desired the muti magic. And every euro or pound she earned was worth twenty times as much back home, where she would soon be the Muti Queen of Jo'burg.

After London, she found herself in Ireland. Her agents advised that she base herself in Limerick, near the growing immigrant population, and the clients would be sent to her.

A house in Moyross was rented for cash, no names, no trails. The crazy man who rented it to her - Mickey Flynn - showed great interest in muti and was excited by her mubobobo. This potion would allow a man to become invisible, so that he could have sex with any woman and she wouldn't even know it was happening. Like a mystical Rohypnol. Flynn used mubobobo successfully, raping a young mother while she slept. So his belief in muti grew stronger.

He demanded more powerful magic. And a Nigerian businessman from Dublin wanted to cure his AIDS. And a woman she'd befriended wanted to entrap a husband for citizenship. And a South African couple wanted their business to grow stronger. All these demands led to one essential requirement: a virgin girl.

Flynn brought the girl, just a child. The ceremony was performed in a field out past Cappanty Woods, at midnight, with a pregnant moon in the sky. All who would benefit from her death were gathered. The mood was nervous, excited. They each took a sip of opiate-laced potion.

After the girl was drugged, the Muti Queen made her incantations. The man with AIDS had sex with her, the others holding her down. And so he believed he was cured.

The Muti Queen opened a big patchwork handbag, drawing a long blade with an evil glint and a heavy meat cleaver. She kissed the blades and made a deep incision on the girl's neck. The girl's screams increased the potency of her parts. She died. Then her chest was neatly torn open and her heart was cut out and given to the woman who wanted a husband.

Then her hands were cut off for the restaurant owners, to attract more customers. Her Atlas bone - which connected her neck to her spine - was removed and given to Flynn. This most powerful of human parts would ensure he had control over the minds and bodies of his chosen women, and give him the strength of a horse.

Then the girl's nipples, tongue and vulva were cut off by the Muti Queen for use in vuka-vuka, sexual stimulant. Finally the bellybutton, which she wrapped with care in a velvet cloth. These parts she put in her case.

Everybody helped cut the child's remains into small pieces. The magic had taken them. The bloody bits were placed in a black refuse sack and the sack was thrown into the rushing stream.

It was over. The Muti Queen was two thousand euros richer. The group dispersed and she went back to her house, where she washed all traces of AIDS-infected semen from the vulva and worked with herbs and spells until dawn preparing the vuka-vuka, which would be worth at least another two thousand up in Dublin. A good night's work.

CHAPTER 23. GALILEO, FIGARO

In the morning, Sara was gone. I woke with confused memories of the seaside. Everything hurt as I pulled the stupid-looking dressing from my brow.

To work. *Thank fuck it's Friday*, my mantra.

Inside the office building's front door, in the grubby hallway, was a list of the businesses that lived there. Including DOYLE & ASSOCIATES. No associates really, it just sounds better. Of the twenty or so businesses listed, I figured only a couple were genuine. The others were fronts for various schemes and scams. Mainly run by Margaret's husband. Margaret, who managed the place, was on her own at reception.

'Morning Margaret, how are you this fine Friday?'

'As in Thank feck it's - ?'

'You better believe it.'

She was fifty-odd, grey-haired and overweight. And she loved her gin, always a bottle stashed in her desk somewhere. Came in handy a few times. Wonder if she ever sussed it was watered down?

'I've to get to the bookies at some stage. I put a few bets on yesterday.'

'Oh? I've the paper here if you want to check.'

She handed me her copy of the *Racing Post*, along with my mail and messages. A fondness for the nags was an interest we shared. I flicked through to the results.

'Yes! Come on baby. Where's number two? Yes! And, incredibly, yes again.'

'Any good?'

'Three winners, Margaret. Three glorious answers to my daily question Do the Gods conspire against me or am I just an unlucky bastard? The answer is a resounding triple-no! How sweet it is!'

'I thought you didn't believe in God? How much?'

'Let's see. On Fat Larry, five hundred, on Fandango, three and on Beach Bum Bono, seven hundred. That's - '

'Fifteen hundred!'

I sang a verse from *Bohemian Rhapsody*. 'Nice or what?'

'Very nice. Will you buy me something?'

'Sure haven't I to pay my excessive bills in this place, Margaret? I'll have nothing left.'

'Just chancing my arm, Charlie.'

'As you must, Margaret.'

Elated, I took my bundle of mail and messages and floated up the two flights of dusty wooden stairs to my office. Three steps from the top, my phone rang. I stopped. I looked at the flashing screen and read NEWCLIENT1.

'Hello, Charles Doyle here,' I said, in my poshest phone voice.

'Good day, Mr Doyle.' She wasn't in great form. 'I need you to go ahead with the job, please. At the price we agreed?'

'Certainly. I'll get started today at the daily rate and report next week. Okay?'

'Very good. Will you please call me if you have any news?'

'I will.'

'Goodbye, Mr Doyle.'

'Have a nice weekend.'

My heart pounded so I could hear it in my head. She called! She'd been in a couple of weeks before. Inquiring about having her husband tailed. Doing the dirt, she figured. She'd left a picture of him and went away to think about it. I'd offered her my highest rates, a grand a day. A gamble. Her tan, her genuine Louis Vuitton bag, her Chanel suit, her understated gold. Real wealth. Her husband was a solicitor, clearly up to his armpits in everything and a bit of fluff besides. I'd get him. And make a fast grand or two in the process. She'd mulled. She'd realised that she was taking a step towards a different life. And she was hot. Mid forties, fit, blond, lovely teeth and a nice smile. A bit of class. Charlie was her man.

As I rooted through my desk drawer for her husband's photo, I muttered the usual Buy a filing cabinet and What a mess. Papers, pictures, betting slips, empty Coke cans, a flick knife, parking tickets, flotsam, jetsam. Gotcha. Old, boring, ugly. Typical. Brian Smythe, if you don't mind. Smythe-Ross solicitors, O'Connell Avenue. Fuck. Best time to start would be after work on Friday. Today.

I rang Dave, who wanted to meet for a lunchtime drink. That gave me half an hour.

The post was all the usual. Final Demand notices from my *How To Be A Private Detective* home study course, junk mail asking me to invest in some African kids or European wine, a bank statement with my balance squatting miserably in overdraft, a bill for the use of the office, three other bills, four final reminders, eight pieces of utterly pointless crap. Filed all under Jetsam.

Paid Margaret a few quid, got out of there.

The streets were busy and the bookies was full. With relish, I counted my winnings, placed a ton on Cleopatra's Ass, Uttoxeter, 2.10, and whistled my way to Dave's. He was quiet, no customers. Fiona stood smoking outside the front door. As usual, she was dressed all in black.

'Hi Fiona. When's the funeral?'

'What?'

'Dave about?'

'The back.'

'Coming for a drink?'

'If he'll let me close. We haven't done a feckin' thing all morning.'

'Let's ask, shall we?'

I knocked at the back office door. Dave shouted that he was finishing my prints and he'd just be a sec. I turned to Fiona, giving her my full attention.

'So, any news?'

'Just about that missin kid. Isn't it awful?'

'What kid?'

'It was on the radio a few minutes ago. There's a kid gone missin in Moyross, just up the road from me.'

'Today?'

'It happened last night, but it only came out today. A girl. Thirteen. Walked to the shop on her own. Never came back.'

'She's probably just run away or something, hiding out in the woods.'

'I hope so. The cops don't sound too happy. Fuckin useless they are.'

'Fuck's sake.'

Dave emerged, looking pale. What happens to people who work in darkrooms. He gave me the prints and I gave him two fifties, insisted he took them.

'Right, drinks,' he said, happy. 'My treat.'

'Fine,' I said.

Fiona looked in good form. Across to the local. The lunchtime news came on the TVs as we tasted our first drinks. The kid was all over it. Witnesses said they saw her being dragged into a white van. Not a good sign. Her picture flashed up, the cops pleaded for information, her mother cried her eyes out.

CHAPTER 24. ESCAPE

So I drank to escape. By two I was half-langers, good feeling. It was the weekend, I had a full wallet and felt a session coming on. While Dave was at the bar and Fiona was in the jacks, I took out my notebook and pen and wrote myself a memo of events before I lost the plot.

Fiona split back to open up the shop.

'So I forgot to ask you about the other night. How was your ladyboy?'

'She was no ladyboy,' Dave said.

'What?' I asked, incredulously. 'She was too beautiful to be a woman, too perfect.'

'She's a fucking lapdancer, Charlie, enhanced in every way. Perfection personified.'

He was smiling now, delighted with himself.

'You serious? A lapdancer? You?'

'What,' he asked, 'can't I score with a perfect babe?'

'Jesus man, you normally prefer a bit of rough. What about those two last weekend? Christ, I'd prefer a ladyboy myself.'

'Whatever.'

We talked about my forehead. We chilled.

'The Flynns are pure mad. *Worse* than the O'Dohertys.'

'Think they're connected?' I asked.

'I don't know. Why?'

'Dunno. Just a niggling feeling in the pit of my langer.'

We laughed, clinked glasses and time passed. The horses were on the box and Dave also had a few bets on. He couldn't believe the luck I'd had and was determined to top me. He failed miserably. I rubbed salt in his wounds when Cleopatra's Ass romped home at six to one. I was elated, yet full of self-doubt. How long could my lucky streak last?

Dave asked 'Have you much work on?'

'I'm supposed to be tailing a guy around now. Fuck.'

'Where to?'

'I'm expecting him to go to South's for a pint after work. Hopefully with a bit of fluff from the office.'

'I can do it for you.'

'What?'

'I'm in no rush home. He cries all the fucking time, I could swear.'

'It doesn't get any easier.'

'Fuck's sake.'

'Sorry. But thanks for the help. Okay. Here's his picture. I want some pics of him with a bird. You know the score.'

'Sound. I'll deal with this, you see if you can reach Pat. Ask him if he can sort you out with a gun.'

So I tried Pat's mobile, pictured him. He was the fast success. I was some kind of slow motion failure. That's why the Sara thing shouldn't - realistically - have happened. I was wrong for her.

Pat was right. But his coolness towards me was starting to thaw.

Got through. Told him the facts and he said Okay, it's time you got a dog.

'So when can I get it?'

'Any time, I'd say. Call this number, ask for Mr White and say Mr Red sent you.'

'*Reservoir Dogs* code?'

'Something like that. Got a pen?'

Took down the number.

'Where is he?'

'In Garryowen.'

'How much, do you reckon?'

'I'd say about four hundred. Be wide, though. He's a cute hoor.'

'How heavy are the others, Pat?'

'Pretty serious. They're not on my side of town, so I'd only know generalities.'

'Such as?'

'Such as there are three brothers. Nobody fucks with them. Worth about two million a year.'

'Not bad. And what about the RA connections?'

'Non-existent, we think. Since the peace process kicked in, anyway. The Flynns were handy at one time, not any more. Now they're a liability.'

'Any connection with the Island?'

'Not that I know. I'll try and get you some current pictures so you can watch your back better. I reckon they'll let it blow over. They wouldn't want to end up getting collared over one little bollock.'

'I sure hope. Thanks a million, Pat. Good man.'

'Be careful Charlie.'

I called the number.

'How are you? I'm looking for Mr White. Mr Red sent me.'

'Riiiiight,' he said.

'Would it be possible to meet up today?'

'Why, kid? Are you in a hurry?'

'Actually, yeah. I am.'

'Do you like dogs?'

'They're alright.'

'Meet me at the track in ten minutes. Can you do that, yeah? Knock at the staff entrance, Garryowen side. Tell them you're seeing a man about a dog.'

He laughed, delighted with his joke. I felt uncomfortable.

'How much should I bring?'

'For a decent dog? Bring a few hundred.'

'Okay.'

'And one more thing. No messin. Clear?'

'Clear.' Cranky old fuck.

He ended the call and I had one more dodgy number in my call register. I got a cab easy enough. We chugged through shitty traffic, past my old cunt of a school - CBS, Christian Brother Sadists, Paedo Central- around by St John's Cathedral, tallest spire in Ireland, and up the hill to the Markets Field. The cab driver asked why I was going to the track, so I told him To see a man about a dog. He didn't laugh, just sneered and stared at me hard in his mirror.

Like he knew what I was up to.

CHAPTER 25. ACE OF SPADES

Landed at the dogtrack. Knocked on the side door and waited. Gazed across at the wide fields in the middle of Garryowen. Pylons crossed the space where football was played, horses were run and heads were broken. Big guy with a black puffer jacket and earpiece opens up.

'How's it going? I'm here to see someone,' I said.

'Yeah? Who?'

'A man about a dog. Mr White.'

'What's your name?'

'Doyle. Charlie Doyle.'

'Over by the traps, so.'

I could hear dogs now, barking, whining. The track was old, decrepit, crappy. Some greyhounds were having a run, the sad hare whirring past, the dogs chasing it stupidly, eyes glazed, tongues hanging. Crowds were coming in the far side, their gates just opened.

The leading dog, totally black, looked handy. He won easily and a guy with a stony look smiled for a second, left the group and walked towards me. My man.

'He's a beauty. What's his name?' I asked.

'Ace of Spades.'

'Nice.'

I didn't know what to say next, so I kept my trap shut. He looked at me closely, searching for signs of excessive nervousness, or a setup.

'I'm Mr White.'

'Nice to meet you. I'm Charlie Doyle.'

With a flick of his head, we went back into the lobby, up four flights of concrete steps and into his office. Old photos of greyhounds on the walls and a nice view of the track. He gestured to a plastic chair, one of the bright orange ones with the tubular metal frame. I sat.

'Right. Three rules. Number one: if you tell anyone where you got the gun, you're dead. End of story. Is that clear?' I nodded *Yes*. 'Two: when you're finished with it, you fuck it into the Shannon. Rule three: refer to rule one and say it over and over in your head. Now, do you still want to go ahead with this?'

'Yes. I don't think I've any choice.'

'Fair enough. Show me your money.'

I went through my pockets and assembled over nine hundred. He smiled and unlocked his desk drawer. He reached in and put on latex gloves. Then he pulled out a revolver.

'Any experience with firearms?' he asked, an eyebrow raised above his glasses.

'No. I've shot a shotgun. Hunting.'

'Did you hit antin'?'

'No.'

'Right, well this shouldn't frighten you too much. Loud as a shotgun, though. This is a snub-nose Smith & Wesson thirty-eight, six rounds. Just safety off and fire. Easy to conceal. And you can see when it's empty.'

He was a persuasive salesman.

'How much?'

'Five. Bullets, two hundred for twenty four.'

'I'll only need six.'

'Right. I'll throw those in, so.'

I counted out five hundred and he showed me how to load and shoot the gun. Then he gave me six bullets in a transparent Ziploc bag.

'Don't take off the safety until you're ready to use it. These things have a habit of blowin guys' balls off.'

Another smile. The guy was warming to me.

'Okay. What's the best way to carry it?'

'Don't, would be my advice. Leave it in your car or your house. Get it when you need it. Then carry it in your inside jacket pocket. And keep a cool head with it. If everyone in Limerick carried a gun, we'd all be fucked.'

'So, be cool.'

'Yeah. Be cool.'

He was right. If I carried this thing around with me, I'd end up shooting someone, anyone. I put the gun and bullets into my jacket pocket. He took off the gloves and locked the drawer, then walked me down to the entrance and opened the door for me.

'When's the Ace running next?' Always looking for a tip.

'Tuesday night. Here.'

'Nice one. Thanks for everything.'

'See you round.'

So I was on the streets of Garryowen with a gun in my pocket. As I passed St John's, Dave rang. In the pub. My stomach growled, needed lining before I met that lush, so I strolled around by Donkey Ford's for a burger and a battered whiting and two battered sausages and chips. Old-school, proper food and all for under a fiver. Two knackers ate their grub on the kerb outside. The gave me dirty looks. I felt for the revolver, sneered at them. Fuck, I wanted them to start. They looked away. I ate on the hoof.

In the bar, Scissor Sisters played loud.

My pulse raced as I put a vodka and orange juice - the healthy option - to my lips. I saw my reflection in the Jack Daniel's mirror behind the bar. My forehead was much better, just a hint of bruise. But everything else was falling apart to my twisted Midas touch, all turns to shit. Maybe it would be easier for everyone if I just made a complete break, got the fuck out of Limerick, set up as a private dick in Malaga or somewhere.

'How'd it go in South's?' I asked.

'Grand.'

'I've something to show you.'

'What?'

I opened my jacket and lifted the butt of the revolver out of the inside pocket.

'Fuck me! Where did you get that?'

'I really, really can't tell. Rule number one. Nice, huh?'

'Deadly, man. Bring on the Flynns.'

'Bring 'em on.'

'Hey, why don't we head out to Moyross and find them ourselves, finish the job?'

'Sure.'

'Any chance of a go?'

'No chance.'

'How many bullets have you?'

'Six.'

'Should be enough. There's only three Flynns.'

'Two each!'

'Haha. I'd rather not shoot it, but if that little fucker from the hospital comes near me, I'll blow his other bollick off. You can chalk that down.'

'So what's the plan?'

'A quiet night in, I reckon.'

'Well I'm definitely heading out.'

'Good luck,' I said, thinking of my couch and a movie and a rest

CHAPTER 26. FEAR AND SMOKING
IN LIMERICK

I called Brian, mentioned greenery and he said Yeah, no problem. I walked towards the evening sun, in good form. But I kept my head down, glancing around and behind every few steps, for once glad to see cops on the beat, in their shirt sleeves, stab vests, shades, living out their *Miami Vice* fantasies. I made it to Brian's without incident. My day was made when I saw his red eyes and he handed me a bank coin bag full to bursting with skunk buds. We skinned up.

Brian opened the windows and the pungent smoke wafted out over the river.

'Do the neighbours ever complain?'

'About the smell? Nah. They'd know better. And I've got even better news.'

'Even better than this mighty fine skunk?'

I was staring intently into the design on the Rizla pack. It sucked me in. Lazy, stoned musings. Musings that felt like a life's work but lasted just seconds. If I chanced upon the meaning of life or a cure for cancer while stoned on skunk, it would have been lost to humanity.

Brian said 'Acid.'

That got my attention.

'Acid? You're shitting me?'

'Check it out.'

Brian went to his kitchen drawer and rummaged about. He had different drugs stashed in different places, mostly in the kitchen. You'd have to be careful if you were cooking there. He pulled out a large, dark Ziploc and, from this, lifted a sheaf of A4s. Must have been fifty sheets. Each sheet was perforated into scores of tiny tabs. Lysergic acid. LSD. The key to unlocking the Doors of Perception. Time to drop out of reality for a while. Perfect.

'It's been fucking ages, man!'

'I know. They're just in from Holland.'

Each tab had a little image printed on it. A cartoon picture of an assault rifle. Underneath, printed in red stencil lettering was AK-47. To me, this was a bit like Alice finding the bottle that said DRINK ME.

I ate an AK. Then one more. Brian suggested I wait to feel the effects before trying any more. Word was, they were mighty strong. He took two as well. When his back was turned, searching for skins or something, I sneaked another two. I like to do hallucinogenic drugs properly, no farting around. I drank some water straight from the tap. My mouth tingled. A strange sensation in my stomach, like being pregnant, maybe. It was anticipation. I lost myself in a shiny haze of wondering what it must be like to be a woman and be screwed. I didn't mention this to Brian in case he suggested I try taking one up the arse.

We chilled and smoked more skunk and had a couple of beers. Miller in clear bottles. We went and stood on the balcony as the day gave up. The evening rush was over and the frantic buzz of traffic across the whistling bridge was dying. The river was extra cool, all oranges and reds from the sky twisting around on the sleepy surface. Herring gulls hovered in the warm evening breeze. Then I saw a gull - a monster - peel off from his mates and make for me like a Jap Zero. He screamed towards me, spitting gull venom and pity. I cowered, crying like an senile fool.

'Whoa, Charlie.'

'Jesus Christ! Did you see that fucker?'

'Me man down below with the mad baldy head?'

'What? The fucking seagull, man!'

'The what?'

'That fucker there, he fucking attacked me.'

Brian leaned over the balcony rail, gazed out at the seagulls, strangely calm. I stayed in the flat, hiding in the kitchen, my tongue hanging now like one of those bastard greyhounds.

'It's okay, Charlie,' called Brian over his shoulder, 'They've fucked off. You're safe.'

It sounded good. But I knew it was just a ploy. Seagulls are very clever birds. And fucking vicious. Ever see their beaks? Hooks on the end, man! *Cut you to pieces.* I cowered in the kitchen on my knees, in the filthy corner where the sweeping brush and the dustpan lived. The evilness of the bird had unsettled me greatly. I saw hatred there, directed right at me. I was a mess. Again.

Brian managed to put on some music and it calmed me some. Ibiza trance, mellow and relaxing to my confused brain. Is this the real life? I made it out of the kitchen and drank some beer. The hallucinations seemed to come in waves. Every few minutes, my mind was seized by convulsions. My deepest memories came to the fore and were warped into new sensations. Sex. Holidays. Childbirth. Jellyfish. Words. All these and more flashed through my head, changing into dark creatures and bizarre shapes from other worlds, other dimensions. My brain was deeply addled. I decided to go for a walk.

'But it's dark out, Charlie,' said Brian.

'I don't give a fuck. I need to get away from these demons.'

'They're only in your head, man.'

'Like the seagulls, is it? I'm off. Bye.'

Brian stuffed the bag of skunk into my jacket pocket and stuck on *Pet Sounds*. He stood in front of the stereo, his body swaying, his arms flapping in the air.

'I can see the music, Charlie. I can see it! Can you?'

'Yeah man, the source.'

I retreated into my brain, the potent chemical having delivered its punch, frazzling my neural connections into clarity overload. Deep inside my frightened mind I made startling connections. I saw fantastic possibilities. I caressed utter madness.

I made all the coming badness possible, maybe made it real.

CHAPTER 27. CHARLIE DON'T SURF

The memory - after the seagull in Brian's - is of me and my gun. Flick out the chamber. Load a single bullet. Give the chamber a spin. Flick it back in. Point at mirror. Aim at head.

And *Apocalypse Now*, first with Robert Duvall and his surf commandoes, falling from the sky all rockets and Wagner and prayer and complex breaks. Then, with Martin Sheen and the riverboat crew, high on LSD, at the Do-Long bridge. A psychedelic battle with a relentless, unseen enemy. Confusion, panic and disorientation. The asshole of the world. Also subtle pains in my skull and a tendency to drop things. And Kurtz. Where's Kurtz? Who's Kurtz?

The moon was there too, laughing, pouring twisted rainbows onto my world where mysterious, lab-concocted lysergic acid was launching my neural pathways into a new place.

He'd been in the desert for days. He was thirsty, but otherwise fine: like he was a ghost, not really there. So the sun beat down by day and the wind howled by night, but still he walked on.

Once, a seagull swooped down out of the blazing sunset and landed on the hard sand just ahead. He walked up to it.

'Hello, brother seagull,' he said. 'Do you know where I can find a drink?'

'Aren't you afraid of me?' asked the seagull, twisting its head.

'No. Should I be?'

'Not really. If you were dead and I was starving, maybe. But then you wouldn't be afraid of anything, would you?'

'I suppose not.'

'Don't you know who I am?'

'Sorry. You all look the same to me.'

'Likewise. I'll give you a clue. I'm famous. I'm in a book.'

'Sorry.'

'I'm Jonathan Livingstone. Seagull. Ring any bells?'

'No. Sorry.'

'You should try to read more.'

'Okay. I will.'

'Didn't you even do me at school?'

'No. I can only remember *Lord of the Flies*. Now about that drink?'

'I can't believe you've never heard of me. I Googled myself and got nearly a billion hits. Impressed?'

'Yeah. Well done. I've a website. I think.'

'Www.lostinthedesert.com?'

'Haha.'

'Okay. Your drink. You see that snow-capped mountain over there?' he asked, cocking a wing towards the horizon.

'The one shaped a bit like a champagne bottle?'

'At the foot of that, you'll find a bar you'll like.'

'Cool. Why will I like it?'

'Because it has drink.'

'Cool.'

'I've to go. Book signings and all that.'

The seagull turned to face the breeze, stretched its wings, then lifted easily into the azure sky.

'Thanks a million!'

'You're welcome. Now don't forget the books.'

She'd just never get it. Ever. Pat was his partner and there was nothing he could do about that. Except get promoted. But that hadn't happened in fifteen years as a detective, so it was unlikely to start now. Anyway, Pat was the one set for stardom, he'd be onwards and upwards in a few months. No doubt there. Meanwhile, she'd have to just put up with the few late nights and the rest.

The rest. That was the main problem. Pat liked to burn his candle at both ends. Nothing strictly illegal as far as Frank knew, just not what he was used to.

Pat was mixing in high circles, mainly through family connections, but also school and rugby and the horses. Sometimes Frank would have to go with him while he fixed something. Pat the fixer. Good name.

While Frank would prefer to unwind with a quiet pint after a shift, Pat wanted champagne and strippers. Christ, what a night. But Frank was only sussed by the wife once. Leave him to it. Bad for the ticker. And the marriage.

Frank had so many things on his mind, he could barely keep up. Murder and carnage on the streets, Liz's moods and jealousy at home.

He checked the digital clock beside the bed. It was nearly six, time to get up soon. So he kept reading. For the eighteenth time in his life, he read about Michael Corleone's sojourn in Sicily, a smile creeping on to his worn-out face.

'I will go to Sicily some day,' he said.

After a minute, his wife said 'Unh?'.

Frank ignored her, kept reading.

CHAPTER 28. LOW

The killer ducked under the shutters and through the door. The shop was dark, Dave in the back office on the computer. Loud music, Bowie's *Low*.

Waiting for the gift of sound and vision.

He held the pistol behind his back, an old Colt.45 automatic with wet suppressor. Because it was in town and that. Closed the door.

'Hi Dave,' he shouted.

Dave turned, frowned, smiled. 'What's the story, man? Good to see you.'

And he was shot dead, a bullet through his forehead.

Dave'd been on the brink for ages. One or two little things would be enough to flip him into breakdown or escape. His mind was too active, too busy, as it tried to come to a decision. *Should he stay or should he go?* The Clash song was always there. Mostly hummed, but he'd break into it out loud when he was on his own.

He hadn't been ecstatic about his life for a few years, finding himself in that rut that hits everyone in their mid-thirties. Is this it? Is this all? Dead marriage, boring job, self-made crappy life, mortgaged. So everything successfully achieved from society's point of view. Except a kid. Okay, let's get one of those so. So. So another thirty, forty, fifty years of the same? No, he finally decided. Jesus Christ no.

But something clicked for him when he was called by the lapdancing club for a bit of glamour work. He thought, Yes I love my job and Now your life isn't so bad, is it? He assumed that he'd add an edge to his dull life, no more. It opened a door into a new perception of existence: a life with no conventional rules, where sex was an omnipresent commodity, where secrecy was critical, where sudden death was never too far away.

She was the third girl to call into him for a shoot. The first two hadn't much English, so they were accompanied by a Russian heavy. The heavy stood around in the front of the closed shop while Dave took some highly professional shots of the women - alone and together - in the back studio.

Woman Number Three called around alone, one Monday evening in winter. Her English was perfect. She was perfect. Stop the lights, thought Dave.

He had no intention trying anything on. The rules of engagement had been made perfectly clear to him. So he just chatted away to her as she undressed, finally revealing a red bra and knickers combo which perfectly complemented her dark hair and pale complexion. His erection was uncomfortable, so he had to lean really far forward into the camera, giving some room for manoeuvre.

'That's lovely. Nice colours.'

'Thank you.'

'So are ye making much above?'

'Not as much as you might think. The club makes a fortune, we get by.'

'I suppose that's the way of the world, isn't it?'

'I suppose.'

'That's it. Now look straight at the camera, hands on your hips. Yeah. Just spread your legs apart slightly. Perfect.'

'There's only one way we can make some extra income.'

He looked at the last few shots on the camera's LCD screen, happy with the levels.

'Lovely.' He looked at her now. 'What's that?'

'We offer our services to gentlemen.'

Dave stepped away from the camera, raised an eyebrow.

'Oh?'

'Yes, full sex for two hundred euro.'

'Two hundred?' he said calmly, thinking, Jesus Christ on a bike!

'For you, one hundred.'

'Let me check the till, so.'

The connection was perfect. Then came the parties. Dave was paid an absolute fortune to edit footage that was given to him by a middleman, someone he knew. He'd clean the footage, edit it and put it onto DVD. About twenty copies at a time. Piece of piss for him, but what an earner. Oh, and keep it to yourself, on pain of death.

The footage was a dream, mainly orgies. Meant he worked nights - when he wasn't on the drink - and weekends. But, as was always stressed, it was nothing illegal.

So he worked Saturday, waited to hear from Charlie who was AWOL. Dave was doing a bit for the Russians, for Leila.

The previous job was a bit of a pain, client wanted the masters. No way was Dave handing them over until he knew what was what and got a decent few quid. It's the professional ethics. He'd hold off for a couple of days yet, then Fox and Smythe would pay up, the rich fucks.

That's what he was thinking, right when his friend called by and the bullet easily pierced his skull and sprayed the whole place red. A bad poet might have called it a brain shower.

CHAPTER 29. DAMAGED

I woke to hot morning sunshine, blood and bullet holes. My head was exhausted, fragments of thought forming into a jungle tiger, a large bird, a machine gun. Then the dreams dissipated and my reality dawned.

Somehow, I'd made it to my own bed. I sat up and broken glass fell from the quilt. My window had been shot through, the glass all over me, curtains in tatters. My forearms were cut, but not badly. Half a dozen deep holes peppered the wall opposite the window. Bullets had whizzed over my unconscious body.

'What the fuck? What?'

Dazed and confused. A sharp but vaguely pleasant throbbing in the back of my head suggested psychedelics. Thought I must still be tripping. I got out of bed and, when I stood on some glass and felt the pain and saw the blood, I figured No, it's real. I looked out the window, saw a police car, a cop standing at the front gate. He saw me, was startled, gestured me down. I threw on my jeans out on the landing and stumbled downstairs, my brain fried stupid. The front door was minced, as was the front room and hallway. Like a bomb went off.

'What the hell happened?' I asked the cop. He was young, a fucking kid really.

'Have you been in there all this time?'

'What?'

'Have you been in there?'

'I was conked out. What happened man?'

'Someone emptied a magazine from an assault rifle into your house, about half seven this morning. Look at it.'

'Jesus H Christ!'

'When we came round the neighbours said the place was unoccupied. We saw the pile of post inside the door. That's why we didn't break in. Forensics are due soon, they would have put the door in. What's left of it.'

'Fuck's sake.'

The house was riddled with bullet holes. Every single pane of glass in the front was broken and the door was in bits too. Lumps of plaster and masonry littered the front garden. Proper bullets.

'And you heard nothing?' asked the cop, incredulous.

'I dreamt I was in *Apocalypse Now*. That must have been it.'

'Are you serious? Were you drunk?'

'Fairly locked.' *You can't handle the truth.*

'Hang on a sec.'

He stepped away and used the radio on his chest to call in and tell the boys back at the station his funny story. Yes, we found the resident and he slept through it. Haha. The talk of the cop shop. The laughing stock. When he came back, I asked if he'd like a cup of coffee, eager to escape the neighbours, a few standing at their front gates, staring at me. We carefully made our way to the dank kitchen.

'You're lucky, you know that?'

'Yeah, so my mam always told me. Instant okay?'

'Fine. So who do you think did this?'

Eager. Too fucking eager for my brain.

'No clue. I've never had this kind of trouble. Ever. I'm a private detective. Could be to do with that. I know a Garda detective, Pat O'Brien. Can you contact him?'

'Pat? He's due in a while with the forensics boys.'

'Forensics? What for?'

'We need to be sure what kind of weapon was used, for starters. Looks like an AK-47, based on the shells. We can try for prints on them and who knows what else.'

He shrugged, nodding his head towards the brass evidence that littered the footpath outside the front garden. Plastic crime scene tape hung limply from fence and poles.

'Any witnesses?'

'The neighbours on your right saw a car speeding off. No real ID on it, though.'

He pulled his notebook out of his breast pocket and started asking me questions. The same ones he'd asked before and some new ones. I needed a joint so badly. Really badly.

'Listen, would you mind if I went up and had a quick shower? Get some blood off me and put some shoes on?'

'No, I suppose not,' he said, disappointed.

'Great. Here's your coffee. There's your milk and sugar. I'll be down in ten minutes.'

I took my coffee to the bedroom with me, strong and black. It tasted like shit. I felt the urge to call Mr White. So I did.

'This is Charlie. Charlie Doyle. I met you yesterday.'

'What is it, Charlie?'

'I'm going to need something bigger.'

'Bigger?'

'Yeah, like I have a Jack Russell but I need a Pitbull.'

'Leave it with me.'

Sounded sorted. I looked out the window again and saw a TV camera and a couple of journalist heads across the street. Scanning, I saw a TV news van with its roof dish. Bullet-riddled houses make good news filler.

'You don't need to be on TV. Christ, once in my fucking life they want me and I can't play ball.'

Then I remembered the gun I already had. Jesus, what kind of fucking dope gets out of his head on acid while carrying a hot gun? My coat was hanging over a chair by the dressing table where my wife used to put on her war paint. I lifted the jacket, half afraid to check the pockets, but the weight told me the gun was still there. I patted it gently and realised that the house would shortly be crawling with nosy cops.

In for a shower. Assessed cuts. Both feet, left arm and shoulder, knuckles on right hand. Only little bastards, but sore all the same. Pain in the back of my head, deep, right at the base of my skull. I put my jacket on, so there was no risk of the gun getting out of my sight and laughed at my descent into chaos. I genuinely laughed.

CHAPTER 30. FORENSICS

My doorbell rang, the cop's way of getting my attention. I went downstairs, my head spinning ninety now.

'Forensics are here,' the cop said chirpily.

An unmarked Transit van had pulled up, darkened windows, new-looking. Two guys got out. Both wore hooded white coveralls, pulled on orange latex gloves. They looked like Oompa-Loompas. Tall Oompa-Loompas. One of them whistled when he got a look at the house.

'You were in there?' he asked.

'Yep,' I replied. 'Up there.'

I pointed at the bedroom window. He whistled again. The other guy picked up a shell, one of the dozens that littered the footpath.

'Jeekist, AK alright. 7.62 mill. Serious. If one of these had hit you, torso or head, you'd be dead.'

'Looks like the gunman got out of the car,' said the other, 'stood about here,' - he pointed an invisible gun at my house - 'let rip and got back in the car.'

'Why did he get out?' I asked.

'Two reasons,' said Oompa-Loompa One, 'better control when standing and no shells or firing residue in the car. Car was probably nicked and then burnt out anyway. All our evidence is right here.

Without a positive ID on the car, we'd have to find the gun in the shooter's possession to make a case.'

'Fuck,' I said.

'What about the bullets?' asked the eager young cop.

'Yeah,' said Oompa-Loompa Two, 'we'll dig a few out of the wall and see if they register on the records up in Dublin.'

'How?' I asked. I had half a notion what he was talking about, but my brain was running on empty.

'Every rifle barrel has little spiraling grooves inside. This rifling makes the bullet rotate before it leaves the muzzle, keeping it on target. Every bullet fired by a gun will have similar marks on it from the rifling. It's as unique as a fingerprint on a person.'

'So,' said the other guy, 'we've got files on every 7.62 round fired in Limerick in the last ten years on computer. If this gun was used before, we'll find out.'

'Sound,' I said, 'so this could lead us to the shooter?'

'Maybe,' said Oompa-Loompa One. 'But I fucking doubt it.'

They both laughed.

'Look lads, do I need to be here? Can I get away for a while? Go for a proper coffee? I'm withered.'

'The detectives will want to have a word with you,' said the uniform.

'When're they due?' I asked.

'I don't know, thought they'd be here by now.'

'Can I maybe give you my number and you can call me when they're on their way?'

He looked a bit confused, unsure what to say. The older forensics guy gave him a nod.

'Okay so,' said the cop.

I fingered the drugs in my pocket and felt the gun against my breast, found a card.

'I'll be on the Dock Road. Two minutes away, okay?'

The cop nodded and went to watch the forensics guys, who were taking photos of the shell casings and the bullet holes. Some neighbours were standing around and the TV crew lapped up the *CSI*-like shots. The neighbours tried to talk to me, but I put on a verge-of-tears act, looked sad and walked on, turning away from the camera.

Stopped in the shop, picked up a paper.

'What's with all the Sunday papers?' I asked.

'It's Sunday,' said the woman.

'Sunday? Are you winding me up?'

She shook her head and stepped back. Nutter alarm.

'Sorry. I'll take one anyway. Sorry.'

Sunday.

I laughed again as I got to the deserted bar and ordered a vodka tonic.

'You're barred,' said the barman.

'What for, man?'

'You don't remember?' he laughed.

'I swear! Please, not now.'

'Go on, so.'

Got through a night and a day and I could remember nothing. I got out my mobile and searched through my call register and texts.

There were a few missed calls, mostly Dave. And O'Doherty. What the fuck was going on? Was someone checking my location before the attack? Did this prove that the Flynns did it? Or did O'Doherty do it? Fuck. I'd need to talk to Pat ASAP. Grateful he'd be the investigating detective.

Messages. One from Sara asking where I was. One from Dave asking where I was. Call register showed I'd been talking to both my wife and Greg O'Doherty. That really threw me.

I drank and leafed through the paper. My photos of O'Doherty's wife and brother getting it on made a big splash, front page and page three. No photographer credit. I glanced around, then laughed quietly. Then Pat rang. He asked me to come back to the house right away. I said I would.

I swamped one more drink and strolled up the road, singing On a Sunday morning sidewalk, wishing God that I was stoned. The sun was out and it would have been a nice day for a barbecue. But that that was something the old me did.

O'Doherty was stuck in the middle of my mind. What the fuck did he want? I still didn't know whether I should call him back to find out, so I long-fingered that one.

Outside my house, Pat stood on the path looking at the shells. The young cop stood by, the forensics guys' van still parked.

'You're some character, Charlie,' smiled Pat. So someone could see the funny side.

'I know, I know.'

'That was a close one. I saw your bedroom.'

'Tell me about it. I actually slept through it.'

'You think it was the Flynns?' he asked, his expression serious.

'I can't think who else it could be.'

He lowered his voice, 'Did you get hold of a gun?'

I nodded.

'It's not in the house, is it?'

I pointed to my breast.

'So what do you reckon?' I asked.

'I reckon you'll have to come clean about the fight.'

'Is there any chance they'd want to press charges?'

'I don't know if they're interested in that sort of justice. Do you?'

'No, but it's a risk, isn't it?'

'Yeah. It's a risk. Did they start the fight.'

I wanted to lie.

'No. I started it. They called a girl I was with a nigger. I was out of it and I lost it. One of them pulled a knife. You'd do the same.'

'Would she lie for you? Say they went for you first?'

'I don't know. I only met her once.'

'Did you shag her?'

'No. She's Catholic.'

He laughed.

'Immigrant?'

'Yep. Fuck. She's married.'

'Fuck is right. Do you have her number?'

'No.'

'Charlie, you're not spinning me a line are you?'

'No, Pat, God's honest truth. What can I say?'

'Is there any way you can contact her?'

'No, but I was planning to bump into her again. With Dave.'

'Dave? How much of this does he know about?'

'Most of it.'

'Not clever, Charlie. You know he's turned into a bit of a tool since the baby.'

'I know.'

'Okay. Here's how we play it. You're going to come clean about the fight with young Flynn and his mates. You say nothing about who they are or what you know about them. I'll put the jigsaw together. Clear?'

'Clear.'

The forensics guys came out of the house, gathered all the shells and left, telling Pat they'd have the bullet analysis in twenty-four. Pat said 'Grand job, you guys are the future of law enforcement and fuck *Robocop*.'

Then Pat's partner came out of the house, a heavy middle-aged guy, thick moustache, Columbo-style coat. Tired eyes.

'Charlie Doyle, this is Detective Sergeant Frank Ryan,' said Pat.

I shook hands with Ryan and he asked Pat what the story was.

'Mr Doyle was involved in an altercation with some youths last Wednesday night,' explained Pat. 'He didn't report it at the time, but he feels that it's the only possible motive for this incident.'

'Why didn't you report it?' asked Ryan.

'I didn't think anything would come of it. Sorry.'

'We'll check with the hospital, see if anyone fits the bill,' said Pat.

'Hang on,' went Ryan, 'wasn't one of the Moyross Flynns in the other night. Lost a bollock or something?'

'Yeah, I heard that. Okay Mr Doyle, we'll check up on this lead. I have your number and I'll call you if we need anything more.'

'What about the house? Can I get it fixed up now?'

'Yeah. Forensics are done. Hang on.'

Pat fished in his jacket for his wallet, found it, then pulled out a business card.

'Here,' he said. 'These guys do a good job fixing up houses after this kind of thing. Give them a call. Tell them I gave you their number. Your insurance should cover it.'

'I'd say they're kept busy,' I said.

'Run off their feet,' answered Pat, walking towards their battered red Ford. He turned to me and winked enigmatically. The uniformed cop took down the crime scene tape and took a lift back to Henry Street station.

Then I was on my own again, realised that I needed company. I felt naked, victimised. Christ, I felt like a target.

CHAPTER 31. MURDER

I called the window guys. Told them I was a friend of Pat's. They said *Yeah, he called*. They were on their way.

They came in a blizzard of chipboard, cordless screwdrivers and ladders. In half an hour, the windows and door were sealed, secure, blacked out. I thanked them and asked how much, sweating. I had no money on me. Just a couple of tenners, that's all. I had an idea that I'd won big on the horses, but couldn't pin it down. Broke now. I'd have to risk a cheque. Would they take it? They said *No, it's a favour for Pat*. I offered them some of my grass. They accepted and were gone.

Trying to find the gambling memory, I remembered the Ace of Spades. Running Tuesday. Sharp dog. Swore blind to myself that I'd get something on him.

I went inside. The house was a fucking mess. With the south-facing front windows now boarded up, there was just a meagre light through the odd crack. It was like being in a tomb after the robbers had been. The air was stifling, unpleasant. Faint chemical stink of cordite, surely my imagination. I had to get out. I put on my shades, walked.

I worried about my low funds situation and figured Dave would be the best to tap until I could get to the credit union, which was up to date. Go Monday, apply for a loan, get me through the current phase of despair. I checked voicemails. One from Dave. Said he'd be in the shop, doing a bit, to call in, something special to show me. Grand. There was a message from my dad, too. He asked if I could call around some time. Said there was news about mam.

So I walked through quiet Sunday streets. Some shops were open early. The Kinks blared from the speakers in the boutiques, women and teenage girls hunting for the shortest skirts. More zombie shoppers lolled about, licking ice cream cones and complaining about the sun, saying *Jesus, it's a dead heat, isn't it?* Most people were off at the beach. Kilkee, Lahinch, Ballybunion, eating periwinkles and dillisk.

Dave's street, just off William Street, was quiet. Everything closed, even the pub opposite. His shutter was half down, no other sign of life. I rapped the shutter. This broke a scab on my knuckle. I left a smudge of red on the shutter and winced with the pain.

'Dave?'

No answer.

I bent to get under the shutter and pushed the door in.

'Dave! It's me, man. You in the back?'

Nothing. The stereo was blaring, some Bowie song I wasn't familiar with. The shop lights were on, little light getting outside. I went to the back office, briefly pausing to admire the bikini-clad model on the cover of Dave's Sunday paper. It lay on the counter along with his bunch of keys and a small bottle of Club Orange, unopened. That was his hangover cure.

The office door was closed. I knocked. He could be developing some black and whites, I figured, or editing. I knocked again. Nothing.

'Dave. You in there?'

Silence. So I opened the door. The room was dark. I fumbled and found the light switch. In a flash, I saw my own downfall, rushing, eager.

Dave sat in his chair, head back. A small, black hole was in his forehead. From it, blood had trickled lazily down his face, then congealed. A lot of blood was splashed across the posters behind Dave's desk. Pictures of sexy girls and sports cars, now spoiled with brain and skull and tissue. I stood, frozen with fear and confusion, unable to look at his face.

After a few long seconds, adrenaline took over. I had to get out. Immediately. Unseen. What about my photos? Oh fuck. His hiding place. That's where he always left stuff for me. Porno movies, drugs, things like that. I'd have to look.

The place had been ransacked, prints and papers thrown everywhere. The killer had been looking for something. I took the Manhattan skyline statue off the filing cabinet, a 9/11 memento from his aunt in Queens. Dave's cousin was a fireman. He died. I shook New York and heard noise. Bingo! The base slid off easily. The photos, in two wallets with my name on them. I glanced inside one. Yes, Smythe. Anything else? A nice little lump of hash and a DVD in a blank case. Probably a porno. Lovely. I pocketed the stuff and remembered my reason for going to see Dave. Cash.

'Dave, I'm sorry,' I said to my friend's body.

I saw his wallet bulge in his shirt's breast pocket. I pulled it out, fearing the body. Inside, I found about four hundred, all fifties, which I took. I put the wallet back. I inhaled deeply and got ready to split the crime scene.

I moved quickly, lifting Dave's bottle of orange. He wouldn't be needing it and I was parched. The street outside was still quiet. Thank Christ. Head down, avoiding street cameras. Crowds coming out from mass. I blended. On towards Arthur's Quay, the riverside park. I sat on a bench and drank. Dave was dead. Butchered while working for me. I thought of his wife. The baby. Fiona. Me. If I hadn't seen it I wouldn't have believed it, not for a sec.

The sun was belting down and swans glided by on the heavy, swirling river. My phone rang. It was O'Doherty.

'Charlie. I tried to call you last night.'

'Ahm, yeah. I saw that. I had a bit of a messy one.'

My voice was cracking. I was in danger of losing my nerve. He sensed it.

'You don't sound so hot, kid. Antin wrong?'

Was the fucker toying with me?

'Nothing too major. I'm okay. Just need a drink is all.'

'I'm havin one now. Why don't you join me?'

'No thanks, I've tons of shit on today.'

'No, Charlie. Now.'

'It's okay. Maybe some other time.'

'Now, right?'

'Okay. Where are you?'

I touched my gun. Felt reassured.

'The pub by the Treaty Stone. Going to a funeral later.'

'Fine. See you in about fifteen?'

'Grand.'

I had no idea what he wanted. Clueless. Was he going to finish me off? Maybe he had nothing at all to do with my house being blasted or Dave getting wasted. Or maybe everything. And now he was pulling me even closer to his centre of misery. So I went.

CHAPTER 32. THE KILLING FIELDS

Looking at the grass, all was a blur, a green shimmer. The shaking in me was bad. Everyone in the car stared at me, smiled. A high-pitched whine in my head shrieked *Flight or fight! Now!* But I could do neither. This was it. I could see where I would die. There, on the Island Field.

Crossing Sarsfield Bridge, I fucked the empty orange bottle into the Shannon. Going along Clancy Strand, I cried two tears for Dave. They came easily enough, with a dry pain in my throat and my teeth clenched tight enough to hurt. I dried my face with my sleeve and stopped off in a little park that juts into the river for a cigarette. I needed to lose the bleary look or O'Doherty would spot it.

I stood and smoked and gazed. I realised, with a grim smile, that this was the very spot where it began. Just four days before, I took snaps of O'Doherty's brother getting a handjob from right here. Now, it occurred, I was on my way to his funeral. Was this karma? Did I make my own fate? Was I in some sort of bad loop and, if so, would the centrifugal force trap me forever? My energy felt very low.

The Treaty Stone sat quietly on its pedestal, just a couple of Americans taking pictures, with

King John's Castle across the river, reminding me of my proximity to O'Doherty's island heartland. The church, St Munchin's, was quiet, so the funeral must be still some time off. I crossed the street, into the bar, a gloomy place which stank of stale beer and residual Saturday night.

O'Doherty sat in an alcove with three mean-looking fuckers. They all wore black, didn't look happy. I figured they were depressed about the funeral, so tried to display some bravado. After all, I had a gun in my pocket. I allowed myself a tiny smirk.

'Drinks, lads?'

'We're alright, kid. Just got a round in, sit down.'

'But I - '

'Sit. Jack, get the man a drink, yeah?'

'What are you havin, shom?' asked Jack.

O'Doherty looked at me. Hard eyes. Someone whose orders were always obeyed. Jesus, he was really starting to come across like Don Corleone.

'Vodka and tonic, thanks.'

'Now sit.'

I sat beside O'Doherty, on the badly-upholstered and stained velvet seat. Jack, who stood out among the goons as the ugliest, most-tattooed - complete with spider's web on his neck and a tear from the outside corner of his left eye - and nastiest-looking, went to the bar, jangling his pocket as he fished for four quid and change.

'You see the paper, Charlie?'

'No, what's the story?'

O'Doherty looked at me closely, as did his two buddies. When Jack returned with my drink, I gulped it. Wasn't quite right. Maybe bootleg vodka. Still I drank. Still they watched me. Uncomfortable.

'Check this out,' said O'Doherty as he flicked through the Sunday paper. He opened it on page three and laid it flat on the sticky-topped table. I'd seen it, but acted well-shocked. The headline shouted.

GANGLAND MURDER VICTIM IN SECRET AFFAIR

That thing where your heart physically lurches happened to me then. The loop got faster. The point of overload came one notch closer. I could feel it click.

All eyes were still on me, so I read the story quickly. They had fuck-all to go on. No surprise.

'How the fuck did this happen?' I asked incredulously.

'You know nuttin about this, Charlie?' asked O'Doherty.

'Nothing. I swear.'

O'Doherty looked around the bar, which was starting to fill up.

'Let's go somewhere quieter. Just for a chat.'

'I - '

O'Doherty must have seen my fear, so he reassured me.

'Just for a chat. Let's go.'

The heavies gathered round me and one put his arm on my shoulder as we left the pub and went around the corner to their car. A big black Mercedes, probably their funeral car. I was put in the back, a heavy on either side, their stink almost raising puke. O'Doherty sat in the front passenger seat, his head turned to me.

'We'll just head to my place for a while. The wake is on there now, but you'll be safe. So don't be worryin.'

We crossed Thomond Bridge, some youngfellas fishing idly for passing salmon. Then left and down the far side of the river, past the broken frames of once-popular diving platforms, now rusting steel poking up like a rotten beached beast. The Baths. I pictured a fifty-year-old Limerick Chronicle shot of dozens of proud swimmers posing before their swanky new equipment. Swimming there now would require tetanus shots.

Rows of council houses stretched off in every direction. Most were small, poor, kept by houseproud mothers, battling against all odds. Litter covered the roads and footpaths. Most council workers afraid to work there, most residents not giving two fucks about the world outside the front door, gave up on it.

Past the houses were open green spaces that served as grazing land for horses and safe drug dealing zones. Beyond the grass was thick undergrowth and the river. I knew it was often used for killings, it was just so far from the system's reach.

When O'Doherty turned his head towards the wasteland, I knew it was where his brother had been killed. I held my breath, fearing the worst. The car slowed and stopped. Nobody around now.

'What's up?' I asked, my mouth dry, head spinning.

O'Doherty turned, faced me fully, eye contact. Fuck, this is it. The gun was in my jacket, but my arms were pinned to me by the sheer bulk of the heavies. Nut the one on the left and grab for it? Scanned the street for police, anyone. Nothing, just a knackered white horse, tethered to a rusty truck axle. Fuck.

He saw my confusion, smiled.

'Just lettin you know what's what, Charlie. You with me?'

'I'm with you.'

'Did you give those pictures to the paper?'

'I swear to God I didn't. I swear.'

He looked into my eyes and I held his stare.

At last he turned and nodded to the driver. We drove on past the Banks, up Googoo's Hill and to O'Doherty's house. I began to breathe, though I still sweated badly.

O'Doherty's house stood out easily. The riches were obvious in the new roof, extensions, tarmacced garden, security gates, CCTV cameras, expensive cars parked outside, satellite dishes and sparkling windows. And they'd knocked into the house next door. Place was huge. About a dozen men hung around at the gate, stepping aside when they spotted our car. We pulled into the drive and stopped beside a beautiful BMW convertible with the roof down. We got out and walked to the house, O'Doherty saluting the guys at the gate, each of them giving me a cruel, interrogating look, saying to each other Who the fuck is that little cunt?

'Welcome to my humble abode,' said O'Doherty to me.

He gestured to the heavies to hang on outside and put his arm on my shoulder as we went in his front door. The front room was full of relatives, mainly grannies, aunts and that. They drank tea or whiskey and every one of them smoked.

He led me through the hall and towards the kitchen, where his wife made sandwiches on a large, oak table. Lettuce and tomato, ham, chicken. At least twenty bottles of spirits sat on one end of the table, along with mixers, a bucket of ice and slices of lemon. Nice.

'Would ye like a drink,' asked his wife, not looking up from her sandwiches. Her lip was split but healing and she had a black smudge under her left eye. She looked like she'd been crying. Her lover would soon be placed in a deep hole, minus his head. When the affair was confirmed, she'd been thumped around, no doubt. I had a feeling that the worst bruises were hidden. She winced as she turned, her ribs sore, if not broken. She straightened and looked at me.

'Yes please,' I replied, my voice faltering as I saw her up close for the first time. 'Got any vodka and tonic?'

'No tonic,' she replied, looking into me with clear blue eyes. Crystal clear, like a fantasy ocean. '7up or Coke any good?'

'Coke would be lovely, thanks.'

'I'm Jean,' she said.

Oh shit, I thought. *You are beautiful trouble.*

She smiled at me, eyes lowered, and I knew I was looking at deep, potentially fatal hassle. Hassle with a history.

CHAPTER 33. PRESUMPTIONS

While she made my drink, half vodka, half Coke, O'Doherty fixed himself a whiskey on ice, no mixer. I figured that somebody would feel the O'Doherty wrath before the day was out. I just had to ensure it wouldn't be me. I felt slightly more relaxed now, drink in hand. Limerick people wouldn't waste drink on someone they planned to bump off. That would be a sin.

'Come on, Charlie,' muttered O'Doherty, leading me to the back door.

'Thanks for the drink,' I said to his wife, who was an oasis in a strange and dangerous land.

She gave me a look that I didn't quite understand. My heart picked up again.

O'Doherty brought me out on to a lovely big wooden deck, and we sat on upholstered wicker chairs. The garden was huge, stretching off towards the river, finishing with a real view of the Clare Hills. A few kids played around at the bottom of the garden, which was littered with Tayto crisp bags and plastic tumblers. It was the kind of garden you'd kill for. Ordinarily.

'So, Charlie, what we gonna do with you?' he asked, smiling.

'I don't know. All I do know is that I didn't leak the picture to the paper. Why the fuck would I?

You'd finger me right away. I'm not completely insane.'

'I didn't think so, to be honest. Now I want you to be straight with me. Who else saw those pictures?'

I drank my vodka, wincing at its strength. I figured that I could deliver Dave up without risking anything. O'Doherty had probably worked it out for himself. He'd probably had Dave killed, the fucker. This was just a game.

'I lied when I said I developed the pictures myself. My mate did it. He has a photo shop in town.'

'Do you think he would have sold the pictures?'

'He never said it to me. But I'd say he wouldn't. He's a bit mad but, again, he's not insane.'

'Anyone else seen the pictures?'

'No.'

'Sure?'

'A hundred and ten percent.'

'Are there any more copies?'

'None. Dave must have made duplicates when he was processing. That's all I can think of.'

'Where's he based?'

I didn't answer, acting as though I was protecting my friend.

'Tell me, Charlie. If not, I'll find him anyways and start treating you like someone I can't trust any more.'

'Are you gonna kill him? I'm not setting up my friend to get killed.'

'And I wouldn't expect you to,' he replied, a coldness in his eyes. 'I just want to have a word, that's all. See who he showed the pictures to. I want to be sure the cops aren't in any of this.'

'Won't they see the paper today?' I asked, trying to deflect his attention from Dave.

'Of course they will and they'll start askin questions. But I'd say they're too fuckin stupid to make it all add up.'

In that sentence, he'd admitted to me that he'd killed Luke and that he was supremely confident of getting away with murder. His wife was hot, granted, but would you kill for her? Your own brother? I didn't know. I felt sure there was something I was missing. I gave him one of Dave's business cards with the shop address on it. I begged that he wouldn't hurt Dave and he smiled.

'Do you smoke a bit of hash, Charlie?' he asked.

I nodded.

'Anything else? Coke? Speed? Any of that?'

I shrugged.

'I take what's going, I suppose. Like anyone.'

'That's very honest of you Charlie, a man in your position.'

What did he mean? My position? Pillar of the community? I think not.

'What do you mean,' I asked.

'I mean your job. You deal with all sorts, I'm sure. You handle lots of sensitive information. Information that could get people killed. But you still like to get out of your head?'

'I do. I don't like what's inside my head half the time.'

'Very honest. Look, hang on there a minute. I'll get Jean out to look after you.'

He disappeared into the house - I assumed he was sending the heavy squad into Dave's - and his wife came out, holding two tall glasses of vodka and Coke.

'I thought you'd need a refill,' she said, handing me a glass.

'Beautiful,' I said, taking the glass and looking down her top as she bent down to me. Unreal. She knew exactly what she was doing and smiled. Women always know. She sat opposite me.

'You goin to the funeral?' she asked.

'I hadn't planned to. Then again, I have no idea what's going on any more. So you never know.'

'Ever feel like a pet mouse in one of those runnin wheels?' she asked, lighting a cigarette and offering me her pack.

'Thanks. I do feel like a mouse in a wheel, actually. More so, these last few days. Why do you ask?'

'No reason, really. Do you have a business card?'

'Yeah, why?'

'I might need a private detective some time. And you're good at your job.'

'There's no way I'm spying on your husband. Not a fucking chance, if you'll pardon my French.'

'I didn't mean that,' she giggled, 'I meant for fun.'

She opened her eyes widely and licked her split lip. Jesus Christ! O'Doherty's wife. Coming on to me. In his house. On the day of her ex-lover's funeral. Are we all mad?

I drained the drink and found a business card in my pocket anyway. Dizzy and half-drunk already, I gave it to her. She put it in against her left breast, winked and went back into the house and its mourners as O'Doherty came out.

'You look a bit cheerier, Charlie. Things lookin up?'

'Yeah, the drink is having the desired effect.'

'Good stuff. Listen. I'm glad you were straight with me. So I'm going to be straight with you. Hold out your hand.'

I held out my hand, palm open. He put his clenched fist over it. When he opened his fist, two small aluminium wraps fell.

'Put those in your pocket,' he commanded.

I did as he said.

'Drugs?'

'Enough to keep you going. Listen Charlie. The shit's goin to hit the fan. Probably this week. All these funerals. All the suspicions. People are lookin for blood. Not just my boys, either. I just want to keep you on my side. That okay?'

'Okay. But the shit's already hit my fan. My house was machine-gunned last night.'

'That your place on the news?'

I nodded.

'Fuck me, Charlie. Who did it?'

'I've no clue. You didn't hear anything yourself, did you?'

He was smiling broadly as he shook his head. I had no idea if he was spoofing me. I asked if he could make some enquiries and he said he would. He looked at his watch.

'Right. Time for us to make tracks to the funeral. You don't need to come.'

'Fine. Suits me. Closed coffin I presume?'

He exploded with laughter, loud enough for the kids at the bottom of the garden to freeze and look in our direction.

'Closed coffin. Very good. I like you Charlie. Look, would you do us a big favour?'

The kids played on.

'What kind of favour?' I asked.

'There's a grand in it for you.'

'Tell me more.'

'It's like this. I don't think Jean at the funeral would go down well. The family's askin questions after the cuntin photos in the paper. So I need you to look after her for a few hours til it's all over. I know I can trust you with her, can't I?'

I gulped.

'Yeah, of course you can trust me. I mean, look what happened to the other guy.'

'Closed coffin,' he laughed, this time with menace. He could switch it on and off like a tap, the bastard.

'Hang on there while I make it clear to Jean.'

He went back in the house and I sneaked a peak inside the packages he'd given me. The first contained a good lump of hash, about half an ounce, the standard Pakistani blend that had flooded the city. The other had uncut cocaine inside, hard and lumpy. A couple of hundred quid's worth by the looks of it. Result. All this and his hot wife too.

Right then, just as all was becoming right with the world, Pat calls me.

'Where are you?'

'On a job.'

'The Island, yeah?'

Shit.

'Yeah. What's up, Pat?'

'Just letting you know we've eyes and ears everywhere.'

Did he slur just there?

'Okay.'

'I know what you did last night, Charlie. I know all about it, buddy.'

'Like what, Pat?'

I didn't know what I'd been up to, so surprise me.

'Like Dave, Charlie. Like Dave.'

And he hung up, leaving me with an open mouth, a dazed expression and an actual, physical sinking feeling.

CHAPTER 34. PICNIC

Bells tolled in the middle distance. For Luke.

'All set,' he said. 'You two hang on here for half an hour. When we're all gone to the church, get out of here. A few of the lads will be hangin around outside. Don't worry about them. Go for some food, go to the pictures, I don't care. You be back here for six or seven, Jean. I'll talk to you tomorrow, Charlie.'

The kids were called, he handed me a wad of fifties and left. Jean brought a small tray of sandwiches out to the patio. The house was now empty but for us, but I had the feeling of being watched, plenty of houses around. I ate in silence. Good bread, real butter, decent Limerick ham. Tasty, but not enough bite.

'Any mustard, Jean?'

'I'll see.'

I watched her hunt around the kitchen, like she wasn't too used to searching for condiments, finally bending over, arse cocked right at me, as she discovered an ancient jar of Colman's English in a press. Christ, what an arse.

She read the label as she brought the mustard out to me.

'Best before date's up. Just a couple of months.'

'Doesn't matter to me. There's nothing in mustard that'll kill you.'

'Unless it's gone green.'

I spread the - still yellow - mustard generously over the thick slice of ham in a new sandwich. My taste buds were in terminal decline from all my smoking, drinking and drugtaking. I needed strong flavours if I was to taste anything. Happens to everyone.

'So what would you like to do, Jean?'

'Jesus, I just want out of the city. Want to go for a bit of a drive?'

'Sounds good, but I'm a bit locked and I've no car with me.'

'Oh no,' she wagged a finger, 'I'm drivin, mister.'

The curvy new BMW Z4 convertible was, of course, Jean's. I'd read about it, seen one or two about. Its body was perfectly sculpted. Three litres, six speed, one hundred and eighty-four horsepower.

'It's a cunt with the petrol, though,' she said, as my eyes popped at the brushed alloy interior detailing.

I had the growing impression that O'Doherty had married above his social standing and was desperate to keep his wife happy. He would give her everything short of the freedom to screw around. She, meanwhile, felt trapped. She told me about the hiding he'd given her after he'd had his brother killed. She'd a cracked rib and bruising on her back and thighs. But she said she was used to it. Ominous.

All this I learned as we cruised out of the Island and on to the Dublin Road. Summery music played loud on the Bose stereo as we inched past the Parkway shopping centre and the gridlocked retail hell that had mushroomed around it. Her dark hair danced and, under her ludicrously expensive Prada shades, I knew that her eyes were smiling. I felt like someone special in that car with her. *Don't matter what I do, 'cause I end up hurtin you*, she sang. I kept one eye on the rear view mirror, but there was no sign of any of O'Doherty's goons tailing us.

As we reached Castletroy, the hill full of the most expensive and exclusive homes in the city, she took a left.

'Where we headed?' I asked. I didn't really care. I enjoyed her company and learned a lot about O'Doherty and his history. My fear of him grew. And my fear for her.

'Plassey,' she said, 'nice and quiet.'

We drove past the monster flagpoles and through the tree-lined avenue to the University of Limerick. There were plenty of students about, studying like fools on a glorious Sunday afternoon.

'You know the study rooms are open twentyfourseven?' I asked.

'Feckin eejits,' she replied.

We went to the car park near the new sports centre.

'We're not going for a swim are we?'

'Not a chance, I thought a picnic might be nice.'

'Very nice.'

We parked and, as the roof went up automatically, she opened the boot and took out a wicker basket and a blanket. This seemed well-planned.

'Do you always carry the makings of a picnic?' I enquired.

'No, this is just for you,' she smiled.

I carried the stuff and we strolled down to the river, passing various lecture rooms and offices. And tower cranes, always tower cranes. We crossed a small steel bridge, got on to the riverside path and turned right, heading further from the city with each step. The fat, lazy river was on our left, blithely ignoring us. A lone sign stood, menaced the place.

VISITORS ARE ADVISED NOT TO WALK
THE RIVERBANK ALONE

'Janey Mac,' she said. 'I thought the Island was bad.'

She took my arm. I switched my phone off. Joggers and walkers passed by every so often. Cute little wagtails skipped ahead of us along the path, playing some bird game, and giant hogweeds towered on the right. We came to the end of the official trail, at the smashed walls of an old castle. Then we were in a meadow, the river on the left, the blank back walls of a massive computer plant far off on the right. We came to a strange bridge which led on to a small island. The bridge had a strong steel framework - all triangles - but nothing to walk on.

'Come on,' she said, clambering on to the frame and edging along.

'Jesus, Jean. I've to carry all this stuff.'

'Come on. I'll make it worth your while,' she laughed.

I needed no further encouragement. With the blanket under my arm, I had one free hand. I sweated, but made it. She led the way through a thicket of trees to a little clearing in the middle of the island. I laid the blanket out on the grass and she opened the picnic basket. I took off my heavily-laden jacket and laid it gently on the grass beside me. Inside the basket, she'd packed some of the sandwiches from earlier, the old mustard, a bottle of chilled champagne - Moet & Chandon 2002 - and two flutes. There was also a bag of cherries and two packs of cheese and onion Taytos.

I opened the champagne, filled our glasses and appreciated the surroundings. The tree cover kept us completely hidden from the meadow behind, but the river was open to the front. Insects buzzed happily in the afternoon sunshine and a steel-grey heron stood motionless by the water's edge.

'This is lovely, Jean.'

'I'm glad you like it. Charlie?'

'Yeah?'

'Would you kiss me?'

I'd been expecting this, but that didn't make it any easier to cope with. I'd figured that, on balance, she would be worth the risk. She had the look. She also had gleaming eyes and, Lord, after the twenty four hours I'd just been through, some affection would be sweet. But I needed to be sure I could trust her.

'What about your husband? Remember why you're here?'

'How could I forget?'

She shimmied across the blanket until she was sitting right up against me. I could smell her now, expensive perfume, Chanel No 5 maybe. She wasn't at all like O'Doherty or anyone from the Island. Her accent was so wrong as well.

'Jean, this isn't a set-up or anything, is it?'

'What do you mean?'

'Like, your husband isn't testing me or something?'

'I hate that prick. Look.'

She whipped off her top. This had the effect of showing me that her husband was, indeed, a brute. Heavy bruises covered her abdomen. She had definitely broken a rib, as a painful-looking red lump testified.

There was a secondary effect. She was down to her bra, a black Wonderbra that pushed her breasts at me, her deep cleavage casting a spell.

'Jesus, Jean. Talk about between a rock and a hard place.'

So I kissed her, felt her, wanted her. She had crisp breath that made me gag at first, and little bits on her tongue, but I soon got used to that. We held back from full sex but, God, I couldn't have stopped myself if she'd said *Take me, Charlie, you fool.*

Tasting her lips, I closed my eyes, felt my idyll. But I couldn't stop worrying. How in the name of

Jesus was I doing this, that and the other with the wife of a gangster who was, at that exact moment, burying his own brother for doing the very same damned thing? And shouldn't I have been mourning my best friend? And what about bloody Pat? Too much, too much. So I eased away from her, switched off, turned on.

CHAPTER 35. TELL ME YOUR PROBLEMS

She always asked about their sex lives, that's what she'd been ordered to do. She was massaging this woman one Wednesday. The woman talked about her husband and how she's tired of him and how his days are numbered and here's his photo.

Etoile took it all in, asked more and more.

'Do you report all this to the doctor?' asked Deirdre one morning, in her pre-orgasmic fever.

Etoile rubbed ylang-ylang into her, relaxing muscles, removing tension.

'Yes. I must complete a report on your karmic state before you see the doctor. It's all part of the cure.'

'And I love the cure.'

'So does Charlie have a future?'

'Not with me. He'll always get by, I suppose.'
More oil.

'What you want Mrs Doyle, is what you need. You must take it. I, too, yearn for something.'

'That's so nice. I like you, Etoile. You have this kind of earthiness, you know? Yearning for something, but sexually evolved.'

'They say humans evolved in Africa. We're all African really.'

'Some day the whole world will be like Africa, I fear.'

So ideas evolved into plans. She had her target. As Deirdre prepared to lay on the guru's bed, Etoile worked out how to get into her husband's. Give him the sex that he craves so badly. Get engaged, get a stay on her deportation, marry him, get citizenship, get him killed. Nobody would miss him, it seemed.

Key to it all was the Muti Queen and her dark strategies. While the office was quiet, Etoile looked over Deirdre's personal file, took notes, smiled.

'My gods are more powerful than yours, Charlie Doyle,' she whispered.

CHAPTER 36. CHASE

To cover any possible sightings of us, we parked outside Castletroy church and Jean went in and prayed for a short while. Sorted, unless her husband smelled me from her. I suggested she have a shower before the night was out. She said she would.

Still time to kill, so I directed her out the Dublin Road and left to Castleconnell. We passed the swans and castle and Sunday afternooners and went straight to the pub on the hill. Sitting there at the bar on rickety high chairs, with a cool Guinness, the sunbeams catching the dust motes, the bric-a-brac of decades, the fishing tackle and mounted giant salmon, the radio playing some music station from another time, Jean sitting beside me, sipping soda water and lime and resting her right hand on my knee, a bizarre feeling crept over me. I wondered if I was dead and in actual heaven.

Two pints later, drove back towards town, stopped by a light. I was hit by a hot, blue funk, faded into the passenger seat. She sensed it in me and asked what was wrong. I told her about Dave being murdered and how I found him. She said *Shit* and I sat quietly with my confusion.

Gazing wearily into my side mirror, I figured that the red Toyota with the twin aerials and the three guys inside had been there for a good while. I looked closer and made their uniforms and the Dublin registration. Patrol cops in an unmarked car.

'Jean?'

'Yeah?'

'Do you ever get pulled by the fuzz or anything? I mean really. Not, you know, euphemistically.'

She smiled and said 'Yeah, they hassle us. Stops, searches and that. Just to annoy us. They can't get to Greg, though. He's got inside contacts.'

'Really? Well I think we've a couple of redneck uniforms on our ass.'

'Fuck. Give us a fag, handsome.'

I lit her a cigarette and then lit one for myself, hands shaking as we rushed smoothly into town.

'Are you carryin antin?' she asked, looking at me.

We got on the Parkway roundabout and took a left up Childers Road, the city ring road that passed by Southill and Weston, two of Europe's most lawless estates.

'Nothing much. Plenty of drugs and an unlicensed gun.'

'Christ. Okay. I'll lose these guys as close to your place as I can. Where do you live?'

'Down near the docks.'

'Perfect.'

She took a right off the ring road, heading down Mulgrave Street, towards town. We sped by the mental hospital, the jail.

'Be ready to jump when I say. I'll call you durin the week.'

'Great!' I was delighted to hear this. She intoxicated me.

'Wait a sec. They might connect you to me if I drop you there.'

'Why?'

'You're in the news, aren't you?'

'I suppose I am the man of the moment.'

'So what do you think?'

'You're right. I don't want to stay there anyway. It's fucking destroyed. I'll stay with my old fellah. There's nowhere else.'

'Sounds good. Where is he?' She kept watching the cops in the rear view mirror. They were stuck to us like flies to a dog's arse. We passed St John's.

'Not far. Just over the bridge. Off Clancy Strand.'

'Cool. You grew up there?'

'Yeah. I used to fish a lot with dad.'

'And is it just your dad there now?' asked Jean as she used the open stretches of street to put the boot down and make some distance. The cops were now a few cars and a good distance behind us. But still on us.

'Yeah.'

'So what happened your mother? She dead?'

I liked her directness back on the blanket. But this line of questioning made me uncomfortable. My palms oozed sweat and I could feel a trickle down my spine.

'No. She's in a nursing home. She went a bit loopy a few years back, on and off. When she can't cope, she goes in the home for a while. Do you find it hot?'

'Oh. That's sad. It's warm alright. Get ready.'

We crossed Sarsfield bridge at speed. Lights with us, Jean took a sharp right on the north side of the bridge, down Clancy Strand.

'It's the little lane just there,' I said.

There was no sign of the cops, so she jumped on the brake. I kissed her hard and jumped out. In seconds, I was hidden in the quiet cul-de-sac and she was half way home. Catching my breath, a strange feeling came over me. I worried about having caught something from her then decided, No, I feel strange because I feel happy.

How could it last?

CHAPTER 37. HOME

Dad's car was there and the windows were open. I rang the bell. Nothing. I rang again. Moving blobs behind the patterned glass in the front door. The blobs become my father.

He opened up, surprised to see me. Wearing his purple leisure suit, brand new tackies and a slightly embarrassed smile.

'Hey dad. How you doing?'

'Hi son. What brings you here?'

'Mind if I kip here tonight?'

'You what?'

'I need to. My house was shot up last night. You must've seen the news?'

'Jesus, Mary and Joseph. Are you okay? I heard it, yeah.'

'I slept through it. Can you believe that? It was like Vietnam.'

He smiled. We shared a love of Vietnam movies. I'll never forget the time he let me stay up late to watch *The Deerhunter* with Robert DeNiro before a Las Vegas boxing match. I was only twelve and didn't really get the film. But it was an exciting night, a pure, glistening memory of childhood.

'*Apocalypse Now* or *Deerhunter*?' he asked, his eyes glinting.

'*Apocalypse Now.* Definitely *Apocalypse Now.* The bridge scene. And I'm now Martin Sheen, in the middle of some shit I just don't understand.'

'It was on the other night all right. I watched it. What about Deirdre and the kids? Are they okay?'

'She left me. Last week. They're all gone.'

'She'll be back. She always comes back.'

'I don't know, dad.'

'Okay son,' he said, putting a hand on my shoulder, 'we'll talk later. Now come on out the back, we'll catch the last of the day.'

He stopped, raised his left arm, rotated the shoulder, grimaced.

'You okay?'

'Just pains in my chest and now my arm.'

'Get it checked out?'

'No. I should.'

I followed him down the hall and through the kitchen. The kitchen table was covered in goodies. Vodka, orange, gin, lemons. I knew the fridge would contain chilled beer, so I grabbed a cold can of Stella on the way. The patio doors to the garden had been flung open since sunrise and, though the sun was low, a decent heat remained. Towels were laid on the grass, a small radio played its tinny music and two deckchairs rested in the shade of my old apple tree. Dad made a call while I had a drink.

We chatted for a short while and I excused myself and went to my room. Just to smell it and to do a quick line. Up the carpeted stairs and along the landing. I peeked into dad's room. The door was half open anyway. The bed was a mess, quilt and pillows on the ground. Tube of KY Jelly on the bedside table. I got a whiff of sex, a primeval tingle in my spine. The crafty old fucker had set himself up as the local widows' stud. But everywhere, overpowering everything else, was the whiff of old age. A bizarre mixture of air fresheners, bowel gases and slow decay. The smell of human life fading.

Grinning stupidly with misguided pride, I went into my room. To think, I spent most of my formative years in this musty little place. Only long enough for my bed, only wide enough for a desk and a wardrobe. The curtains were closed, so I whipped them open and tried to encourage some dust out by opening the window. The view was the same as always, the blank gable wall of the neighbours' and, on the far left, a little patch of river, bridge and sky.

My little old Aiwa stereo waited patiently before me, so I turned it on. There was an actual cassette tape in it. I missed tapes, so I hit play. *The Joshua Tree*, U2's first classic. *Where the Streets Have No Name*, what pure class. I increased the hissing volume, no Dolby.

My phone beeped a text message. It was Jean, asking if I'd made it in okay and telling me she loved me. She was infatuated with me. Fuck it, I'm probably like the most urbane sophisticate next to the Neanderthals that surround her. How bad? I told her that I was safe and that I enjoyed the day. I couldn't risk sending her a filthy message in case her husband spotted it. For all I knew, the cheeky fucker could have sent me that text himself. I'd always been fairly carefree, naive even. Now I questioned everything and everyone. It's called survival instinct. I saved her number anyway.

I hid my contraband in the secret compartment behind the desk, the place where a dozen Playboys and Penthouses had done time, where I used to hide cigarettes, for Christ's sake. Now I'm hiding a gun and cocaine. Is that growing-up?

I went into the sunny, yellow bathroom and washed my face. In the mirror, I saw a wreck of a man. But at least the headbutt bruises were almost gone.

Fuck it, you'll be grand. Back down to the garden. Dad had cranked up the gas barbecue and the smell of old grease burning made me salivate.

'Fancy a steak, son?' he asked.

I said 'Does the Pope shit in the woods?'

'Did you turn the immersion off?'

'Yeah. Don't panic.'

Two decent steaks were dropped on the grille. I sat on the grass with a fresh beer and watched as my father nursed the grub.

'I just wish your mam was here.'

'Don't worry about mam. You have to get on with your life. It wasn't your fault.'

'Maybe it was.'

'What do you mean?'

He looked at his feet.

'I was doing the dirt behind your mother's back since the day we were married.'

I was shocked. I'd never dreamed it was that bad.

'Constantly,' he continued. 'I have some kind of sex addiction, I suppose.'

'Yeah, yeah. Did mam know about this carry on?'

'Only much later. She caught me in bed with another woman. Right upstairs.'

'Who?'

'I can't tell you. I feel like such a flute about it.'

'Who, dad?'

'Later. She was never right anyway. Not since you were born.'

We ate in silence and I had a doze on the grass. I woke up an hour later, dinner just a residual smell and the garden in full shadow. The sky was that intense electric blue after sunset. A star - more likely Venus - twinkled on its own. So I made a wish. I wished that I could get out of my hole and find true love. Really.

Dad had moved inside and it took me a minute to get my bearings. For a sec, I thought I was a kid again.

Then we sat in the living room. He opened a bottle of Paddy whiskey and we drank until I puked.

He told me about how he'd shagged his wife's sister, my auntie. Bitch. Bastard. I couldn't believe it and accused him of driving my mother crazy. He denied this but I didn't care.

'And there's something else, Charlie.'

'What the fuck else could there be?'

'I had to get your mam taken out of the nursing home.'

'So where is she? Is she coming home?'

'Not for a while. I had to get her signed into St Joseph's on Friday. It's doing my noggin in.'

'The nuthouse? Are you for real?'

He nodded, resigned to taking it from me, knowing there was nothing I could actually do about it.

'Well fuck that for a game of soldiers,' I said.

I went to my room in a temper, snorted some cocaine, then sat on the bed for an hour, spitting my dinner and a pint of acidic yellow bile into a plastic bag.

And that was my best day.

CHAPTER 38. TINGLE

He was still in his black funeral suit, pissed out of his face. Even more repulsive than usual, asleep and snoring, legs up, in his Italian leather recliner. *The Sopranos* blared from the Bang & Olufsen flatscreen TV.

She'd been in the house for ages, waiting for him. She'd showered all the contact from her body so all that remained of the day was a distant tingling in her belly.

He'd come in from the garden after midnight, sent his cronies home.

'So was he okay? Did he try antin on?' he slurred.

'He was fine. He tried nothin. I'd say he's straight up. I'd trust him.'

'Okay. Give us another whiskey there, love.'

Shit, she thought. Don't tell me he's going to try and ride me. I don't know if I could take it. Or another hiding.

She took his tumbler and went to the kitchen, filling the glass almost to the brim. Then he drank greedily while she prayed he would pass out on his armchair. With the funeral over, maybe they'd get back to normal soon. Simmering resentment, casual disrespect and shouting matches, but nothing more.

But Luke was gone, her second lover to be murdered by her husband. New Guy Charlie could be handy to get her through and, if she kept him on a tight leash, maybe he'd be good for a lot more. She'd see. And if he copped it, well, that's an occupational hazard for desiring a gangster's wife. Didn't he know full well what he was getting in to? Actually no, he only saw the tip of the deadly iceberg.

Then Greg droned. The funeral, the pubs, the fights and the singing, how he did it for her, his own brother and all. Then his glass fell off his lap, spilling the dregs of his whiskey on to the deep, white carpet. She looked at him with resentment, considered getting the bread knife from the kitchen, pictured it stuck in his chest. But, too tired, she just went upstairs to bed.

His day would come.

CHAPTER 39. LEGACY

Later. Stomach emptied, my old room stopped spinning. I felt a little better, found some soluble painkillers in the bathroom cabinet. It was crammed full of dozens of medications. Old people like to hoard medicine. Sense of security. The large tablets fizzed excitedly in a glass of water, then slid down my parched throat like manna from heaven. Half came up again, but enough stayed down to make a difference. Downstairs to the kitchen for coffee. I sat at the kitchen table and filled in a Proust Questionnaire in the back of an old person's magazine. Made me think.

In walks dad.

'I just wanted to apologise for earlier. Sorry for messing your head up like that.'

He was watching the kitchen TV. CNN on Sky Digital. He was as obsessed with the news as I was. Mosque bombings in Baghdad, numbers raced across the screen, scorched flesh in bloody piles, splashes of crimson.

'It's okay,' I said, sensing his remorse.

'Bad business.'

I pressed on.

'Listen, dad. You couldn't do me a favour, could you?'

'You need money?'

'What else?'

I'd a grand and a half in my pockets, pretty much all of which would go on a machine gun, I figured. If I could score another grand, I'd be covered until the shit blew over or I got some cash in from other jobs. I was owed on a few and could get something in from the Smythe job this week if I pushed it. Dad said he'd help out and went off to the cash machine while I sat on the back porch and went through the photos from Dave's. Dave. I'd managed to block out the vicious murder of my best friend.

The pictures were dynamite, a fitting legacy to his skills. Smythe was in about a dozen. Must've been Saturday, while I was totally out of it. In some, Smythe chatted in a restaurant with businessmen, suits, freaks. Some I recognised, but one jumped out, setting off a million alarm bells in my numbed brain. It was Dr Robert Fox, one of the very richest dudes in town. He'd made his fortune in pharmaceuticals, invented some kind of fat-eating enzyme - morbidly huge in America - and now spent it on buying up the city and sticking a fat finger in every pie. He was a creepy-looking fucker, overweight, slick grey hair in a ponytail, trademark dark glasses, obvious smell of money. In the pictures, he and Smythe were obviously having a super time. Best of pals.

More pictures, more quality work from Dave. Smythe with a woman in South's. There they were, real chummy. And in a quiet doorway somewhere in town. He had his tongue down her throat and his hand on her tit. She was hot for him. It didn't add up, but it was enough for me get paid and wrap the job up.

The remaining dozen pictures were a different ballgame. Fiona. Luscious Fiona, former assistant of Dave. Naked as the day she was born and without even a trace of shyness. Christ! Seeing her bending over, arse into camera so you could literally count her pubes, I was getting hard. My heart couldn't cope, labouring in my chest.

The pictures got dirtier. Fiona, clearly in Dave's back office that was also a mini-studio, letting the camera look inside her, to her sex soul. It was almost hardcore stuff. I had the feeling that I was looking at professional porn, not just some messing around. I wondered if Dave could have been into this deeper than he let on. I knew he loved porn. Maybe too much. He'd done some glamour work, for sure, but I always figured that was just so he could screw around more.

As the newsreader droned on about the Middle East's descent into chaos, I got a call from Pat.

'I'm sorry about Dave, Charlie. Really sorry,' he began, like his earlier call hadn't happened.

'I know, man. You better get whatever fuck did this, Pat. Promise me,' I stammered, continuing the pretence.

'I promise, Charlie. We'll get the bastard. Any ideas? Was it whoever riddled your house?'

'I can't see it Pat,' I said, working it through in my head. 'Dave had nothing to do with the fight. He could've been seen with me, but I don't see why the Flynns would want him dead.'

'Well I thought you'd want to know straight away. His PC was full of porn. Hardcore stuff.'

'You looked at his PC?' I asked. I played dumb well.

'Obviously.'

'So what kind of porn?'

'All sorts. Mostly straight hardcore, including the women from Pussy Galore. Then there was some sadistic stuff too. Not my cup of tea.'

'Yeah?'

'Bad news. Really bad news.'

'Fuck it Pat, what is it?'

'I'm sorry bout this, but there was some child porn there as well.'

'You're fucking kidding me.'

'I'm not. I'm not sure how young they are yet but let's just say they weren't eighteen.'

'There's a chance that he was being given footage by our Russian friends,' I said, proposing a credible solution. 'Dave would do the editing, put it together for DVD duplication.'

'What I was thinking,' replied Pat, 'was that he found out something about the Russkis. Something they didn't want him to know. Maybe he was making movies for them, maybe just taking promo shots, I don't know. But he found out something. Somebody arranged to meet him at the shop on Saturday night or Sunday morning, then shot him.'

'Any time of death?'

'Inconclusive,' he said glumly.

'Inconclusive? How could it be inconclusive in this day and age?'

I needed to know when Dave was shot so I could strike myself off the suspect list.

'Any news from the CCTV?' I asked.

'One of them was broken and I'm still waiting on the other. I'm so fucking annoyed about that. Forensics showed up dozens of DNA traces. It's a shop, so that's no good. Nothing on the body. Only lead is some DNA off Dave's wallet and his hiding place. Oh yeah, and the outside shutter.'

My heart froze. That was my DNA.

'Really? You got a sample?'

'Yeah,' he smiled. 'All it takes is one cell from one drop of sweat off your finger and we can isolate it. The wallet only had Dave's DNA, plus one more. We found the one more on a stash box as well. Lucky the bastard had sweaty hands. The shutter's the best, though. Blood. Fresh blood. The best source. All matching.'

I couldn't answer. I glanced at the scabs on my hands.

'Still doesn't give us enough for a case though,' he continued.

'Really?' I breathed again.

'Yeah. A bit light. I could do with a solid suspect. Then link the DNA. Bingo. You know what I mean.'

'Shit.'

'Where were you again on Saturday night?' Before I could stutter an answer, he changed tack. 'Have you gone to see his missus yet?'

I hadn't even considered visiting Dave's widow. And we knew each other years.

'She doesn't like me,' I answered. 'It might be better if I went with you.'

'Maybe you're right. When would be good for you?'

'Any time tonight, I'd say. Best to get the condolences out of the way.'

'Grand. Be over in ten.'

'Cool.'

I fixed myself a light gin and tonic and smoked a mild joint. The drink tasted horrendous, but stayed down. Dad came back and handed me seven hundred - maximum withdrawal - in cash. I thanked him and told him about Dave's murder.

'Mother of God, I'm sorry for your troubles, Charlie. I'm hearing about it all day. I didn't know who it was. Oh Jesus.'

He was concerned that I might be involved in something dangerous. I told him not to worry.

'Jesus, Charlie. Dave. Your best pal all your life. Dead.'

Pat came into the house for a few minutes, to have a good natter with my old man. They'd always gotten along well and my dad was fascinated by police work. He asked a lot about Dave and the other murders and searched for a connection. Pat said he didn't see one, that it seemed to be more about a jealous husband or boyfriend or something. Or plain robbery.

Pat said the whole shop was being done over by the forensics boys, the Oompa-Loompas. He said that initial results were good, with prints, DNA and material evidence. Even blood. Pat glanced at me and grinned when he said that.

He said that Dave was still in there, his rigid body still thrown back on his chair. The blood from the bullet wounds would be congealed black by now, flies would have laid tiny eggs on him, the bacteria colony inside him would be cannibalising itself or trying to find a way out. I saw this as a technical event, not an emotional one. The curious detachment returned.

The thought crossed my mind again: Did I do it? I managed to dismiss that fear, but an awkward uneasiness stayed lodged in my guts.

CHAPTER 40. BOYS IN BLUE

Pat's police radio crackled, spat out bits of information. Units were on the lookout for a handbag snatcher on William Street. There were two gangs of drunken teenagers causing aggro on O'Connell Street. A few burglaries around. Domestics. The usual Sunday night shite.

Driving through town in the unmarked police car was an unnerving experience. Whenever we stopped or crawled through traffic, we were made for detectives immediately. People looked at me, stared at us. I turned my face, afraid that someone from O'Doherty's gang would spot me and make a connection.

'Can we go any faster, Pat?'

'The looks, ha?'

'Yeah. The looks.'

'Hang on.'

Pat grabbed his blue light from under his seat and plonked it on the outside roof, its coiled wire crossing his body to the dash. He flicked a switch on the dash and the light flashed and a siren wailed. He pulled out sharply as the immobile traffic ahead made space.

So we were there in a couple of minutes. Dave lived in Raheen, near the sprawling Crescent shopping centre and the hospital. Though it was late, the sky an ever-deepening blue - almost black - there were a few cars outside the house. Parking, Pat said that he'd do the talking and I nodded dimly. It was starting to hit. Inside, a few shocked relatives sat in the front room, drinking coffee and eating from a tin of Afternoon Tea biscuits. We both shook hands with Tina and gave her a hug. She took us out to the back garden, where she lit a cigarette.

She knew nothing. Dave and his wife had been living separate lives for months. They never had sex, never went out together, never talked. All this I knew. She mentioned his appetite for pornography and how he even asked her to pose naked for his new camera, just to test it, like. Other than that, no leads.

'And then there was the other prick, his partner in crime,' she said quietly.

I nodded and said nothing. God only knew how many times Dave had used me as an excuse when he was having affairs. No point telling her the truth, just rubbing salt.

'And he even wanted me to go swinging,' she said, full of poison now. 'Can you believe that? The very idea makes me sick to my stomach.'

Pat glanced at me, then stared at the floor.

The baby - Peter or Paul - suddenly began to wail from the next room. Tina didn't budge, wasn't interested. Her mother went and fussed, changed the nappy, got the bottle. Yes, Dave was gone, but his genes lived on.

Pat thanked Rita for her time and consoled with her again. He asked if there was any way we could help with the funeral and all and she said No thanks, all done. The body would be released tomorrow, so removal from funeral home to St John's Monday night, church to graveyard Tuesday morning. Plenty of drinking opportunities. Jesus, death in Ireland is such a boozy drag. I said nothing.

Pat said Dave's phone would be returned as soon as they'd finished checking its logs. Shit. There'd be plenty to and from me there, including on Saturday night into Sunday morning. Bollocks! Realised what a fucking dope I was not to have taken Dave's phone for my own leads. I wasn't half as sharp as I cracked on.

Driving back into town, I made up my mind.

'Pat, listen,' I began, as we crossed the new bridge, the oddly futuristic hotel and office block beside us making the scene like Poor Man's Miami.

'Yeah?' he seemed lost in thought.

'We have to get whatever bastard nailed Dave. Between us. Me and you. For our mate.'

'I agree. I've officially got the case. Well, me and the team. We've a meeting later.'

'Good. Then there's time for you to follow up a lead.'

'Which is?'

'I got some pictures off Dave on Saturday. He was doing some surveillance for me, a bit-on-the-side job. Interesting one. I'll tell you about it some time. Anyway, Dave dropped them off to mine about eight and split off straight away before I could check them. He'd only just taken them?'

'And where were you on Saturday night?'

'Like I say, at home.'

'All night?'

'Yeah, now can I please get to the point?'

'Fire away. Which way we headed?'

'Kileely-ish. Anyway, Fiona is, or was, Dave's hot assistant. Model material, I'm not joking you. Dave only told me last week he was shagging her.'

'Dirty bastard. And with a lovely wife at home?' he laughed. 'I'm only messing. I met her once or twice. Nice. Pity about the mouth on her.'

'So there were pictures of Fiona in with my ones. Porno pictures. Taken by Dave. In the shop.'

'Fuck. That's a good one, Charlie. Porn and the sex trade in general are fucking massive right now. These eastern Europeans are masters at it and they're pushing their weight around to take over. Even here. Where's Fiona? I've got to talk to her anyway. See who was in to see Dave and that.'

'That's the problem, Pat,' I said, gritting my teeth.

'Why?'

'She lives in Moyross. Feeling brave?

'No, my machine gun's back at the office.'

'So call your buddies with Dave's phone. Get them to send you Fiona's number. It has to be in there.'

Pat made a call and, within two minutes, had the number.

'I'll talk to her,' I volunteered, figuring I knew her better.

'Fine,' said Pat. He keyed her number into my phone and gave it to me to press the green button. She answered immediately.

'Charlie!' her voice excited.

'Hi Fiona. How did you know it was me?'

'Dave gave me your number. Made me save it. Oh Charlie, what'll I do?'

'Take it easy, Fiona. You're okay. Can we meet up? I know it's late. I'm with Pat. We're going to catch whoever did this.'

'I can meet you in ten minutes. That little hotel on the Ennis Road with the nice garden? The Woodfield? They've a late bar.'

'Beautiful. See you then. How will you get over?'

'I'll call a hackney. It'll only cost me a fiver.'

'Great. I'll fix up with you for it. See you soon.'

'Bye Charlie.'

'She sounded rattled,' I said.

'Could she be the key, do you think?' asked Pat. Maybe he could sense the promotion potential in solving a mysterious murder and busting an international sex ring into the bargain.

'Maybe,' I replied, keeping the O'Doherty photo connection to myself for a little longer. That would have been enough to warrant a bullet in Limerick. More than enough. I'm lucky it wasn't me that copped it.

Pat became quiet again, thinking about the permutations and taking the odd note in his little cop notebook. As we drove to the Ennis Road, Pat told me more about the sex traders. They came from all over. It was an all-encompassing racket for milking the biological need for sex. Prostitution and the exploitation of women was its bedrock, but its profits came from pornography, slavery and paedophilia too. You couldn't have one part of the sex trade without all the others. Everything was connected.

And it was, of course, one of the three highest-grossing industries on the planet, the others being drugs and weapons. Again, all connected. If Dave had gotten in with any of these characters, even on an innocent level, he'd be fair game if anything made them suspicious. Anything. Even like knowing and socialising with Pat, a known cop.

We passed Thomond Park rugby stadium, floodlights blazing, the Munster team preparing already for next year's Heineken Cup.

A call came through, general announcement. The remains of a child - butchered - found in a stream outside the city, past Moyross. No ID yet, no leads. The radio operator sounded pissed off.

'Fuck it,' I said. 'It can't get any worse now, can it?'

CHAPTER 41. SHATTERED

Ever feel like there was a little man inside your head, chipping away at your bits with a blunt icepick?

'That's her,' said Pat angrily. 'Shit!'

'Fuck it. A fucking childkiller on the loose on top of everything else.'

This wasn't a pleasant or helpful event. As a human being - whether animal or divine - I was sickened to my core, worried for my own kids, wherever they were. And resources would be shifted from Dave's investigation to catch the child's murderer. It might be up to me and Pat now.

My worst fears were confirmed when Pat got an order over the radio to get back to the station to help set up an incident room. He confirmed receipt of the order and said Fuck.

'Sorry Charlie. Can I drop you and you talk to Fiona.'

'No worries.'

'I trust you on this one, Charlie,' deadpan as usual.

'We're doing this for Dave,' I said as he screeched to a stop at the kerb opposite the hotel. I leapt out and slammed the door and Pat was gone in a second, his hand waving out the window.

I skipped through the traffic, relishing the prospect of a chat with Fiona. I checked around the packed bar and the outside seats. No sign of her, so I ordered a vodka and tonic and bought some cigarettes. Taking a corner of a bench out in the night, I smoked and went over my texts, looking for clues. Fiona arrived soon after, giving me a kiss on my cheek. She smelt good. I ordered her a rum from the waitress. When the drink arrived and I lit her cigarette, she began to lay her life with Dave bare, speaking quietly, fidgeting often.

'Dave and me had the hots for each other. I was only with him six months. He knows me father, that's how I got the job. He started tryin to kiss me and rub my arse on me second day. I gived in. He was nice to me. He brought me out for lunch. Once we even locked up early and went to the pictures in the afternoon. Can you believe that?'

'I can.'

'Then we started havin it off. First it was only in work, early or late or at lunch hour. He wanted sex all the time. It suited me. I really liked him, plus I could do what I liked at work and he paid me well.'

'Your candour is refreshing, Fiona. So what happened?' I asked, calling the waitress again. Fiona stayed quiet until our drinks order was away.

'We were out on the piss one night. Dave was blowin some cash. He'd coke and all sorts.'

'He was a right blackguard. I'll miss him.'

'So we were sluggin champers in one of the lapdancin clubs,' she went on. 'Dave was in top form and some guys came and started talkin to him. Said they heard he was a photographer and would he do pictures for the club. He said Of course. The girls there were all rides.'

'Any idea where from?'

'I thought they were all Russians. Anyway, by the end of the night, Dave is these blokes' new best friend in history. They gave him ten minutes in a private room with his favourite girl. And he fucked her too. He told me. I didn't care.'

'Can you describe the guys?' I asked, wondering about murderers.

'Not really. The place was dark and they all look the same to me.'

'Where, exactly?'

'Pussy Galore.'

'I know it. So did Dave do the work for them?'

'He spent a few afternoons at the club doin publicity shots. Then it turned into porn in his studio. The lapdancers make extra cash posin for hardcore shots. They're sold on. Then Dave branched out into findin local girls who'd pose for a few quid. Fast, easy, dirty.'

'Did he ever ask you to pose for him, Fiona?' I watched her closely, wondered if she'd lie to me.

'Yes,' she replied, without batting an eyelid. 'Once. I would only do it for Dave. Plus I made three hundred for an hour's work. We had sex afterwards.'

I'm sure.

'So Dave was supplying the porn pictures to these Russians?'

'I suppose so. Can you get us another drink, please Charlie? Dave forgot to pay me on Friday. I was supposed to get it Monday.'

'Jesus. That's rough. Can I give you a few quid to keep you going?'

'No thanks, I'll find a job soon enough' she said. And I knew she would, with her face and her figure. Plus a sharp head on her shoulders.

'You could always work for me, you know? I need some help with my filing,' I blurted.

My dick had taken over from my brain. But my brain began to see the potential as well. Worst case scenario, I find out if she's connected to Dave's death. Best case scenario, she'd be handy, do a good job and maybe fall for her new boss. What a sleaze.

'You mean as a private detective?' she asked. 'Really? Wow, that would be pure cool! Are you serious?'

'That depends. How much was Dave paying you?'

'Two fifty a week into my hand for thirty hours.'

I watched her eyes closely. She didn't seem to be lying.

'Well I can match that for now. If you can help me organise myself, I'll get more done. You can pick up some tricks of the trade as well. Before you know it, you'll be helping me on jobs. More jobs, more pay. How does that sound?'

'Great. Thanks Charlie. I appreciate it.'

'No problem. You're a sound girl. I hate to see you stuck because of what happened to Dave. He wouldn't want you to be not taken care of. I'm sure of that.'

'He was a sound man. I'll miss him.'

'Sound as a pound. I'll miss him too. So you free to start in the morning?'

'Really? Yeah, of course. Isn't your office down near Baal's Bridge?'

'Yeah, Riverside. Call in around eleven. You can meet Margaret, the receptionist and owner of the building. She's gas. I'll show you the ropes and you can get cracking. Any idea about computers?'

'I did a European Computer Driver's Licence course in the community centre. It was cool. I learnt all about Word, Excel, you name it.'

'Fuck me. Maybe you can help me computerise my jobs?'

'We'll give it a go anyway,' she smiled.

'See you in the morning so.'

We talked on. After one, she said Is that the time? and called a hackney on her mobile.

I gave her twenty to cover her cab home. She kissed me on the side of my mouth. Her kiss lingered for a second longer than was required by convention. I walked towards town, my head buzzing from drink, my thoughts erratic, everything leading me towards Fiona's altar of sex.

Found my way back to dad's.

'Shattered now,' I said to myself. And 'Can't take much more of this.'

CHAPTER 42. BISCUIT

Dr Robert Fox was born rich, stayed rich. As he dressed in a sober grey Armani suit, starched white shirt and cold blue tie, he considered his position. He was about to progress from being filthy rich to obscenely rich, thanks to his old school pal, Smythe, and some Russian money. And Pat, his latest MVP, another alumnus.

Adjusting his tie in the kitchen mirror, Fox's mind drifted back to boarding school - as it always did - to where he first met Smythie over a game of toss the biscuit. They were first years, totally naive, virgins. The older boys in the dorm say Come on, it's fun, you have to or you'll be sorry. So they play. It's still so clear in his mind.

Six boys kneeling in a circle, a digestive biscuit in the middle. *Go!* Each boy drops his shorts and starts to masturbate. One by one, they come.

But one boy doesn't. The loser. The biscuit a soggy mess, swimming in a pool of semen. An older boy carefully picks it up with thumb and forefinger and orders the crying Smythe to open wide. The soggy, disgusting biscuit is forced into his mouth and a hand held in place until Fox's friend, gagging, swallows it.

Fox lay in bed that night with a curiously elated feeling, smiling as he listened to the wretched sounds of vomiting from the toilet. He had enjoyed seeing Smythe eat his spunk, eat everyone's spunk. Fox would never lose a game. He'd been tipped off and had started rubbing himself in the toilet beforehand. Family connections. Everybody played it at boarding school, didn't they?

There were countless more games of toss the biscuit during those five school years. And more, much more. Mutual masturbation between boys wasn't seen as anything weird, so it was normal behaviour. Some of the queer boys did more, but away from the dorms. Some of the boys had relationships with the staff, male and female. It was all perfectly normal. Helped to pass the endless winter nights, fill in the weekends.

Now his old school chums were the pillars of society - the high-flying lawyers, judges, bankers, accountants and politicians that called the shots - the very system itself. It was understandable that, having experienced boarding school puberty, one's views on sexuality and morality would be unconventional.

This explained how rapists escaped with three year sentences. How paedophiles often got off scotfree. How women were sometimes judged to have invited rape. How some of the obviously guilty never came before a judge. How the rich and privileged looked after the rich and privileged. But the proles would never understand the true complexity of power, the system.

So Fox got on with his career after university, doing very well in business relationships with Smythie and the other alumni. Thanks to that first night of soggy biscuit, Smythe would always be beneath Fox - lesser - it was an unspoken law.

Fox thought about his childhood games every day. They never left him. They had shaped his personality, his sexuality, his success in life and brought him, now, to the edge of something vast and powerful.

He dunked a digestive, finished his coffee, looked forward to Karpov's party. The party of the year is how the *Leader* or the *Post* would describe it.

CHAPTER 43. HANDY

The intercom on my desk buzzed. Margaret announced Fiona's arrival. She had a quick look around and said You seriously don't have a PC?

'So how much is one going to set me back?'

'To buy, about a grand. We'll get a deal with printer and scanner thrown in.'

'You know how to work all that stuff?'

'Piece of piss. Or we could try an alternative supplier.'

'Such as?'

'One of me brother's mates works out in Dell. He gets stuff out the back door.'

'I thought that was impossible.'

'They watch um like hawks, for sure. But these boys have the best scams goin. They always get stuff out.'

'And how much?'

'About four hundred.'

'That's worth a risk.'

'For sure. You'd have to be pure mad not to go for it.'

'Pure mad?' I laughed. 'Can you give him a call, please?'

Fiona got on the phone and I looked through a catalogue full of office crap. I found a filing cabinet I liked the look of, so I ordered it for next day delivery. I made it clear that the cabinet would have to be brought up into my office if they wanted COD. No way was I putting my back out with a fucking filing cabinet. No fucking way when my sex life was finally starting to pick up.

Fiona's brother had a full system, boxed, ready for delivery. He said he'd be about in the afternoon and to have the cash ready. Progress. I used the time before lunch to talk Fiona through the cases I was working on and the ones that'd just been wrapped up. I left O'Doherty out of it. She was quick and took notes without being asked. She hit me with twenty questions about my procedures on cases. My head was spinning as I'd never had to try and explain my procedures to anyone. She seemed a bit confused, not surprisingly, so we knocked off for lunch.

Then the PC arrived and she set it up.

We went through the Smythe case and she began drawing up the invoice. I called his wife and told her I'd like to meet her. She said fine, she'd bring cash with her. I wanted to get her out of the way, so pushed for an immediate meeting. She said *One hour, the coffee shop in the Parkway*, a city limit shopping centre.

'Fiona,' I said, 'I've to do this and follow up on a couple of things. Would you be okay without me?'

She gave me a silent look, one eyebrow raised. She finished the invoice, printed it. It was perfect.

'Oh Charlie!' she cried as I was stepping out the door.

'Yeah?'

'Dave's removal from the funeral home. It's tonight. Seven.'

'Fuck's sake. I thought he was out of my life.'

CHAPTER 44. POSH

I drove east. The sun beat down, blinding me. I'd forgotten my shades. The road was backed up badly and the journey was a nightmare crawl.

Eventually, the Parkway loomed ahead on my right. The crazy roundabout was a test. By the time I parked, my mood was black.

I found Mrs Smythe at a quiet table in the coffee shop. A look from her made me smile. She had a cappuccino before her and stirred it anxiously as I approached. I shook her hand and ordered a Lavazza Americano from the waitress. My hands shook a little, but less than the day before. I ordered a large bottle of mineral water too. The Evian and coffee were delivered quickly and then I gave her the pictures.

'Do you think it's serious?' she asked calmly.

'I think the photos speak for themselves. In my professional opinion, he's having an affair. I'd say there's a lot of it going on at work.'

'Why do you say that?'

'He was socialising with his colleagues. I get the impression that the secretaries do the rounds.'

She looked closely at the pictures, her face registering disgust.

'I see. Well, you've done a very good job, Mr Doyle.'

'Thanks. What are you going to do?' I asked, though it was none of my business. My guess was Nothing. She thought for a moment, putting the pictures into her Chanel handbag.

'Nothing,' she answered, smiling now. 'I have no interest in him. Sexually anyway. I keep myself amused elsewhere.' Her eyes flashed, for the briefest instant. 'If I ever tire of him, this is my escape clause for a new life on the Med with half his fortune,' she continued. 'This has actually cheered me up. Thank you. Now, your bill, please.'

I gave her the envelope which had her neatly typed bill inside.

'Very professional, Mr Doyle,' she said, all business, examining every detail on the invoice. 'Excuse me while I go to the ladies.'

I half stood up out of manners and watched her, very fit for her age, as she went to the jacks to count out the cash for me. I finished my coffee and started on the water. She sat back down and handed me an envelope, different to the one I'd given her.

'Two thousand,' she said in a whisper, winking.

'Two? The bill is only one and a bit,' said an astonished me.

'One for a job well done and one for keeping quiet about it. I think that's fair.'

'But surely you know that, as a professional, I'm not going to blab about this.' I acted hurt.

'I fully accept that. This is just to cover all eventualities. Just take it Charlie. I like you.'

'Do you know a Dr Fox?' I asked, suddenly remembering his photo with Smythe.

'Only on the surface, socially. My husband does some work with him.'

'What kind of work?'

'I really don't know. Money games, golf.' She paused. There's just one thing.'

'What is it?' I asked gently.

'This cannot ever be repeated by you, do you understand?'

I nodded gravely. She moved her face close to mine, her smell sophisticated and understated. Her eyes showed emotion. Sadness there.

'There have been rumours going around about Dr Fox for years,' she began, glancing around the cafe. Then her eyes rested on mine. 'People say that he likes young women. The younger the better.'

'Kids?' I asked incredulously, that dead girl flashing into my mind.

She nodded, unable to say it. She said that she kept Fox at arm's length and just didn't want to know anything more about him. I sensed that the dead child had rattled her too. Maybe that's why she let this slip. I left a tenner tip because the service was good and I was now a - temporarily - rich man. So make someone's otherwise crappy day.

We shook hands at her flash car, a black Saab, and she thanked me again. I headed back into town, no traffic in that direction, thankfully. The call I'd been waiting for came while I passed the creamery on Clare Street, so I pulled in outside the art college.

It was the man about the big dog.

CHAPTER 45. FLIGHT K235

Karpov was pissed off. The Moscow airport authorities had delayed his flight on a security pretext. He knew it was done solely to annoy him, to squeeze an extra bribe. He finally got clearance to leave for Ireland an hour late. They would wait for him, it was his presentation after all, but he didn't like being late.

His private Boeing 737-800 - brand new - taxied to its takeoff position and, after another delay, darted into the black sky. As he crossed Germany, Karpov adjusted his watch to Irish time. His assistants worked on his speech and Powerpoint show, while the girls - ostensibly secretaries - who would work in Ireland for three months, chatted nervously.

'Sir, would you like to eat now?' asked his stewardess, a beautiful young woman from St Petersburg.

'What's on the menu, Katherina?'

'What would you like, sir?'

'I'd like you to come to my quarters with me. We have a shipment of the purest cocaine I have ever known. Let's try some.'

So they landed at Shannon Airport, passed near the US Military Zone, witnessed a CIA Gulfstream prepare for take-off, saw scores of Iraq-bound soldiers disembark from a huge transport for a last taste of the West.

'I feel sorry for them,' said Katherina.

'Why? They're getting paid, aren't they?'

'It's always the pawns that are sacrificed so that the kings may conquer,' she said sagely.

Though he was now very late for the presentation, he was in an increasingly positive frame of mind. The customs officials - who were on his payroll - nodded, had a cursory look over the plane and the mountains of luggage, gave clearance. *I love this country,* thought Karpov. *Money talks here.*

An airport greeter escorted the group to the arrivals hall, pointing out that Irish Coffee was invented in Shannon Airport as a means of warming up the transatlantic passengers from America back in the forties.

'Though they might dispute that over in Foynes.'

'Oh?'

'That was the first transatlantic airport, flying boats.'

Karpov smiled graciously, always the benign billionaire in public.

His security detail was waiting and, within minutes, he left the Shannon Free Zone in a convoy of armoured jeeps, headed towards the buzzing city that would soon be his.

CHAPTER 46. MADE IN CHINA

Mr White looked me straight in the eye, all serious. Alarmingly so.

'Who did you shoot, Charlie?'

'You what?'

Was this proof that I'd killed Dave?

I'd pulled up to the quarry gates after half-two. A deep rumble nearby. Like thunder, only deeper. I beeped. After a minute or two, a guy in dusty overalls came into view. He eyed me closely as he walked slowly out.

He quizzed me, let me in, pointed towards two huge steel silos, each with a huge excavator arm towering overhead and piles of rock on either side.

'Rock grinders,' said my guide. 'He's back there.'

The racket made me wince and I hurried after my guide, towards a long, low building to the left of the tower.

He took me through oily rooms of machinery and parts, then down a stairway and under the ground. We were in a more comfortable space, done up like a freakish lounge. A mahogany bar unit contained glasses, bottles of spirits and a little fridge with bottles of Budweiser inside. Three leather couches were arranged around a low coffee table, again mahogany. Posters of naked women draped over heavy earthmoving equipment covered the walls and the light came from a single, bright bulb hanging from the rough ceiling.

'Take a seat,' he said, keying a code into a door at the far side of the room, 'I'll get the boss.'

Mr White came through the door after a couple of minutes, wearing his trademark flat cap, this time with bright orange ear protectors over it. He smiled in greeting and beckoned me towards him.

The other room was a firing range. I was stunned. We were directly under the rock grinders. As long as they were on, you could fire an RPG down here and nobody'd hear. It was perfect, beautiful. A long, wooden bench went the length of the back wall. A variety of guns, including an AK-47 rested on it. Three firing posts were before the bench, each with a shelf for holding bullets and stuff. Beyond the firing posts was a thirty metre open space, with three targets at the far wall. They were of the standard torso and head outline like you see on TV and each hung from a wire. This was the real deal and Mr White looked quite proud of himself. Sure I'd taken it all in, he stood by the bench, pressed a big red button on the wall and waited. Then the roaring from above stopped, but it still echoed in my ears.

'That's better,' he said, lifting his hearing protectors off his ears. 'So you want somethin bigger.'

'Yeah. Whoever shot up my house is well-armed. The cops reckon it was an AK-47. I figure I need something heavy as backup, y'know?'

'And what about the revolver?'

'I'll give that back to you.'

I stood there while he thought about it. He went to the bench and pulled a canvas sheet over something he'd been working on, a mess of wires, cans of chemicals, batteries, an odd metal cone. He picked up a little machine gun.

'This is an Uzi. The cops use it.'

He put down the Uzi and picked up another familiar-looking submachine gun.

'Heckler and Koch MP5. Restricted to military and police use. The ERU has these. Nine millimetre again. Lovely gun.'

I held it, it was surprisingly light.

'Now, try this one. She's the best.'

He put the MP5 back on the bench and picked up the AK. He handed it to me with some reverence and I accepted it like I was being handed a new baby. An actual AK-47! It was a heavy fucker. Serious and mean.

'Kalashnikov?'

'Right, made in China. This came in with a shipment from Ghaddafi back in the eighties.'

The gun had a symbolic value that even outweighed its deadly performance. Osama bin Laden always has one in those grainy videos from Afghanistan. Every Vietnam movie, every clip of the IRA, every episode of the news, every child soldier in Africa, the AK is always there. It's the key product design of our time. Already the design icon of the twenty-first century.

He went through the essentials of the thing and how to shoot. Took about a minute.

'Six hundred rounds a minute, so you'll get through a mag of thirty in three seconds on full auto. Okay?' he said, nonchalantly.

'Okay,' I replied, trying to sound cool. I was shitting myself.

He handed me the gun and a full magazine. My hands shook as I fitted the magazine of gleaming brass bullets into the gun. I adopted firing position before a fresh target.

'Don't forget to cock her,' he reminded me.

I'd completely forgotten about that. Could be a fatal mistake, Charlie, I warned myself. So I pulled back the cocking handle, released it and then it sprang back home. Safety catch off, automatic selected, ready to go.

I pulled it tightly into my shoulder and gently squeezed the trigger. The gun exploded into life and my body shook. The noise, smell and recoil were overwhelming. Almost too much. And kids in Africa fire these? Four rounds had been fired in a fraction of a second. I checked the target, no contact.

I focused on the sights and fired again. This time I was delighted to see the target shake. Again and again I fired until the magazine was empty. Dead. It felt like I was firing for ages, but it couldn't have been more than ten seconds. I put the safety on and handed the gun to Mr White. He smiled and pressed a button. The target whirred towards me. I tasted the rounds in my dry mouth. The smell was horrible and exciting at the same time. I was delighted to see that I'd put eighteen of my thirty rounds on target.

'Not bad for your first go,' he said.

'So how much?'

'These are twelve-hundred normally, includin a couple of mags. If you give me back the revolver, we'll call it a grand. You didn't fire it, did you?'

'No, never even came close.'

'Good.'

'Right. Now, do you need another go or are you happy?'

I checked my watch and saw that the afternoon had slipped away from me.

'I've to get to a funeral, my best pal. I better split.'

'Fair enough. Give us the revolver and the few quid and I'll pack this up for you.'

He had a heavy canvas bag ready and loaded the rifle and two full magazines into it, after wrapping each item in a lightly-oiled rag. I put the revolver on the bench and counted out a grand from my healthy wad. Mr White checked the revolver and sniffed the barrel.

'Who did you shoot, Charlie?' he asked, all serious again.

'What? What are you talking about?'

'There's only five bullets here. I can't tell much from the smell, but this could've been fired. The empty cartridge is gone as well.'

'Fucking hell,' I blurted, surprised and confused. 'I've no idea, really and truly. I didn't shoot it, I swear to God.'

'Was anyone you know shot recently?' he asked, a mischievous grin on his face.

'Yeah,' I answered gravely, 'my best friend. Shot in the head. The weekend.'

'And where were you the weekend.'

I shrugged my shoulders, must've looked guilty as sin to the man.

He just nodded, smile gone. This was bizarre. There was no way I'd have shot Dave. No fucking way. But doubts lingered. The acid and all. There were maybe thirty blank hours. But no. Not possible.

'I need to know, Charlie. If this gun can be traced to antin and then to me, you know you're a fuckin dead man.'

'I know, I know. Trust me, I didn't shoot the damned thing.'

He stared me in the eye for a long few seconds. Then he nodded and handed me the bag with the AK-47.

'I believe you Charlie. Or at least I believe you're not lying to me. Find that bullet, will you? I won't be able to relax until I know where it is. You with me?'

'Yeah.'

'Well I won't be done for no fuckin murder so find me the bullet or we'll have to do somethin else about this.'

I prayed that it had just fallen out of the gun while I was arsing around with it, playing Clint

Eastwood. *Make my fucking day.* He counted the cash, then put his arm on my shoulder, easing me towards the door.

'Why did you show me all this?' I asked, curious.

'You remember rule number one, don't you?'

'Yeah.'

'That and the fact that this'll all be gone soon.' He gestured to the room. 'Things are changin for us. This is the past here.'

He sounded a bit down. I figured he was an IRA quartermaster and, if they made good on decommissioning, he'd soon be out of a job.

'One more ting,' he said. 'There's a few fuckers screwin around with you. I can't tell you any more. Just watch your back.'

'I kind of guessed that. Can you tell me anything at all?'

'All's I can say is it's about to get very bad.'

He walked me to my car and I was away in a cloud of dust, marvelling at the IRA operation, wondering just how much Pat knew about it.

Time sped by. I didn't have time to stash the gun or freshen up, so I went straight to the funeral home, my hands oily and an assault rifle in the boot. It's called showing your respects.

CHAPTER 47. ALLEY

The funeral home was near Garryowen, on a dying street in whose many side alleys lurked rapists and muggers.

A crowd had gathered, all hushed conversations about how nice Dave was and an eye out for the widow. I spotted Fiona right away and went to stand with her. Dave was dead. The outside chance that I'd killed him wouldn't go away. A lingering, bitter taste in my mouth.

Tina arrived, looking deathly pale in her black outfit. Pat was with her, sober black suit and expressionless face. Tina held his arm for support.

She took her place inside and people began filing in. We joined the line and shuffled into the gloom. It was slow progress. We eventually reached the coffin, top half open. I looked at the corpse and shuddered involuntarily. It was like somebody'd made a wax copy of him. I guess that's what death does to you. Only the husk remained. His forehead was lumpy, like the bullet hole was filled in with putty. I guessed it really was.

We commiserated with Tina. What a couple. The best friend who took Dave away from her and the employee who shagged his brains out. I felt a pang of guilt in my gut, put it down to hunger. Glad that Tina didn't spit her usual dirty looks at me. She seemed resigned now. Going with the flow, playing the dutiful widow, the survivor.

A sudden wave of claustrophobia and nausea overwhelmed me. I had to get out. I nodded to Pat and whispered to Fiona that I was going for air. She stayed with Tina. Outside, I leant against the railings and smoked a cigarette. It tasted like shit, so I went to my car and rolled a joint as discretely as possible. I walked down a litter-strewn, stinking alley and smoked it. Feeling a lot better, I went and waited at the railings again.

Then the coffin came out, supported by Dave's two brothers, his dad, Pat and two guys I didn't know. The coffin was placed in a hearse and the procession to the church began. They were walking behind the hearse, the church just metres away.

My nausea returned, so I decided to skip the rest of the proceedings. Waited at the church door until all were in, sat in the car. Then, like when low tide exposes the river's secrets, I got to see some of the truth. A list of victims tied Greg O'Doherty into most of what had happened, which I knew. But there was also some unseen force at work. A dark, sneaky-as-fuck force.

When I factored my fucked-up house into the equation, that unknown force showed its hand. Those fucking Flynns, they were the killers, their shitty hands were all over the case. And I'd been too stoned, too dim to spot it.

O'Doherty is using the Flynns to do his dirty work. Chances are they've always worked together.

Jesus, how did I miss it? They're so close together, they would have killed each other long ago if it wasn't for some sort of pact.

All I was missing was a reason why the dark force hadn't made sure to kill me stone dead.

I went home, stuck on the *Lost In Translation* soundtrack, smoked some joints, fondled my gun, tried to come up with a reason for the Flynns to kill Dave. Nothing. I put Dave's DVD in my player, thinking a wank might take my mind off stuff for half a minute. Only it wasn't regular porn, more of a home-made job, regular people, group sex. I jumped ahead again and again. It got filthier, weirder, scarier. What in the fuck was Dave doing with this shit?

More confused than before, I slipped into sleep on the armchair, the AK in my lap. *This is hard.*

CHAPTER 48. MYSTERY TOUR

Woken an hour later by the phone. Pat said We're going out tonight, get organised. I had a pain deep in my thighs from the damned gun. Stashed it in the closet under the stairs. Put the DVD away in my jacket. I smoked three cigarettes and drank a cup of black coffee. No milk.

I groaned, body clock confused. Then I shaved with lukewarm water.

Ready by nine, smelling good. Pat came. I asked him about the girl, *Any news?*

He said 'Nothing major, forensics were after the killer's DNA, nothing yet'.

I feared a serial killer on the way back up to my room. I snorted deeply, quietly. The rush was intense and I felt awake. Bounded down to Pat.

'All set?' I asked, eager to go.

'Yeah, just a sec. I've something to show you.'

'What?'

'Poop sheets on the Flynns. Interested?'

He took a bundle of rolled-up A4 sheets out of his jacket's inside pocket. He held them out to me, grinned.

'What's so funny,' I asked.

'Take a look,' he answered. Not much of an answer.

I took the sheets and sat on the couch. I lit a cigarette and studied the first page as Pat looked through my CD collection. Tony Flynn, twenty-nine, leader of the gang, served two years for the manslaughter of a rival dealer in Moyross. The Flynns came from the poor side of Moyross, Glenagross. A wasteland of burnt houses, shaven-headed kids and mean teenagers on every corner. Horses and Mercs, conspicuous wealth beside abject poverty. Tony Flynn was the brains behind the operation and had succeeded in building a drug business worth seven figures a year. No wonder he also owned the flashiest house in Killaloe.

His brother Mickey was a year younger and more brutal. He was the gang enforcer. He'd done four years in Limerick Prison for killing a traveller boss who got in their way. Mickey was a certifiable mental case. Oddly, he didn't look at all like his brothers, who were ugly as fuck. Mickey was good-looking, in a mental kind of way.

Pat stuck on a Thin Lizzy album, selecting *Whiskey in the Jar*. Classic.

Young Sam Flynn, the one I'd kicked the bollick off, was only fourteen, but already a handful. Involved in all sorts of petty larceny, fights, minor dealing and using insulting or abusive behaviour, you could see that the cops were already exasperated with him, but couldn't nail him on anything. It was clear from his sheet that this kid would eventually kill people, but there was sweet fuck all anyone could do to prevent this.

'What do you think?' asked Pat, who'd been watching me while I read.

'Not very pretty, are they. I mean, look at Mickey's haircut. Is this a mullet I see before me? And a lazy eye? Fuck me.'

'We reckon they've got about a dozen foot soldiers. Most of them would pull a trigger without hesitation.'

'So blasting my house would be no big deal?'

'Like a walk in the park. Just the outside risk of getting caught with the gun. In fairness, if any one of these fucks was ordered to get you proper, you'd be dead by now.'

'Jesus, thanks Pat.'

I didn't need the truth told so bluntly.

'Sorry. Just to let you know the gravity of this fucking mess.'

'Jesus.'

'Oh yeah, the boys in the station say Thanks.'

'For what?' I asked.

'With the two little langers you hospitalised off the streets, muggings are down twenty percent.'

'Are you serious?'

I stared at the photos of all three Flynns, imprinting their ugly mugs on my brain. I'd have to be able to spot them automatically if I was to have any chance of defending myself. Pat said I could keep the sheets, they were just copies. I folded them up neatly and put them in my jacket pocket, right beside the weird porn DVD.

Pat smoked another cigarette and brought the talk back to Dave.

'I'm just worried,' he said. 'If we can't turn up something concrete, I'm just going to make it fit somebody, anybody.'

'What? It was obviously a hit, wasn't it?'

'Maybe. But there's also evidence for the robbery.'

'Like what?'

'Like Dave's wallet was emptied. It looks like someone went through his drawers as well.'

'You kidding? What about the gun?'

'It was used in an armed robbery on a post office a couple of years back. Nobody was hurt and they got away with fifty grand. They fired a round into the ceiling to shut everyone up.'

'Shit. That can't be it. It can't be.'

I was worried. Dead worried that whoever killed Dave would get away because of my stupidity. The porn lead had to lead me somewhere.

'Oh yeah,' he said, 'Dave didn't give you any DVDs lately did he?'

'No. Why?'

'You sure, Charlie?'

'Sure I'm sure.'

He looked at me blankly, watching my reaction. I gritted my teeth and, to myself, said *Fucking hell, where's this going?*

'Cos I'm definitely going to have to pin this on somebody,' he muttered, only half to himself.

CHAPTER 49. STALKED

We drove into town in Pat's car. He was scanning, alert. I was half-worried he was driving me to the station to charge me with Dave's murder. Would he have his man, though?

'I thought we were going out, Pat.'

'We are. Relax Charlie. I'm working, but you do anything you want. Anything. Okay?'

'Mystery tour or what?'

'You got it, man. You got it. Time to kill, first.'

We stopped off for a pint in Nancy Blake's. No sooner had we grabbed a pew out back, than Etoile appeared beside me. With her aunt over from Africa, Emily.

This was a surprise, but not exactly a problem.

'Pat, this is Etoile, who I was with the other night.'

'Yes, Charlie defended my honour. My man.'

'Very good,' said Pat, winking at me.

Then Pat took a call and had to split back to the station. So I was left with the ladies.

Etoile was full-on, staring into my eyes and rubbing my thighs. My *Fatal Attraction* alarm bells began to ring, off in the recesses of my twisted skull. I didn't hear them. Her aunt was gas, not bad-looking for her age, wicked cat's eyes, full of gold, splashing the cash, rubbing my head. They flattered me and I asked them a hundred questions about Africa. After a while, we strolled up town for some grub. I sensed a long night ahead.

I texted Pat to find us in the Chicken Hut and that I'd get him a snack box. We walked the short distance and joined the long queue. I attracted a few dirty looks from little knackers. I sneered back, they turned away. After the previous week's fiasco, I figured that if anyone else started on me over Etoile, I should just kill them stone dead. Get it over with. I felt myself for the revolver. Gone back. Shit. I stopped sneering.

The queue moved quickly, so we got four snack boxes and found a table upstairs, with a great view of the night mobs as they searched for food, sex or fights. The gravy, a salty sauce with the look and consistency of pale diarrhoea, was not to the girls' taste, so I scoffed it all.

As we took our Formica seats, Pat came and tucked into his chicken.

'No gravy?' he asked, disappointed.

'All gone, man,' I said. 'Anyway, it's got to be bad for you.'

The girls smiled. Etoile kept looking at me and laughing to herself, touching me under the table. Nice, but I didn't really feel up to playing games. Pat devoured his food, licked the grease from his fingers.

'So ladies, will we walk you to your taxi?'

'So early, Charlie? Do we bore you?' said Etoile, pretending to be highly offended.

'Now, now. Don't cast aspersions on my manners. You have to get home to your husband, don't you?'

'Not really.'

'Why not?'

'I'm not really married. I'm sorry I lied to you. I say it to every man I meet. I have to.'

'Jesus.'

Pat winked at me again.

Etoile stared into my eyes, a wide smile on her lips. I couldn't decide whether this was a good or a bad turn.

'I've an idea,' began Pat, nodding at me. 'Myself and Charlie were going to go and check out a lapdancing club for an hour. Would you like to come along, see what it's about?'

Then they both said Yes and we were on our way. I wasn't sure about any of it. The city streets buzzed with drunks. Still very mild, t-shirt weather at ten. A glow to the west.

Etoile linked her arm through mine. I held a cigarette with the other and inhaled its ghastly smoke while trying to smell her hair. The club was just a block away and they joked, mixing English and French, about whether they'd dance for us or not. How cosmopolitan is that? I asked Pat if the club allowed this and imagined Etoile sliding down an oiled pole, glistening in the half-light. Began to feel more positive about it all.

The club was halfway down an alley off Thomas Street. A cluster of people waited at the entrance, which was well-lit, bright red. Discrete sign on the wall, cut-out metal letters, silver against the red brick wall. When it opened first, they had a big fat neon sign. People complained. They changed the sign. By then, everyone in five counties knew about Pussy Galore in Limerick. Pussies Galore, they called it. Two clean, smiling bouncers checked people, padding down some punters. Whether they were looking for weapons or camcorders, I do not know. They sounded Russian.

Inside, the club was dark, humid, jangling noises of strained conversations. And the odd yelp. Loud music, Coldplay's *Yellow*, pounded from unseen speakers as we passed through a narrow hall, framed photos of naked women, nipples and pubes hidden by fruit and other props. They were dancers in the club. Maybe Dave's work. I was simultaneously paying homage to the man and trying to discover why he died.

We found a dimly-lit booth and Pat ordered a bottle of white wine. Squeezed into the padded seats, Etoile's thigh pressed against mine. A dancer performed on the pole just in front of us. She looked Czech or something, tall, blond - long and dead straight - hair, fantastically built and not a hint of shyness. My kind of woman. She wrapped her legs around the pole, making eye contact with me straight off and licking her lips. Etoile saw this and took my chin in her hand. She twisted my face to hers and planted a wet kiss on my lips, while simultaneously rubbing her hand along my inner thigh. The tinted glass table did a good job of hiding my erection.

I'd been semi-hard since I walked in the door: the smell of sex, the idea of lapdancing. Now I was stuck in my seat until the blood in my engorged cock figured that the rest of my body needed a visit. Could take a while. Etoile took her mouth off me, flicking her tongue as she went. The pole dancer wasn't deterred. By now she was wearing only a red thong, her enhanced breasts calling to me, the crowd cheering her simulated sex acts. Lewd and I loved it. Sad fuck.

The blond finished her dance and there was a lull. People talked and drank. After a while, she came to our table and asked me if I'd like a lapdance. She spoke perfect English, in a clipped, direct tone. Like she was German. I looked at Etoile, eyebrows raised. She shrugged, knowing she couldn't stop me even if she'd wanted to. I said I'd need a voucher and the blond signalled to a guy waiting at the bar. He came over and sold me a voucher for twenty quid. This system was to stop the girls ripping off the club. No matter how many dances they did, they could take only vouchers. At the end of the night, they'd swap vouchers for cash, less the club's fifty percent, of course.

I gave her the voucher and asked her name. Leila. Just in from Moscow. She stood before me, a chiffon wrap over her red bikini outfit, tapping her feet, waiting. Other dancers who'd scored also waited with their punters. The DJ, hidden somewhere in the back, watching his monitor, took the cue and put on a dance track. Dance tracks were engineered to get straight into the song, then wrap it up after three minutes. That's what you got for your twenty. The song was from an Austin Powers movie. *I Touch Myself.* Christ above.

Leila rocked her hips in every direction, legs well-spread, then whipped off her wrap, bringing her perfect, firm curves within inches off my face. After much finger-licking, which - momentarily - brought me back to my fried chicken, she took her bra off and fondled herself.

Christ, she was perfect. I was in a reverie, her sexuality firing at me on every possible level, firing only for me. When I think about you, I touch myself.

As Leila played with her thong, pulling the sides up to give me a flash of trimmed pubes and turning around to stick her perfect arse in my face, the music faded and abruptly stopped. Game over. She gave me a kiss on the cheek and whispered in my ear.

'See you around, big boy,' she said, looking me straight in the eye. I wanted her so badly I couldn't speak.

She gathered her clothes and went out back to get ready for the next dance session. Meanwhile, background music filled the small room and another dancer took to the pole.

'Nice one, Charlie,' said Pat, his eyes gleaming. 'She's a beaut! I'd eat chips from her knickers.'

'Jesus.'

'I thought I was your girlfriend, Charlie,' said Etoile, not so happy now.

'What?'

'Do you know how demeaning it is for me to sit here and watch your behaviour with that whore?'

'Sorry, but - '

'This is your final warning, Charlie. I won't be treated with this disrespect again.'

She signalled her aunt, who gave me a stare that would knock a horse, and they stood up. They both said something in some African dialect. It sounded like a damned curse or something. Gave me the creeps. I hoped I wouldn't see them again, feared there was something going on with Etoile, something I didn't want to get involved with.

CHAPTER 50. TO BE RICH

So they left, hissing.

'What the fuck?' I asked Pat.

'I don't know where you get them from Charlie. But we're probably better off. You'll see.'

Confused to hell, I drank and looked around for Leila, my eyes resting on a tough dude with an elbow on the bar. He looked familiar. He drank a bottle of Heineken and seemed taken with the pole dancer, sweating profusely with his black leather jacket still on. Then I remembered. It was one of O'Doherty's goons I'd met in the pub the day before, Luke's funeral. He seemed to be just a punter, but I was learning fast that you don't take things at face value if you value your hide in this town. He hadn't spotted me.

I saw the manager of the place, who went behind the bar and emptied the till of fifties and twenties. He counted the money and stuck it in his inside pocket. The goon watched him closely, either eyeing the place for a hold-up or acting as muscle. When the manager came out and walked to the back of the club, where I figured the offices were, O'Doherty's muscle followed him. Leila was there too.

'Jesus,' said Pat quietly, 'that guy with him is one of O'Doherty's men.'

'O'Doherty?' I said.

'Yeah. I didn't know he had any connection with this place, though. Could be collecting protection money or something. I'll have to have a word with vice.'

Pat pondered the development. I made the connection. The dismembered bodies of two unidentified eastern European men had been found down the Shannon Estuary a year before, a mess of decayed flesh and sun-bleached bones on the mudflats, grub for the gulls. Once the lapdancing business had got going, O'Doherty must have forced his way in for a piece of the action. The Russian boys had a tough reputation, but they were on foreign soil and there was no way they could get to O'Doherty in his Island fiefdom. They must have bitten their tongues and allowed him in. I'd have to talk to Jean about this. And soon.

We relaxed over our beers and the place died down. Leila was gone, only one or two dancers remained.

'Time to go,' said Pat, checking his watch.

We drove out the Ennis Road in Pat's work car, the radio keeping us up to speed on the night's stabbings, muggings, rapes and shootings.

'You carrying Charlie?'

'No. I got rid of that.'

'So you've nothing?'

'Nothing at all, clean,' I lied. This was my friend, but I was still concerned. Cagey, worried about something as yet unclear.

'Okay. Clean.'

We drove out past the Two Mile Inn, heading towards Shannon Airport. The road was quiet, the moon nearly full. We turned at the Radisson, heading up Cratloe Hill. A mile or so up the road, we turned left into a private driveway, through a densely-wooded area and into an open clearing before a huge old house perched on the side of the hill. Floodlights lit up the freshly-painted house and a few people stood before it. Off to the side, I spotted a car park, full of gleaming Mercs and caterers' vans. Plenty of heavies lurking purposefully around the place.

I had a wrap of coke on me and figured it might make an appearance sharpish. Something big was happening.

We parked and merged with the group of people who were standing around. A few cabs pulled up and out popped Leila and a gaggle of excited lapdancers.

'Jesus fucking Christ, Pat! What's going on?'

'I figured you'd enjoy this.'

'Say, man. Whose party is this anyway?'

'It's in honour of a visitor from London. Well, he's from Russia, but he mainly lives in London now. Mikhail Karpov. Very nice man. Very rich. You could call him a tycoon. He should be here soon. He's flying in from Moscow. I'm here to keep an eye on him, casual like.'

'Nice.'

Pat led the way up the wide stone steps. Three heavies waited by the entrance. They stopped me. They weren't your standard rugby-playing muscle.

They were older, Russian, fit. I figured them for ex-military or KGB. They wore formal jackets with telltale bulges and earpieces. Two used handheld scanners to check me for weapons while the other watched. I was passed; Pat was just waved through. They knew him.

In the entrance hallway was a huge crystal chandelier, a rug on the floor: some sort of Russian crest with a mermaid, and a woman in evening dress with a tray of champagne flutes. Two guys in servant outfits took our jackets and the woman gave us a drink. Leila and her friends looked absolutely stunning, wearing obviously expensive evening dresses, dangerously high heels and dripping in gold. Leila wore red. Her colour.

We walked through the hall and into a reception room. The house was a big Georgian job, high ceilings, plaster details and the smell of money. The crowd was mixed: plenty of Russians, a few local yokels and many more with permanent suntans and smug expressions.

Limerick was a natural base for the Russians. Aeroflot had been flying through Shannon, en route to Cuba, for years. Perfect for smuggling in both directions, coke one way, guns the other. Plus, Russian coal ships delivered to the Moneypoint power station just down the estuary. You could bring in a tank on one of those fuckers. Ireland was seen as a soft touch by international criminals, with its dysfunctional state apparatus and sleazy corruption at every level of society. Our Russian friends must feel right at home here.

'Hi Leila,' I said, after I made my way around the room to her.

'Hello. Nice to see you again.'

'I'm Charlie Doyle.'

'And I'm Leila, but you know that already.'

She offered her hand and, on impulse, I kissed it. This made her laugh. She had an easy laugh.

'Let's stand over there,' she said, tugging my elbow towards a quiet corner. A grand piano sat there, pregnant with sound, while a string quartet filled the air with class. No sign of Pat.

'So how's Mr Karpov so loaded, Leila?' I asked.

'Oil,' she replied, 'He bought stakes in three oil companies, right when the old regime collapsed. His stakes are now worth many billions of dollars.'

'Jesus.'

One of the richest men in the world, right here. I'd never seen a billionaire but I liked him already.

More people arrived and trays of caviar and foie gras on fancy crackers did the rounds. Whenever I emptied my glass, a woman with a bottle - Dom Perignon no less - was at my shoulder. It was certainly the classiest party I'd ever been to. Many people knew Leila and she introduced me to most of them.

One guy dragged me away from Leila and led me to the vodka table. Stolichnaya, the finest Russian vodka, served ice cold. I had a couple of shots, toasting our host. Then a nice long - really long - vodka tonic with ice and lemon. Perfection.

Smythe arrived with a girl on his arm. Not his wife.

I met Leila again and we found a baroque chaise longue to sit on. I asked questions. She had a degree in Russian literature and business from Moscow University. A first.

'Tolstoy, Dostoyevsky, Chekhov. The greatest writers ever, the Golden Age of Literature. Just look at Chekhov. He invented modern literature with all its petty obsessions and inconclusiveness before Joyce even thought about *Ulysses*.'

I admitted my ignorance of Chekhov.

'And wasn't *Ulysses* just a rip-off of a Greek myth? Do you know Dublin much?'

She was animated, interested, holding my elbow with her free hand, though her bright eyes constantly darted around the room.

'You see this glass of champagne?' she asked, holding her bubbling nectar up to the light. Chekhov wrote a story about the effect it can have. Like I'm feeling now.'

'Really? What's it called?'

'*Champagne*. Look it up. You can get a collection of his stories in most bookshops for about two euro. New. The cheapest culture ever. I must mingle. Back soon.'

My head was light, happy again. I decided that sport, kids, DIY, shopping, golf, drinking, work or religion wouldn't do it for me, wouldn't fill my life, the long empty years stretching ahead. Golf? It would be books. Reading first - so many books, classics, I've never even picked up - then I'd write.

Crime thrillers, maybe. Christ, you couldn't make up my life.

Leila flitted around the room, connected with everybody, only a couple of dozen yet. She made her way back to me. I told her I'd just decided to become a writer.

'So what would you like to write?' she asked. 'Something based on your own experiences, maybe?'

'Maybe. But nobody'd believe it. Anyhow my memory's fucked. I've had such blackouts lately you would not believe.'

'And what would be your quest?'

'Quest?'

'It's said that all fictional detectives are on a personal quest, that the case is just a means to an end.'

I'd never thought about that. We drank more and a crowd of people appeared suddenly, all suits. The music faded and the chatter dropped away.

From a far doorway, not the one we'd used, came Mikhail Karpov, flanked by two serious-looking bodyguards. There was a smattering of gentle applause. Karpov was not at all like a little Leon Trotsky, which was how I'd pictured him. He was tall, a bit chubby, but well-built, clean-shaven, bald. He wore a tailored suit - got to be Armani - in light grey, a white silk shirt and a mint green tie. Immaculate. I figured his outfit to be worth ten grand at least. A Rolex peeked from under his sleeve and his fingers were adorned with heavy gold rings. Karpov raised his hand and addressed us, again in perfect English.

'My friends,' he began, 'I am so happy to be with you, this wonderful night. Ireland is my second home now and this special house, where I am free to entertain you all, is one of my favourites. I trust you are all being looked after?'

There was an enthusiastic murmur of affirmation, a round of applause.

'Good, good. Now, to business, which won't take long. I have made this special trip tonight to tell you of my newest project.'

He nodded at someone off to the side and, with a quiet whirring, a projector screen slid down from the ceiling as the lights dimmed. An image appeared on the screen, Karpov's logo, a mermaid, Russian text underneath. It was like the bad guy's logo in a James Bond film.

I felt like I was in a damned movie.

CHAPTER 51. MASTER PLAN

The logo faded, replaced by a shot of a computer-generated low-rise building, all glass. It was maybe five stories and had choppers swirling around it. The viewpoint changed and began to swing around and through the building, showing luxury rooms, gyms, pools, a clinic, golf courses, forests and the ocean. The film paused on a frontal shot of the building, big graphics.

ATLANTIC RETREAT - A KARPOV DEVELOPMENT

Everyone applauded. Karpov held his hands up for silence and continued his presentation.

'This will be the most luxurious hotel in Europe,' he said. 'It will meet the most exacting standards in architecture, construction and facilities. Every room will have a view of the Atlantic Ocean. For relaxation, for doing business, for leading edge surgical procedures, for pleasure. Atlantic Retreat will cost three hundred million euro to build and equip. One of our main target markets will be Russia, so we will use many staff from my homeland. We will target the richest men in the world and offer them the finest destination on the planet.'

A new slide appeared on-screen, showing that all roads - South American, North American, European, Middle Eastern, Asian, African - will soon lead to Limerick.

He was beaming now, his cool front slipping. A trace of megalomania bubbled to the surface. He paused for effect.

'I could not hope to complete such a huge task,' he went on, 'without the assistance and partnership of one man. A man who has the power and connections to make our goals achievable. Ladies and gentlemen, I present to you my good friend and partner, Dr Fox.'

Fox left Smythe's side and walked up to Karpov. They shook hands like old friends. I spotted Pat standing beside the stage, scanning the room, but avoiding eye contact with me. Fox said a few words about how delighted he was to be involved and looked forward to the fancy Chamber of Commerce dinner the following night. Karpov, enjoying the limelight, then went on at length about how fabulous Ireland was and how he was applying for citizenship.

I had a feeling that the hotel development could be just a fresh cover for getting women, drugs and guns from eastern Europe and Russia into the EU by the back door. Karpov and Fox could be building the world's most exclusive knocking shop, with a little extra on the side for the richest perverts in the world. A scary thought. And Putin was putting pressure on Russia's oil barons, looking to take the industry back. Oil wealth was fleeing the Russian taxman. I wondered if Karpov was the moneyman behind everything going on in town. King Perv. And Fox his crown prince.

Then Karpov wound up the presentation and ordered everyone to enjoy the rest of the party. In the nicest possible way, of course.

Waiting staff reappeared and offered silver platters of caviar, king prawn in tempura batter and sushi. I tried a prawn. Best one I'd ever tasted. I tasted caviar for the very first time. Odd stuff. What a fantastic party.

I whispered into Leila's ear, enjoying her smell and asking if she'd like to do a line. She nodded.

'Come with me,' she said, taking my hand and leading me out of the room and towards the stairs. A heavy stood at the bottom of the plush stairway, blocking our way. Leila smiled at him and said a few words in Russian. He smiled back and stepped aside.

'What did you tell him?' I asked as we ascended.

'I told him I was taking you upstairs for a fuck.'

CHAPTER 52. COITUS -

I followed her up the wide stairs, admiring what looked like genuine Impressionist paintings on the wall. A Monet, for sure, now a Van Gogh. On the landing, she took my hand and put her finger to her lips, silently advising me to keep quiet. I nodded and we passed down a hallway with ornate doors on both sides. The first few doors were closed. We came to a door which was half ajar. She peeked inside. Nobody. She pulled me in and closed the door quietly.

'Closed doors no good,' she said. 'Open doors are free rooms.'

'You've done this before?'

She smiled and switched on the light. The room was like the Presidential Suite in a top hotel. The bed was huge, soft, white. Antique furniture and fittings, plus a well-stocked bar, added to the feeling of luxury. I strolled around and took it all in.

'Jesus Christ!' I exclaimed. 'Is that a Picasso?'

'Probably,' said Leila.

She walked over to me and we admired the early Cubist sketch of a woman carrying a jug of water.

'Yes,' she said then. 'It is a Picasso. Good, yes?'

'Fuck me, he could draw. A Picasso in a guest bedroom. A guest bedroom! How's that for class?'

Amazed by the wealth that surrounded me, I rummaged in my pockets and found the cocaine and began cutting it up on a silver tray. Leila sat on the bed and took her heels off.

'That feels better,' she said, laying back and feeling the soft quilt.

'All set here, Leila.'

I gave her a rolled-up fifty and she snorted two lines. I took the note back and inhaled some of Colombia's top export. Mighty. Seconds later, she was on top of me. She pushed me on to the bed, lifted up her red dress, then sat on me, grinding hard against my crotch. I tried to pull her down for a kiss. She resisted.

'My make-up, Charlie,' she protested.

'Hooker sex, then?'

'Hooker sex,' she laughed.

She stood up, released a hidden catch and her dress slid down to the floor. She wore red knickers and bra. These came off too. Her nakedness was astonishing. Even though I'd seen most of her before, the sight of her clipped, blond pubes made me as hard as a Russian bodyguard. She undid my belt and slipped my trousers off. The coke coursed through my veins with my sex hormones. The anticipatory delight was almost too much. My heart almost exploded. I could feel it. She pulled a condom from a pile on the bedside table and unrolled it over my pulsing penis. Then she got on the bed, ready to sit on me.

A knock at the door.

Christ!

Her face was in mine, nostrils flared, breaths shallow. There was a look too. I hoped it was disappointment.

More knocking, sharper, and some words in Russian.

'Da,' she said.

Then, without saying a word more, she raised herself, picked up her clothes and went into the bathroom. I took the disappointed condom off. I had a hint of her smell, complex and evocative. I regretted not having gone down on her - instead of farting around with the coke - and prayed to the God of Sex that I would, some day, be given the opportunity for cunnilingus with Leila.

I sat on the bed, waited for her, smoked a cigarette. My heart pounded on, confused.

Leila came out of the bathroom after a minute.

'I am needed. I will see you.'

She returned to the party, leaving me with a hard-on that could sink the Titanic and an indelible memory of her nakedness. What an idiot.

CHAPTER 53. HEARTBURN

After a little more coke and half a stupid inkling to lift the Picasso, I went downstairs. I joined a group of well-pissed suits, but the conversation centred on the hotel business. I laughed when everyone else laughed and nodded when they nodded. But I couldn't take my eyes off Leila as she flitted around the room. When she took the hand of a clammy suit from the Chamber of Commerce and led him from the room, jealousy welled up inside me. At least with you it was for pleasure, I told myself. Little consolation. Christ, I'd never felt this jealous before.

I wrote some mental notes, Karpov and every other name I heard. A beautiful Asian woman in blue silk handed out brochures. I took one.

I found a quiet spot in the conservatory and sat down to think things over some more. My conspiracy theories were beginning to gel. A waiter kept my glass topped up. What lives the rich lead.

I found myself sitting on the patio after five as the sun came up, a bottle of Dom Perignon in one hand and a cigarette in the other. From behind me, the sun cleared the ridge, illuminating the vista to the west, in front of the house. A flowing ribbon of pale grey burst into life as the sun rose over the hills. Patches of mist shimmered. Misty blotches became defined. The river glistened, showing off her lazy, serpentine curves as she neared the Atlantic.

Truthfully, a wonderful location for a swanky hotel. Wasn't Dromoland Castle, Ireland's most exclusive venue, only down the road? Bollocks or not, Karpov's grand plan at least had a ring of authenticity about it. Clever fuck. I guessed you had to be a clever fuck to become a billionaire. I wondered if I was up to all this. Could a drug-addled private dick from Limerick really hope to take on this guy? Self doubt, always self doubt.

I gazed at the stunning panorama, wondering if I should split, when Leila came and sat beside me. I offered her my bottle, which she took and swigged from.

'How are you?' I asked.

'I'm good. This is beautiful, isn't it?'

'Yeah, beautiful. Leila, do you mind me asking you a personal question?'

'No. If I can ask you one, too.'

'Okay. So, why is such a beautiful, intelligent girl like you, working as a lapdancer?'

'You mean a hooker?' she laughed.

'Well, you said it.'

'For the money, Charlie. For the money. I imagine we just don't have the kind of sexual hang-ups you have here. We never had organised religion under communism. No guilt, no sense that sex is dirty or wrong. And our history is very depressing. So we do what we must and we grab joy any way we can.'

'I can bring you joy. What's Russian for cunnilingus?'

'And in a couple of years, I'll have enough money to own a business back home.'

'Oh yeah? What?'

'Maybe a brothel, maybe a bookshop. I haven't decided yet.'

'Okay. That's a good answer. Now ask your question.'

She thought for a minute.

'Charlie, why are you not married?'

Jesus!

'I was married. It all fell apart. I suppose the main reason was me. I have this addictive, compulsive personality. Sex, drugs, booze, whatever. I just want the experience of the instant, the moment. I'm a selfish prick, really. I've fuck-all to show for my life. Fuck-all. I don't know where I'm going. All I know is I'm happy when I have sex or get high. Pathetic, really.'

'It's not pathetic. At least you're honest with yourself. You just have this Catholic guilt thing. There's nothing wrong with wanting to enjoy sensations. Living for the moment is actually an excellent philosophy. Just get over the guilt. Guilt is terrible.'

This made me feel better. Then she rested her head on my shoulder, which made me feel a bit special.

'I think I love you. That or I've heartburn.'

I don't know if she got the joke, she just smiled. We sat for a while and savoured the view.

Then everyone was called for breakfast. Full Irish, huge plates alive with delicate pork flavours and saltiness and delicious grease. It was served on long tables in a huge dining room out back, glowing in the midsummer morning's sunshine. Karpov - still wired - shook hands with everybody who was left. The man had a damned strong grip.

Then taxis arrived. Leila stayed on. I took a cab alone, Pat having disappeared during the night. It felt surreal, driving into town at nine on a Tuesday morning, after that bizarre and amazing and terrifying party. The car was quiet. But my head was buzzing, filled with hidden enemies, unseen killers and the awful awareness that I was hurtling towards some kind of resolution. And I finally realized the worst truth: someone else was behind everything. There was a missing link, someone close. But who was it?

I wrote some shaky notes as the cab belted in the Ennis Road. I felt alive and bright and the fog in my head began to fade.

CHAPTER 54. IF I WAS

Straight to the office, to find my new assistant at work. Fiona had the computer connected to the internet. She gave me a ten minute demo that made my head spin. She showed how to do Google searches, look up city maps, access newspaper archives, the works. I had an urge to look up seagulls, put that down to excessive drugtaking.

'Fucking CIA or what?' I laughed.

'Watch this,' she said. 'Microsoft Works projects.'

She'd set up project management files for jobs, linking all the bits of clues and background together off one page. I was amazed. She was good.

'You look rough.'

'Up all night. Here, have a look at this brochure, Karpov's new hotel. Maybe check on his business partners, Fox and the likes. I've to go home and freshen up.'

'Don't be late, Charlie.'

'I will in my hole be late for my best friend's funeral.'

She stayed on and I strolled up to my kip of a house. I made some coffee, feeling depressed at everything the day held in store. I showered and put on a charcoal grey suit with a blue shirt, no tie. I did a line of cocaine and rolled up half a dozen joints, which I would need just to get through the shit. I put the rifle back in the boot of the car, along with my heavily-laden jacket, and drove to the church.

Parking in the shadow of St John's spire, I hurried into the church right on ten-thirty.

The day was bright, clear, warm. Dave would have liked it. The priest was kicking off, Dave's closed coffin on a stand before the altar. There was a good crowd and I took a pew at the back. After some standard funeral prayers, the priest launched into a homage to Dave. I smiled when he spoke of Dave's teenage years and his prowess on the rugby field. Then he studied photography at art college - where I met him - and set up a successful business, providing well for his wife. He said that we should be grateful for the time he gave us and his legacy, a son. At this, Tina broke down in tears and had to be supported by her sisters, one on each side.

More prayers and then his younger brother said a few nervous words. I gazed at the coffin, imagined Dave's already-decomposing body, how easily a man could die. Just one little bullet, one killer, one reason.

I felt misplaced, left the church. Met Pat at the doorway.

'Have you anything?'

'Nada.'

'Really Charlie? Nothing? You surprise me,' said Pat, curious at my lack of ideas. I was normally the ideas man.

'Sorry man,' I apologised,' I've just been fucked up by this you know? It still hurts. And this paedophile thing has me in a daze, I swear to God. I don't know what the fuck is going on. Look, just a guess, right?'

'Yes?' he asked, happier now. We moved away from the door as Tina came out, crying like a child, eyes red. I blessed myself, displaying petty comfort in mystical tradition.

'How about if Dave was given some footage to put together for a DVD for paedophiles? Maybe by the Russians, maybe not. He sees someone he knows, maybe someone famous. Blackmails him, gets whacked.'

Pat nodded more and agreed that this would be plausible.

'I'll get someone to take a shot of every face on all his footage, men and women and children.'

'I don't want to see any of that stuff, Pat.'

'I know, just the faces. I promise.'

'Cool. I have to take my car. I've stuff in the boot.'

'Okay, pity,' he said. 'That everything?'

'I swear.'

He went to his work car and I went to mine as the car park filled with people wearing black. After a couple of chaotic minutes, I eased out on to the choked street and waited in line behind the hearse, which was moving ahead slowly. I put the radio on and lit a spliff. My mind was fixated on the notion that Dave had been given the paedophile footage, was disgusted and threatened either whoever gave it to him or someone in it. Or did he make it? If he had, I'd've killed him myself.

The DVD might contain a clue. I'd have to watch it closely, wait for Pat to get the face prints done up. Time of death inconclusive? Who the fuck are they kidding?

It was slow progress up past the jail. I lit up a second spliff as we passed the grey stone blocks of St Joseph's, unchanged since Victorian times, the four-faces of the clock stubbornly frozen at half-one. I imagined my mother at one of the windows, gazing blankly at the unmoving clock from her padded cell, thinking that time had actually stopped. This brought me closer to tears than anything else. I made a vow to go see her soon and mused that the one street contained the city's jail, mental hospital and graveyard. Always best to just pass through Mulgrave Street.

I parked beside the Munster Fair Tavern and snuck in for a fast vodka while the funeral got into position beside a hole in the ground. Used to be the Fair Green across the road, horse fairs, circuses, all that stuff. Duels to the death in the olden days, when wigs would fly. DIY superstores and council houses now.

Around to the graveyard, Mount St Lawrence's, biggest in town. You'd only get in there now if it was a family plot. Tina figured Dave would be happier with his parents than waiting for her, the one he'd lost so completely.

The graveyard was what you'd expect, ancient names and crumbling crosses. Flowers in all stages of decay, big trees, ash and sycamore. Heavy clouds gathered in the open sky, their edges glowing gold. A sense of calm. I like graveyards.

Pat found me and we stayed at the edge of proceedings. Dave's hole gaped, waiting. The priest started talking and there were plenty of Amens. *This is the end, my friend, the end.*

'I called the station on the way. I should have those stills later on,' said Pat.

'Great,' I said. 'What poor sap has to look at them?'

'We've two guys who've seen everything imaginable over the last few years. Doesn't seem to bother them. They did some course on it in the States, detachment training they call it. And a shrink checks them out every few months, makes sure they're not losing it.'

'Mad. Then what?'

'Then we look at the faces, show them to Fiona. There she is,' he said, waving.

Fiona left the crowd and walked over to us, on the gravel path that ran between rows of graves. She looked great, a black silk dress that stopped just below her knees, showing just a glimpse of shadowy cleavage up top.

'Hi,' she said as I kissed her lightly on the cheek.

'How are you doing?' I asked.

'Fine,' she said. 'Better today.'

'Good,' said Pat. 'We're making progress on finding the killer. We should have a lot more by the weekend.'

'You dig up anything?' I asked Fiona. Maybe the internet had thrown up something. Fuck, there was so much I knew and just couldn't tell him.

'Yes,' she answered brightly. 'Good stuff. The Pussy Galore site has links to all sorts of European porn sites. Most of them need your credit card number before they even let you in. Serious operations. Then there was a bit of a weird thing.'

'What?' I asked.

'I just done a general search of Pussy Galore, in Google. Besides all the James Bond connections and porn, I found a couple of news reports to do with our club.'

'How?' said Pat.

'Russian news sites with archives. There was a double murder in Moscow a few months ago. Really nasty it was, an all. Two young ones had their throats slashed in a brothel. Their families said they were goin to Ireland, to work in Pussy Galore, which they were told was a model agency.'

'Jesus,' said Pat, astonished. 'Far as I know, nobody got on to us about that. I'll have to check it out.'

'Probably didn't bother because they got their man. Right Fiona?'

'Dead right, Charlie,' she said. 'The guy was collared within twenty-four hours. Confessed it all. The Moscow law probably thought Fuck Pussy Galore, case closed.'

'Who was he?' asked Pat, pressing for everything.

'The guy worked in the brothel.'

'Well done, Fiona,' said Pat. 'This could tie our boys into international people-smuggling. Sounds like the standard slavery scam. Those women were conned into coming here for modelling work, given a few quid up front, probably complained when they discovered that they'd be sex slaves, got the chop.'

'Fucking scum,' I said.

Fiona nodded, her passion raised by her research.

'These guys are for real. If Fiona's lead is kosher, they've been getting away with murder,' concluded Pat. 'Human trafficking is the biggest racket of all and Europe is where it's at.'

'Fuck's sake,' I said. 'First we have to get the gowl that killed Dave. Let's get over. He's in.'

We moved closer to the graveside. Dave's coffin was lowered into the hole, the attendants puffing in their battle against gravity. Then the priest threw in a handful of earth and blessed everyone. Tina didn't bother with the token dirt or jumping into the grave and left immediately with her sisters. Then I threw in some earth, as did some of Dave's other friends and relatives. It rattled off the coffin, scuffing its deadly sheen. The reddish brown soil clung to my sweaty hand and, trying to wipe it off with the other, I ended up with both hands filthy. Fiona gave me a make-up wipe from her bag. It helped.

Looking around at the sadness - maybe eight people crying openly, maybe fifteen more truly gutted - I feared that killing would be easy. To me, the whole funeral affair was old-fashioned, pointless, overblown. If I was the killer, I would relish the power to unleash emotion, to release my own bitterness, to do what everybody else is scared to. If I was.

We drifted out and away. Fiona took a lift from me and we drove back down the road towards town. Everyone stopped off in Jerry O'Dea's pub for tea and ham sandwiches. I had a pint of Guinness. I saw that Tina was drinking brandy. Get locked, girl. Best thing for you today.

Everybody seemed to settle after the first drink and a bit of grub. It would turn into a session: what Dave would have wanted. I figured I'd ditch the car and the gun, get langers safely.

I explained to Pat and Fiona about the car. Pat said he'd stay with Fiona until I got back, but he had to get to the station then for a meeting about the dead girl. Forensics reports due any minute, he said. I promised to be quick.

Straight to the office. Nobody lurking at the entrance, so straight in with the gun in the bag, bold as brass. Margaret put on a sad face and consoled me on losing my friend. She liked Dave, he was always pretend-flirting with her, dropping filthy double-entendres. I shared her grief for a moment then slowly climbed the stairs.

I looked around for a suitable hiding place. The gun was long enough and bulky. I put myself in the mind of a thief and wondered where I'd miss if I was turning the place over. I figured behind the new filing cabinet would be good. It was in a corner, tight. I pulled it out a couple of inches. The gun went in snugly and got lost in the shadow. I found an old flipchart and jammed that in there as well, then put some dead fluorescent tubes leaning against the gap. Looked like plain old office clutter. Perfect. I'd have to warn Fiona to not go there, allude that I'd porn or drugs or something hidden.

Everything else looked fine. I left the car around the corner. Then I caught a hackney back up to the pub.

The wake was in full swing by now. Another funeral party had descended on the place since and they were going at it full pelt. A sing-song had started among the oldies. I joined in for the Fields of Athenry while waiting for my Guinness to settle. Spotted Fiona and Pat down the back, chatting with Tina. She looked completely locked already. Christ.

Got my pint, finally. I gently eased through the dense, swaying crowd. People I didn't know spoke to me and touched my arm. Dave's aunties and uncles, I figured. Most were well on it by then. Funerals. I smiled and nodded stoically at each one, my brain obsessing over the terrible fear that I'd caused it all.

CHAPTER 55. THE LOOKING GLASS

Greg O'Doherty rarely felt nervous. But his palms were sweaty and the back of his neck itched as he put the chalk to the tip of his cue and lined up the break.

The bar, a popular spot on the New Road in Thomondgate, was quiet enough with just a couple of seasoned drinkers nursing their pints of Guinness at the bar. Down the back, a couple of barwives drank cider over ice while their barkids guzzled Coke and munched crisps. It was a kind of no-man's land. But still O'Doherty carried a gun.

'Age before beauty,' said Mickey, pouring peanuts from the bag into his mouth.

Greg broke, potting a red and a yellow.

'Two shots,' said Mickey. He turned to the woman behind the bar. 'These cuntin things are dry. Have you the salt?'

She didn't answer, busy pulling pints.

'Have you the cuntin salt?' he shouted.

'There's no need for that sort of language with kids in the bar,' she said, placing the glass salt cellar on the wooden counter, slapping it down.

Mickey poured a lot of salt into his peanuts, slammed it harder on the bar, went back to the game. He scanned the table and selected a yellow.

He potted it easily, the ball crashing into the worn pocket.

'I'm on yellows, so.'

He potted two more. Greg stared through a poem painted on the wall, the adventures of Drunken Thady.

'So what's the score, Greg?'

'Just a couple of things,' said Greg, looking around to ensure they had no audience.

'Go on.'

'There's a lot of shit goin down at the minute. I just want to see if you know antin about it.'

'Love to help you, Gregory. But I'm under strict orders from Belfast. Low profile and all that. Can't do shit. Cunts have me under their thumb. You wouldn't believe it. But I don't give a fuck as long as they pay me. Tiocfaidh ár lá.'

'So you're not up to antin?'

'Just the usual. Have to make a proper few fuckin quid, don't I?'

'Course. By the by, here's that'

Greg handed Luke a folded paper bag from his inside pocket.

'Muchos gracias, my man. Twenty?'

'That's all of it.'

'Cunt!' screamed Mickey, missing an easy pot.

The guys at the bar glanced over, swiftly turning back to their pints. The woman behind the bar consciously ignored the pool area, thinking *Fuck off out of it, you gowl, I've a pain in my head looking at you.* Mickey swamped his pint of Carling, then fixed his hair in the mirror by the blackboard. Greg thought

Look at the cunt, thinks he's gorgeous. Doesn't he know he has a lazy eye?

Greg lined up a shot.

'Mickey?'

'Yeah?'

'Know antin about that kid gone missin up your way?'

'How the fuck would I know antin?'

'Your patch, isn't it?'

'I haven't the time to be worried about little sluts, have I?'

Greg potted the ball, a nice shot.

'So you haven't been up to your old tricks then?'

Mickey whacked his cue off the table. His eyes were wide, crazy.

'Don't even go there, Greg. I'm fuckin serious, right?'

'Alright kid. Calm down. Fuck's sake.'

'Fuck this. I'm off. I've to see a man about a dog.'

He threw his cue onto the table and marched out the door.

Greg took the discarded cue off the table and finished the game quietly, thinking *Yes, I've some business to see to as well, you cunt.*

CHAPTER 56. MATINEE

My eye was caught by a stunning face across the bar. It was Jean. She'd been watching me and caught my eye as soon as I looked in her direction. I scanned the pub on my way over to her, noting no sign of any goons or gangsters.

'Hey Jean,' I said, happy to see her, 'you on your own?'

'Yes. All on my lonesome,' she answered, staring hungrily into my eyes.

So I kissed her on the cheek, putting my hand on her waist. I felt a tremble.

'You okay for a drink?'

She held up her glass of white wine. We toasted Dave. She became downbeat.

'What is it, Jean?'

'Somethin about Dave. I heard talk.'

'Can you tell me?'

'That's why I'm here. They were drunk the night of the funeral, last Sunday. Our day out.'

She smiled a proper smile at this memory. I joined her.

'They were completely langers, sittin around the garden at midnight, whiskey,' she continued. 'So they start talkin about how everythin's goin accordin to plan and how they were goin to take over the whole town.'

'Did they mention Dave specifically?' I asked, 'Or the sex business?'

'The sex business? Sure, Greg's always been in that. For years now. He's into antin dirty, in all fairness. As long as there's money in it.'

'Go on.'

'He owns two knockin shops, one on the northside, one on the southside. And he has a half share in a lapdancin club in town.'

'Pussy Galore?'

'Yeah. He thinks the name is hilarious.'

'Anything else?'

'I think he's been fuckin his prostitutes and maybe the lapdancers too. If they're not prostitutes as well. I know he's been to some mad parties with all sorts of high flyers. He's a bit of a perverted bastard.'

I drank my pint as I took it all in. Deeper and deeper. I ordered more drinks and she hit me with the biggest bombshell.

'He's into swingin as well,' said Jean, taking her eyes off mine for the first time, now studying the bar counter. 'I've been to swingin parties with him. I don't care, I just want to fuck someone else every now and then. He's fat, ugly and useless in bed. Just gets himself off as fast as he can, game over. Anyways, they were braggin about the guy they shot on Saturday night. I thought it might be Dave.'

'Bastards.'

So Jean was a swinger too. Was she in my DVD? I'd have to have a close look. Idea.

'Jean, would you do me a favour?' I asked.

'Go on so. What is it?'

'Just say it if you think it's perverted.'

'Charlie, come on, spit it out.'

'I have this DVD. I found it at Dave's. I haven't seen it yet, could be nothing. Would you mind looking at it with me? Maybe you'd recognise someone.'

'Is that all? Jesus, we'll have to sort out your shyness. When do you want to watch it?'

'I've always been shy,' I said, pretending to be hurt. 'You free for long?'

'You mean now? What about all this?'

'I've had enough. He's dead, end of story,' I said flatly. 'I could handle watching dirty movies with you though.'

She nodded, downed her drink and shook her car keys at me.

'One more thing,' she said.

'Go on.'

'That guy back there who keeps lookin at us.'

'Pat. He's a cop.'

'Greg knows him. Well.'

'Figures.'

Fuck.

Out the door and to her car. Thankfully she hadn't brought the flashy convertible. My heart couldn't handle another police chase. Today's little number was a sober blue Volvo estate. Plenty of power under the hood, but concealed nicely.

We drove to my car and I retrieved my jacket from the boot. Stopped off at Tesco in town for champagne, strawberries and balsamic vinegar. We fought over paying, but I won. Home to a welcome mat of a pile of bills and the smell of ruin. Opened all the back windows and curtains. The champagne was chilled, so we opened it right away.

'It's pronounced *mwet*, by the way.'

Then I sliced up the strawberries and sprinkled some of the vinegar over them.

'That's disgustin,' said Jean. 'I'm not touchin them now.'

'Relax baby. I thought you were so open-minded and everything. Trust me, they taste delicious. Sure, why would I possibly want to make you sick?'

'Okay. I'll try one.'

Then she tasted it and laughed, amazed. We toasted Dave and put on the DVD. We sat on the couch. She rested her free hand lightly on my crotch. For comfort. I stirred.

The film started out promisingly enough, clearly made locally. I could tell by the accents. It was a swinging story, with couples meeting up in a big, flashy mansion and then fucking in a variety of positions. It was professionally edited. Looked like reality TV.

The crowd was mixed, maybe ten couples in all. Some hogged the limelight, enjoying the porn star fantasy. Others stayed in the shadows. The woman were drunk or on coke or both. She watched the film intently, commenting on the sexual antics, most of which she'd tried at one time or another. After a few minutes of girls pleasuring girls, some men came into the picture. She didn't recognise anyone she'd swung with, but her eye was caught by a big vase in the background.

'I know that vase from somewhere, that big white one with the blue pattern.'

'Is it Delft or Ming?' I asked, casually displaying my entire knowledge of ceramics.

'Oh, Ming. Definitely Ming. I saw it in the house of a rich prick. My husband knows him and we were at a swingin party in his place once.'

'Oh?' I sat up, really interested.

'Yeah, it was full of drugs, everytin. Most of them were doin lines and drinkin champers. Endless supplies of everytin. I was so hammered. I came to and found myself bein banged up the arse by some old cunt at seven in the mornin, surrounded by a twisted mess of bodies. I got out of there.'

'Doesn't sound pleasant at all.'

'It wasn't. I don't like that shit any more. But I remember that vase. I know I do. The owner made sure to tell everyone not to mess with it, it's worth a million.'

'Who was he?'

She thought about this for a second, not sure if she should tell me. She finished her champagne and gently rocked the glass in my face. I got the bottle and topped us up.

'There he is. Look,' she said, pointing at the screen.

The scene was disturbing. Three men having sex with one woman. She looks in some pain, as her lovers screw her almost to death. People sitting around, watching, laughing, applauding. One guy in particular. He sits on a gilded Louis XVI chair, one that Marie Antoinette's own derrière had once warmed. His figure is in shadow, but he is close to the centre of everything. He leans forward, elbow on lap, chin resting in hand, taking it all in. His face catches the light. It's Dr Fox. Rich man, property tycoon, bigwig, pervert. Would he kill to protect his reputation? Maybe he would. When the sex act is over, the girl goes to Dr Fox, who puts something small into her hand. We can't tell what. I see her face and commit it to memory. Change of scene to a mass orgy, much later in the night. Some kind of Roman theme. Togas, grapes, not too many virgins. Camera stationary from well back, capturing the scene, too far for facial recognition. Lots of them wear masks. Fucking odd.

'Fox,' she said.

'My God,' I said to Jean. 'This is fucking huge. How many people know about him?'

'I don't know, maybe a few dozen, tops. But they're all from his circle, corrupt and perverted themselves. The rich protect the rich, else there'd be a revolution.'

'Bring it on. Tell me, would there be hookers at the parties too?'

'Of course,' she said. 'Lapdancers, hookers, sex slaves, they'd all get fucked at Fox's parties.'

'Jesus Christ. What about kids?'

With a look of disgust, she shook her head, no.

'I wouldn't put it past him. He rode me twice. I couldn't say no. Insisted on not usin a condom. I couldn't refuse him.'

'What? Are you insane?'

'I was on too much drugs to care.'

'That's fucking crazy debauchery, Jean. You could get AIDS off that fucking gowl. He's twisted. Or what about getting pregnant?'

'The pill, of course. I've been on it all my life. No way I'm having kids with Greg.'

'How did you end up with him anyway?'

'Not now, Charlie. That's a long story. Let's finish the champagne and go upstairs. To bed.'

I swallowed hard.

'Really?'

She took my hand and put it between her thighs, brushing her fanny, then put her hand on my cheek and kissed me in answer. I was ready.

Then she checked her watch, said Sorry, gotta go, Greg's waiting. She kissed me hard on the mouth, stuck her tongue in, apologised again, then split.

I was left alone, pointlessly aroused, again. And stunned by the news that I had, at last, a motive for Dave's murder.

I wondered if the longest day would ever end, daydreamed of sleep, feared a bullet in my forehead. Then I imagined my funeral and who'd be at it.

CHAPTER 57. HAWAII 5-0

I sat on the back step with a vodka - no ice, no lemon, no tonic - and listened to the one o'clock news on RTE One. Top headline was something I'd been half-expecting. The girl. Autopsy showed she'd been sexually tortured, raped, chopped to pieces while still alive. The details were almost too gory for a daytime news report, with a butcher's cleaver mentioned. And it was only radio. Police feared that the killer - almost certainly a male sexual predator - would strike again and warned parents to be vigilant. No news on DNA. The cops did seem satisfied that she was killed someplace other than where her body parts were found, caught by a fallen tree in the river. If not for the tree, she'd have gone into the Shannon, then the Atlantic, maybe never've been found.

The coverage went on and on. The brutality of the killing seemed to have stirred the nation. People were angry, sick and tired of it all. This murder brought clarity. Nobody cared about gangland killings any more. My life crystallised in an instant. Maybe for the first time, I knew that justice depended on me. To bring peace to Dave's memory, I had to nail his killer. I finished my drink and made another. Dave was mentioned in the report, along with the week's other bodies, but the cops saw no connection with the girl. A cop said that they were following definite lines of enquiry. We'll see, I thought.

The news changed to talk about Israel, Iraq, standard everyday bollocks. I went and shaved and took my shower. It was glorious. My choice of the best things in life varies constantly. It depends on what I'm enjoying at the time. When I'm in the shower, it's my favourite thing.

Then Pat rang to say he was on the way with the screen shots.

He was a bit pale around the gills, but happy with a ham sandwich and a cold beer. We made small talk for a while, mostly about Karpov's party and the funeral. On the surface, all was fine between us. I couldn't make him out, couldn't even guess at his motivations.

There were about forty faces captured from what was on Dave's PC. Each face was blown up to fill an A4 colour page. The graininess was exaggerated and the colours saturated. A dark shadow ran across everything. The pictures could have been taken at the bottom of the ocean, or on another world.

I looked at faces contorted in pleasure and in pain. My heart jumped when I saw the woman from the swinging party, the one who'd been fucked by three blokes. I recognised her face, her look immediately. Same footage, no doubt. I kept looking, waiting for the shot of Dr Fox, millionaire pervert. Nothing. I reached the end of the pile.

'This everyone?' I asked, 'That them all?'

'That's all. Turned out that there wasn't that much stuff at all. And nothing illegal either, if you know what I mean. I was wrong.'

So Dave wasn't a paedophile. That must be good news. But where was Fox? I knew now that either Pat was covering for Fox, or someone above him was. This was a fucking bad development. I kept my cool and played the fool.

'I don't see anyone I know.'

I got more beers.

'How's the head, Charlie?' he asked, noting my shaking hands.

'Pretty bad, Pat. Funerals and whiskey just don't agree with me, y'know?'

'I know. I'm the same. Don't know why I drink it. Makes me go a bit mad, sometimes.'

So I said, 'Ah, it's genetic. Makes every Irishman nuts.'

'Okay,' said Pat, putting the pictures back in a large manila envelope. 'Pity we couldn't get more from this. I still need to get my hands on that loose DVD. Badly. Oh well, what can you do?'

'What can you do?' I echoed, my mind racing. 'So what's next, Pat?'

'Well the DNA and a partial print or two are there. Now we just need to test them against a suspect. Motive is still hazy, but we'll get someone.'

'It's all fucked, man.'

'Fuck, I've just been totally wound up by this child murder. They're screaming for a result. Any gangland murders now would probably slip between the cracks, nobody'd give a shit. It's the ideal time for hitmen, actually. We're fairly stretched as it is.'

I felt that Pat was trying to tell me something, but in a very oblique way. Was he inferring that if I had anyone to kill that now would be good? Hardly. But what was he trying to say? That it would be a good time to kill me?

The sun emerged from behind a sooty cloud, blasting us with intense radiation.

'It's like being away foreign.'

So Pat asked me about my ex-wife. Ex. That's how I saw her.

'How is Deirdre?' he enquired casually.

'Deirdre? Oh, fine. As far as I know. Haven't seen her in eleven days now. You know that.'

'I do.'

'So she's probably still pissed off with me now. Nothing new there.'

'True. She hardly needs the aggro though, does she?'

'Probably not,' I agreed.

'And what about the kids?'

'Ah, I do miss them. Sometimes. And sometimes I don't.'

He'd become all serious. Melancholy. They say most cops become alcoholics, or worse. God, the relentless negativity of the work must be soul-destroying. The scum you have to deal with every damned day.

'Maybe you're better off.'

'Maybe. Would you like tea?'

'That's probably the meaning of life right there. Share a pot of tea with a pal. Trust. Yeah. Go on so.'

Pat's mobile rang. *Hawaii 5-0* theme of course. Work. I went and made a pot.

Pat finished the call and gratefully took the tea.

'That was work,' he said, 'Karpov needs me. He's doing a function in town later and wants some extra armed protection.'

'No better man.'

And he was gone, just as I was warming to him again, convincing myself that he couldn't be the one: the question mark.

Then I was struck by the fear. I imagined the childkiller, saw him stalking my kids, pictured him as a stereotype in a parka with the hood up full, darkness inside, just two red eyes shining out. A demon, walking the streets of Limerick.

I feared what I would do if I met the bastard.

CHAPTER 58. YOU'RE SO FINE, YOU BLOW MY MIND

To the killer, it was just work. He'd had a busy few days. Driving the van to the latest job, the warning still rang in his ears: *Don't kill him unless you have to.*

'Fuckin DVD,' he said as he pushed in the CD he'd made, one song over and over.

'Oh Mickey, you're so fine, you're so fine you blow my mind,' he sang, tapping the steering wheel with his fingers.

Busy fuckin week, but worth it. Cuttin off Luke O'Doherty's head was a strange one. But fuck it. He did it and now Greg owed him big. Really fuckin big.

Fuckin loads of cops around this evening, sirens galore. What the fuck were they up to? His piece was under his seat, held up off the floor by a special bracket. Safe enough, but all the cop activity made him nervous anyway.

Then the kid. The whole business gave him a hard-on. He caressed the leather pouch that hung around his neck, the pouch that contained the key to invincible power.

'Hey Mickey! Hey Mickey!'

What was the big fucking deal about a cuntin porno DVD anyway? Didn't fuckin matter. All that mattered was getting the cunt and knowin that now, as long as he didn't go too fuckin mad, the cops wouldn't go near him and the boys. Fuckin ever. Then O'Doherty would be fucked. Big time. He'd probably cut that cunt's head off as well, just for the laugh. Then the Flynns would be top dogs. Top fuckin dogs over all of Limerick. He'd have to beat the women off with a big stick. Such a sweet, sweet plan, made real by a dirty cop. Would you fuckin credit it?

He pulled in near the office. More fuckin squad cars! He got his gun, a Browning nine-mill, cocked it and stuck it down his crotch, inside his shirt.

He felt hungry and figured he'd grab a pizza after the job was done. Then find some young one, always that desire.

'Oh Mickey, you're so fine, you're so fine you blow my mind,' he sang quietly, focused now on the job at hand. And he waited.

CHAPTER 59. SAME OL', SAME OL'

Time for food before anything else. What to eat? Chinese. Up to the Happy World sit-down, old-style Chinese restaurant. Nostalgia food.

'Nee-how. Table for one, if you have it, please,' I said to the ever-smiling waitress.

'We have it,' she said, waving her hand at the busy restaurant.

She led me to a little table at the back, beside a huge fish tank. It was perfect. The place was full of young couples, filling up before a night on the town. Later, there'd be middle-aged couples, for whom the restaurant itself was a night on the town. I checked the menu, but already knew what I wanted.

A waitress came to me within seconds and I ordered a Tiger beer, not strictly Chinese but Oriental all the same. When she brought the bottle of beer I gave her my food order, which she scrawled on the paper tablecloth as well as in her little order book. I slugged my beer as the sweating kitchen staff got to work on my grub.

There was a pleasant buzz in the place. My starters arrived, some spring rolls and dumplings, lovely chilli dip. I licked my fingers and remembered how I used to be there with Deirdre. When we were dating first, we'd often go for the old-fashioned kitsch look and quiet privacy. She'd rub my thigh under the table and give me that coy look from under her fringe. God, she was beautiful. My main arrived, deep-fried prawns in batter, fried rice, noodles in sauce on the side, more dips. More beer.

I stuck a napkin on my lap for spillages, damn chopsticks. So I tucked in, savouring the delicately-flavoured prawns, like smelling the sea from a great distance. They weren't as good as Karpov's, though. People came in and went out all the time. Place is a little goldmine.

I watched a couple over at the far side. They paid their bill. The woman was tall and dark-haired, with her back to me. She wore a tight dress, showing off a dynamite figure. I knew that ass. She rose, turned to take her cardigan from the back of her chair. It was Deirdre. She glanced in my direction, smiled. No eye contact, but she knew I was there. She knew it. She turned back to her company. A bloke.

My eyes flitted about the restaurant, resting on him every other second. He was a lot older than her, fifty maybe. Hair thinning on top, glasses. Wearing a tweedy jacket, shirt open at the neck to show some sort of silver medallion. The guru! I couldn't fucking believe it and had to restrain myself before I made a complete ass of me. Fuming, I drank beer and they went, out to who knew where. Now she's gone.

When Deirdre and I ran in to our marriage difficulties - months, maybe years before - she embarked on a quest for spiritual development. She said she wanted to fill her empty life with something positive. I chose to fill mine with drink, women and drugs. Different strokes.

She did yoga, pilates yoga, power yoga, every damn kind of yoga. She started reading books about Yogis, spiritual masters from the east who claimed to know the answers to everything. She got into herbalism, homeopathy, anything to do with the opposite to conventional wisdom. I'm happy to go with the flow, eat, have sex, get stoned, die, that's me. She wasn't satisfied with that. But I didn't stop her, no way. I even went along with her tantric sex. I couldn't handle that though, too slow. Just wanted to get on in there.

Even when she discovered her guru, I left her off. A doctor of psychiatry, Dr John was recommended to her by one of her twittering, tree-hugging friends from yoga class. This guy offered hands-on training in unleashing the true you. Pseudo-scientific, Post-Freudian nonsense. She fell for his scam hook, line and sinker.

She went to his practice every week and sometimes off on group retreats to some shitty camp in the middle of nowhere in the Burren. I gladly went along with it all, minding the kids, wishing her well. I was supportive. Then she came home from a session on the Thursday. The kids were asleep in bed and I was drunk. She told me that her spirit was trapped in our marriage. I said Yeah, whatever and fell asleep on the couch, watching late night Italian league football. I went to work next day, came home, and she was gone. Kids, everything. Bitch was out of my life.

I should've seen it coming, but didn't. I got mad and threw some stuff around. I tried to call her, but her number was out of use. I figured she was at her parents' pad and nearly went out there to cause a scene. Instead, I had a drink. A week of drinks. Now, here she was, out with the fucking guru, the bastard who told her to leave me in the first place. Fuck's sake, that kind of shit just isn't fair. My hunger was gone and I couldn't touch the rest of my food. I was disgusted with myself. Now it all made sense. How dumb are you, Charlie Doyle?

I asked for my bill and fidgeted, fuming. I called the waitress back and asked for a double brandy as well. I sussed Dr John right away. He didn't need Deirdre for sex, he'd have plenty of that, with his posse of bored housewife nymphos. So he was after her money. That or he loved her. I wanted it to be the money and felt sure I had him sussed. My brandy arrived and its warm glow behind my breast bone helped me to relax a little.

I paid the bill, twenty three quid, and left a tip of seven. I got smiles from the waitress on the way out. I bowed and said Konichi-wa.

The streets were busy, drinkers buzzing into town and office clowns stumbling home for a bollicking for getting locked after work. There was no sign of Deirdre and her guru, thank fuck: the AK had flitted across my mind. I strolled towards home, down William Street and up O'Connell Street in just a few minutes, slowing to admire the gorgeous young ones waiting for their dates outside Brown

Thomas. Glad to see micro mini skirts making a comeback.

I had to get it off my chest, so I called Pat.

'I was up having a Chinese and who did I see with a bloke, only Deirdre.'

'Fuck, who was he?'

'Her fucking guru,' I said, disgusted.

'You mean that cunt was using his influence to take your wife away?'

'Something like that.'

'That fucker deserves to have his legs broken.'

I half-hoped he'd say that. Half-hoped he'd do it.

'Fucking gowl.'

'Later, Charlie.'

'Later.'

My first reaction when I saw them in the Chinese was anger. That had subsided, in tune with my general laissez-faire attitude. But Pat had brought rage to the fore again. I clenched and unclenched my fists, cursing my stupidity. Duped, and so easily!

CHAPTER 60. HOUSE GUEST

I switched on the radio to catch the seven o'clock news headlines. There had been another murder. One of O'Doherty's goons had been found in an alley with a bullet in the back of his head, execution-style. I figured this was revenge for his gang's double killing. A police helicopter buzzed overhead as the newsreader announced that the heavily-armed Emergency Response Unit - paramilitary police - was back on the streets of Limerick. This was standard cop reaction. I'd have to be extra careful driving about, as they tended to set up snap checkpoints, checking for unusual reactions as they stuck their machine guns in your face. Hardly rocket science.

I wondered how O'Doherty would be dealing with this. Likely, he was holed up in his Island fortress, planning a counterattack, aiming to wipe out the opposition. My mobile rang. Surprise, surprise, it was O'Doherty.

'Hey Charlie. Hear the news?'

'Yeah. Nasty. One of your lads?'

'Jack, my right hand fuckin man,' he said. He actually sounded upset, an emotion I wouldn't have associated with him.

'Jesus,' I said.

'Yeah. Look, I can't say too much over the phone, but the shit's about to hit the fan. I'm worried about Jean and I want her out of here in case they come gunnin for me. Anyway, I just haven't the time to be thinkin about her. So I want to hire you.'

'Go on,' I said, elated - throbbing - at the prospect of seeing Jean.

'I just want you to look after her for a couple of days max. That's it. I'll pay you a grand a day, plus expenses. I'm preparin for the worst.'

'Okay, so. What's the catch?'

'If antin happens to her, you're dead.'

'That's some catch.'

'I just want you to be on the ball. Deal?'

'If anyone comes after her, I can't defend her.'

'I'll look after that. Deal?' he sounded impatient now.

'Deal,' I said.

'Okay, I'll send her to you in a taxi. Now. Where do you want to meet?'

'Can you send her to my place?'

'The house that got shot up?'

'Lightning rarely strikes twice,' I said.

'For your sake, I hope that's fuckin true. Good luck.'

And he hung up. I stood in the garden, trying to think the scenario through. Worst case, O'Doherty would win the gang war, Jean would go home to him and I'd be a couple of grand richer. Best case, O'Doherty would get nailed by the opposition or the cops and then some totally new scenarios would present themselves. Not bad. Jean getting killed while in my care wasn't a possibility worth considering. I'd have to die defending her, if it came to that.

I did a quick tidy-up around the house. As I splashed some after shave on my face and chest, a car hooted outside. I peeked through a gap in the boards. It was a cab, Jean in the back seat.

I jumped down the stairs in three bounds and was out the door to her. She got out of the cab, carrying two bags. The cab split and I took the bags. I made no effort to kiss her until we got inside. I dropped the bags on the couch and kissed her. She kissed back hard, squeezing my arse. I got lead.

'This is for you,' she said, handing me the smaller bag.

I unzipped it. Inside was a thick wad of cash, two grand I guessed. There was also a plastic bag, taped up, with something heavy inside. I ripped the plastic and found a gun. A revolver, thankfully. I opened the cylinder. Loaded. I made sure the safety was on and stuck the gun under my belt, covering it with my shirt. Bit of a deluded expert.

'Do you think anyone's going to come after you, Jean?' I asked.

For the first time, she looked a bit scared.

'I don't know,' she said. 'Jack gettin killed was a fright for us all. A right fuckin shock. Greg thought he'd the other gang pretty much wiped out. This wasn't supposed to happen.'

'Is he sure it was the other gang?' I asked.

'Sure, who else would it be?' she asked.

'I wonder. Drink?'

She nodded, so we went into the kitchen. I mixed a couple of vodka cranberries. She took a call from her husband.

'He asked if you were treatin me okay,' she said.

'I hope you said I was.'

'I did. But if you don't give me a cuddle, a proper cuddle, I'll tell him you whipped me.'

'Oh yeah?' I laughed, 'Show me the bruises, so.'

She sat forward and pulled her top up at the back. There were five or six heavy bruises on her, on that lovely curve of her hips, like she'd been battered with a length of lead pipe. Nasty Cluedo. They were fresh.

'Did he do this?' I asked, staring at the wound.

'Yes.'

'Was it because of us?' I asked, confused as to why he'd send her to me if he knew about us.

'No. Over Luke. Again. He tells me that even though he loves me, he has to punish me. Says it's only right. It'll go on and on.'

'Jesus Christ,' I said, feeling like a prick for giving her this pain. At the end, it was my fault.

'And Charlie -'

'Yeah?'

'I'm beginnin to think he's right.'

I put my arms around her and my face in her hair.

'He's not right,' I said, 'He's a psycho. I don't know why you did it with his brother, but that's no excuse to beat you. He's a prick,' I said, 'And he deserves to die.'

'Well he thinks someone's gunnin for him, that's for sure.'

'Jesus, how many murders have we had now in the last week? Six? Must be some sort of record, even for Limerick.'

'Life is cheap.'

'I wouldn't be brave enough to put a bet on the final tally, though.'

'And you a gamblin man and all.'

CHAPTER 61. THE CALM

When my phone rang then, the real world sank its teeth into my heart, making it colder still.

'Hey dad. What's up?' I said, confused as to why he'd call me, scared. Normally it was one-way traffic, me looking for money or whatever.

'Bad news, son,' he said, sounding like he'd been crying, 'It's your mam. She tried to kill herself.' Silence.

'Jesus Christ, dad. Don't blame yourself, man. You didn't do it. She doesn't know what she's doing.'

'I do blame myself, though.'

'Well don't.'

I was in danger of losing my temper with him, so I calmed myself down a bit, lighting a cigarette.

'She wants to see you,' he said.

I'd been meaning to pay her a visit. Just it was so easy to put off.

'Okay. I'll go see her. I'll head straight away.'

'Fair play, son.'

'How did she do it, dad?'

'Tried to cut her wrist open with a broken bottle.'

'How the hell did she get hold of a bottle?' I asked, angry that she couldn't have been properly looked after.

'Don't know, son. They're trying to suss that out. She keeps asking for you, though.'

'Okay. I'll get there ASAP.'

'Good boy. I'll probably see you there later, then.'

'Okay so. Bye.'

He hung up and Jean turned to face me. I was thinking, trying to cope, to understand.

'Bad news?' she asked.

'Yeah. Bad news. My mam tried to kill herself.'

'Jesus.'

I told her the latest about mam and how I figured her experience had maybe fucked up my own ability to have a proper relationship.

She said 'An I thought my life was in the shit,' which made me smile, then she let me talk, smoked her cigarettes.

We drove to the hospital, Jean wasn't leaving my sight. Anyway, she didn't mind. I stuck my new gun in the glove box. Passed through fairly serious security doors and a fat guy in a pseudo-cop outfit. He looked a bit mad himself. I supposed if you work around mental people all the time, a bit of the craziness must rub off on you eventually. I told the woman at the desk who I was and she said Isn't it awful? She pointed us to a waiting room and said that someone would be out to me in a minute.

Then a male orderly came in and asked me to follow him. Jean waited in the strange little room with the old magazines. I figured she'd be safe enough there.

I followed the guy through another security door and down a long corridor. I had fear in the back of mind, that the thing about my mam was all a ploy to get me here and that I was about to be shown my new home, my very own cell.

My fear evaporated when we entered a small nurses' station. Single rooms, all with their doors locked, radiated from the round central area, with its computer screens and transparent drawer units filled with plastic tubes, syringes, medication. I saw my mother through the glass of her door, the tough glass with diamond patterns of steel wire through it. She was sitting up in her bed, playing cards.

She saw me too, all smiles and waves and bandages. The orderly left and the nurse unlocked the door. Christ, how did it come to this?

'Charlie, my boy. Come give your mother a kiss,' she said, her voice cracking, strained.

I sat on the side of her bed and gave her a hug and a kiss. She was weak, fragile. I worried that my hug could break her. Her hair was long and grey, unbrushed, wild. She'd lost a lot of weight and her hospital-issue nightdress hung from her shoulders like it was on a clothes hanger.

'What are you playing, mam?' I asked looking at her cards.

'Oh, it's not a game, Charlie. It's the tarot. I've been doing a reading for you.'

'Really? What's the story so?'

'Not too good, you poor crater. Not too good. Still, it might point you in the right direction.'

'For what?'

'The truth,' she said, staring into my eyes, a hint of madness about her. 'Isn't it the truth that you're after?'

'Yeah. Of course. Can you be more specific.'

I was entertaining her in her confusion, not expecting to hear anything much.

'Your first card,' she began, 'is The Tower of Destruction, the past. A great revelation, truth shattering an illusion. You must be very careful, son. Expect the unexpected. Change is afoot. But be confident, as the changes will be to your advantage.'

'Okay. What else?'

'The Hanged Man, the present.'

'Oh Christ, that's all I need.'

'It's okay, son. This doesn't symbolise your death or anything. No this says that you are now in a moment of calm. All will change for you. And soon. This is your time to prepare, physically and mentally.'

She'd started getting into the tarot just before she'd lost it completely. Dad thought the cards had helped tip her over the edge. I wasn't sure. But I could see that they certainly animated her. There was life in her eyes now, a life I hadn't seen in a long time.

'Another thing about The Hanged Man,' she continued, 'Don't relax your guard. Someone is working against you. A rival. Or maybe a friend will blackguard you.'

'Well I have felt as though everything is stacked up against me,' I confessed. *Fuck, could she be on to something?*

'Finally, Charlie, The Wheel of Fortune. Your future. This is all about change. You're coming to the end of one cycle and entering another. I hope it represents success for you. You deserve it.'

'Thanks, mam. You've given me a lot to think about.'

'Ah, this is only rubbish, Charlie. You know that. All it does is help us to shine some light on the darkest parts of our hearts. All the answers are within,' she put a hand on her bony chest, 'not in some old deck of cards from the Middle Ages.'

Lucid, smiling, she lay her head back on her mound of pillows, looking exhausted again.

'And how are you, mam?' I asked, taking her so-skinny hand.

'I'm fine. Just passing the time.'

She didn't look at me, just stared at the ceiling.

'If you're going to keep cutting yourself, they'll never let you out. I mean it.'

Now she looked like a kid again, being scolded by a parent, half smiling to herself.

'Okay,' she said, eventually. 'I'll stop. I promise.'

'Do you mean it?'

'Yes, Charlie. Thanks for coming to see me.'

I felt like a shit for not having been to see her before. The suicide attempt was probably just a cry for help, looking for attention, wanting a visit from her only son. You cunt, Charlie Doyle, after all she's done for you. Jesus, I almost cried with self pity. I cleared my throat, so I could make a commitment to her.

'Look mam,' I said, 'If you promise to be good and do nothing stupid, I'll come and see you every day. I promise. How's that?'

'And will you bring me something nice, son?'

'You know I will.'

Then the nurse came in and said it was time for mam to take her medication. She'd doubtless be tranquilised to the gills, knocked out for her own good. But I felt that maybe I'd helped, just by coming to see her. I resolved to be less of a shit in future. I asked the nurse if I could see her doctor. She said *Not today, maybe tomorrow.* I gave my mother a kiss and said I'd see her tomorrow. Then I waited outside, out of her sight. I glanced into the other rooms. In one, a young woman, maybe twenty, sat on the edge of her bed, staring at the palms of her hands. In another, a woman about my own age lay on her bed, covers off, staring up at the ceiling, unaware of me. She was attractive enough and I wondered if those stories about orderlies screwing drugged-up patients at night were true. Poor woman. The nurse came back out and I had a quick word.

'So how bad is she?' I asked.

'Oh, not bad at all. She barely broke her skin. It was just for attention, really.'

'Well it worked.'

'I can see that.'

'I promised her I'd come see her every day.'

The nurse raised an eyebrow.

'That's good,' she said, 'If you mean it. Giving her false hope wouldn't be good. Most of the poor souls in here deteriorate rapidly once the visits stop. And they always stop.'

'I suppose it's not easy coming in here from the outside world. I know I'm freaked out. If you don't mind me saying it.'

'Not at all. If it didn't freak you out, you should be locked up yourself,' she said, smiling at me for the first time.

'What about my father? Has he come to see her?'

She checked through the visitor book on her desk.

'He's been here every day since she came in,' she said. 'Some days, she won't see him. Some days he just sits in there with her for hours. He's very good.'

He's very guilty, I thought. Guilty as sin. I thanked the nurse and said I'd see her more often. She buzzed for an orderly to take me back to reception. Back down the long corridor, with its smell of bleach and hidden secrets.

Jean wasn't in the waiting room, the woman at reception pointing a finger outside. I passed through, observing that the security goon had his eyes planted on Jean's lovely arse. Dream on, twat. She was on the phone, smoking a cigarette. I lit up and waited for her to finish. Christ, we were both smoking like troopers.

'Your husband?' I asked as she hung up and put the phone in her pocket.

'The one and only,' she said. 'He thinks he knows what's really goin on.'

'What?' I asked, excited at the prospect.

'He wouldn't say,' she answered. 'He just said to keep a low profile and that he'd be in touch with you himself.'

'Maybe mam was right.'

'About what?'

'The Wheel of Fortune. Ah, it's nothing. She's mad, God love her. Let's get out of here. This place gives me the creeps.'

CHAPTER 62. FRIENDS LIKE THAT

So Pat rang and said he wanted to drop around. For a chat. Sounded ominous, but I said *Come on over.*

The radio news babbled as we drove to my place. There had been a hit and run in town. A man was smacked by a fast-moving car. He was thrown on to the bonnet and then bounced on to the road. The car fucked off at speed. The victim had a smashed hip and two broken legs, but would survive.

Jean went to the bedroom, locked herself in.

Pat arrived and I made fresh tea. He was quiet, his face set, like he was trying to keep something in. We sat in the garden, on white plastic chairs. Evening stretched on.

'Charlie,' he began, 'I need something from you.'

'Anything Pat,' I said.

'The DVD. Dave's DVD. I know you have it and I need it.'

This hit me hard. He stared me straight in the eye, watching my every reaction. I flinched at the shock of the question, betrayed my position. And he knew it.

'What?' I said.

It was all I could muster, my heartbeat pounding in my ears.

'Charlie, we're friends and I don't want to change that. But I have to get the DVD.'

There was a hardness to his voice now, a stiffness in his expression. He was serious, scarily serious. I expected him to nonchalantly flash his gun at any time.

'Jesus, it's hot,' he said, standing to take off his sports coat and put his shoulder holster and automatic pistol on display. No fucking around.

'What DVD, Pat?' I asked, lighting a cigarette with trembling hands. I offered him one but he didn't take it.

'Porno movie, Charlie. Dave was putting it together for some friends of mine. But there's stuff on the disc that shouldn't be there. Dangerous stuff.'

'Powerful friends, maybe?' I asked.

'You know exactly what I'm talking about,' he slapped his thigh, smiling now. 'Just hand it over, will you?'

'What makes you think I have it, Pat'

'Please don't play with me, Charlie. Please.'

He stood in front of me, hands on hips.

'Okay,' he sighed, 'Dave's phone records show multiple calls to and from you in the twenty-four hours before he was killed. I can guarantee that the DNA and partial prints we found in the shop will match yours. Also, there's a bit of CCTV, taken around the corner from the murder scene. You're on it, moving quickly away from the shop.'

I nodded, dumbfounded. He'd known all along. I tried to think where I'd left the revolver

O'Doherty'd sent with Jean. Couldn't remember. *Fuck.*

'So,' he continued, 'you went to the shop on Sunday morning, having planned to meet Dave there. You saw the body and took what you could, figuring his cash would be no more use to him. Am I right?'

I nodded, dumbly.

'Good,' he said. 'So you spotted the DVD as well and took it, thinking you'd have some new wank material. I can see it was an honest mistake. So now, you just have to give it to me and we're square. I've even done you a favour already, as a thank you. We are friends.'

'What favour?' I asked, confused.

'Your wife's guru. The prick had a nasty little accident, didn't he?'

'Christ. That was him? You did that?' *You're insane!*

'All I'll say is that one good turn deserves another, Charlie. I could've got Deirdre as well. But that would've been a waste, wouldn't it? She's a sweetie. Now, the DVD. Please.'

'What if I don't play ball?' I asked, wanting to see how desperate he was.

He shook his head and tutted.

'Don't even go there, Charlie.'

I looked at him blankly, insisting that he spin it out for me.

'Okay,' he said, 'We can place you at the crime scene with forensics. Plus, I know you had a gun at the time, the same kind that was used to kill Dave. I also have a witness, your little druggie friend Brian, who will testify that you were out of your head on acid late Friday night. He'll say you were delusional, waving your gun around, making stupid threats. That kind of thing.'

'In all fairness Pat, what was my motive so?'

'Anything. Maybe the drugs made you crazy? Maybe you were arguing with Dave over a woman? Fiona, maybe? Most motives are mixed anyway. People kill their friends all the time.'

This struck home like he'd held a gun to my nose. He didn't have to say any more. I knew I was dead unless I handed over the DVD, which was sitting in my jacket, in the front room. Or I'd have to kill him myself. Time to buy some breathing space.

'What's in it for you, Pat?' was all I could muster.

'I'll make it fit. Capeesh?'

He was right. I was well-fitted up.

'Capeesh.'

'Good. So where is it?'

'Not here,' I said, holding my hands out, palms upwards. He relaxed.

'Good man, Charlie. Where?'

'In a safe place. It'll take me a while to get it. Can I meet you later?'

'Okay, where and when?'

'My office, ten?'

'Okay, fine. I've to get back to work, big night tonight with my new buddy the billionaire.'

He winked at me as he picked up his jacket and headed into the house. I started to get up. With difficulty.

'I'll see myself out, Charlie,' he said. 'One more thing,' he said, deadly serious again, 'Don't fuck with me, Charlie. I mean it. Okay?'

'Okay.'

'I'm just looking after number one, kid. In the end, that's all that matters to me. You should try it some time. I'm going to be a very rich man soon, so just don't get in my way, okay?'

I was getting sick of being threatened.

'See you later. Oh, one last thing.'

'What the fuck else could there be?'

'The Flynns have no clue who you are. No clue.'

'So you're the question mark.'

'What?'

'Nothing.'

And off he went, to protect the decent people of Limerick from the scumbags. Only he was the biggest scumbag of all. But how would the endgame play out?

Jean came down and we smoked cigarettes. I filled her in.

'What a complete cunt,' she said.

Then O'Doherty rang me. I jumped when I saw his identity flash up. I was nervous, surprised at how badly I'd done reading Pat, confused by how many people were fucking with my head.

'Evenin, Charlie,' he said. 'How we doin?'

'Not great, truth be told.'

'Listen kid, I'm about to fuck your head up a bit, okay?'

'Shoot.'

'Okay. Know your pal, the cop?'

'Pat, yeah.'

'He's playin you for a fool.'

CHAPTER 63. CLARITY

O'Doherty's story had the unmistakable ring of truth to it. No less stunning for that.

'What? How do you know?'

'I think the fucker's been playin every side in the game.'

'What game?' I asked, my confusion growing, my stomach falling, my head heavy.

'Ah, just a bit of a power struggle. I've somethin goin on with the Russians. It turns out we've been fucked around with. Remember the little incident with my wife in the park? I was told to contact you and only you, Charlie, and tell you where and when to take the pictures.'

'By Pat,' I said.

'Yep. Told me he was doin me a favour, the prick.'

'He was working for you?'

'A bit. He'd give me the odd tip-off before a raid or warn me about what the other gangs were up to. He never pulled a trigger for me or antin. I paid him well. You can never have too many cops on side in my business.'

'Jesus Christ,' I said.

'Yeah. It's always cat when you find out what your friends have been hidin from you.

'So why did he tip you off?'

'Probably to fuck with my head and maybe use me to rub out the other gang before he fixes me.'

'Fixes you?' I asked.

'Yeah. That was, like I say, a distraction. The real game is with the Russians and their buddies. Their powerful buddies.'

'Go on.'

'When the Russians moved in a couple of years back, I muscled my way in. Made them an offer they couldn't refuse, and everytin was fine. I protected their sex operations, even did some work with them in drugs and guns and that. But they made their own contacts too, playin for time. Now some big rich cunt from Russia has bought in and they've decided they don't need me any more.'

'Karpov,' I said. Pat's new buddy.

'That's the cunt,' said O'Doherty. 'But they're not goin to have it their own way. No sir.'

'What have you planned?' I asked.

'Let's just say that your pal won't see tomorrow and Karpov won't be buildin any fuckin hotels here.'

'You're going to kill Karpov?' I asked, incredulous. 'He has heavy security. Ex-army types, I reckon. I'd say they're well-armed.'

'Not a bother. I've twenty good men if I need um, plus somethin special in reserve. He won't know what hit him.'

'What about Pat?'

'He's bein watched. He was at your place a while ago, wasn't he?'

It was another one of those defining moments, when all my smugness was blown away. I was the amateur in all this. I decided to be straight up, to use O'Doherty.

'Yeah. I've this porn DVD that he wants. This fucker called Dr Fox, Karpov's local contact, is in one of them, doing some perverted shit.'

'Fox,' he said, 'Yeah I know Fox. He's dirty enough.'

'Planning to kill him too?' I asked.

'That I haven't decided yet,' he said. 'I put all the blame squarely at Karpov's feet for now.'

'But is he giving Pat his orders or is Fox? Like, Karpov wouldn't know or care about porno, would he?'

'Probably not. Probably not.'

'We'll have to keep tabs on that cunt Fox so,' he said. 'Just in case. Thanks Charlie.'

Fox was too close to Pat not to be involved in the greater machinations for control of the city's vice trade. Plus, there was a good chance he was a paedophile. I'd cry no tears for him.

'Pat's meeting me at my office at ten tonight, to collect the DVD,' I said, hoping that O'Doherty would take care of the dirty work.

'Really?' he said. 'That's good, Charlie. Very good. That suits, that suits. Have you still that gun I sent you?'

'Yeah, somewhere.'

'Keep it on you. Okay, that's all for now. I'll call you back by nine, let you know the plan. That okay?'

'Grand.'

I filled Jean in on all the shit. We sat in the garden, smoked like troopers, enjoyed the evening heat.

'So what would you do if you knew you had only a couple of hours to live?' I asked her.

She got her bag, took out a bottle of chilled Dom Perignon and a blanket. We put the blanket on the grass, drank the Champagne from the bottle.

'Sit here with you, maybe.'

'Same,' I said.

I was getting nervous, my palms sweating. Time passed slowly as we sat in silence.

'And make love to you, maybe.'

She stood up and pulled down her skirt. Then she took off her knickers and sat on my knees. She bent down and began to lick and suck and nibble. I was stiff in a millisecond. She moved up my body and kissed me on the mouth, her lips with the salty sweet flavour of champagne and me. Then she sat back up and reached across for her handbag. She found a condom and ripped the pack open with her teeth.

As she prepared the condom, I fondled her breasts and her nipples became as hard as my cock. She sat back a bit and unrolled the condom over my penis. Then she lifted herself and, holding me from behind, came down slowly, gently guiding me inside her. She pushed her pelvis down hard and I was in deep. She rocked up and down and began to groan involuntarily. I kept my hands on her and she put hers on me. She pushed down really hard, so hard I was afraid she'd damage her ribs more. She wasn't in pain, her eyes closed, her mouth open.

After a long minute, she lay down fully on me. Her tongue was in my mouth, touching every tooth. This was a perfect opportunity to fondle her arse. I grabbed a cheek in each hand, pulling her vagina down around me.

'What will the neighbours say?' she breathed into my ear.

'Fuck them. No, fuck me instead.'

So she did.

I felt a subtle trembling inside her. She was hot. She jumped up off me and turned so she was on her hands and knees, her wet pussy almost in my face.

'From behind, Charlie. Doggy-style, please,' she gasped, her breathing fast and shallow.

I struggled into position, got a view that almost made me cry.

At last, she began to cry out, wordless sounds that meant she was close. I pulled her tighter and pushed more. Then I grabbed her breasts and roughly twisted her nipples, all the while marvelling at her arse as a grateful me slid in and out between her cheeks. With a scream, she came. Then I could let go and my orgasm erupted deep inside her, her vagina pulsing with pleasure. We panted like greyhounds. Then I grabbed the base of the condom and withdrew slowly, tingling intensely.

I fell back on to the blanket. She turned and fell beside me, then rolled her side of the blanket around her. I found my cigarettes. I lay beside her on the blanket and smoked. The betrayal was complete.

'Doggylicious,' I said.

Right then O'Doherty rang, like he knew. The hairs on the back of my neck stood up.

'I'm dealin with the other in a minute. You go ahead with your ting and we'll be waitin outside. Stick her in a hotel room, stay low. Got that?' he breathed, his voice low, controlled.

'Got it.'

End of conversation.

'What's the plan?' Jean asked, looking a little worried as she lit a cigarette.

'You've to wait in a hotel. I've to go ahead and meet Pat at ten. They'll be waiting for him.'

'They'll kill him.'

'Probably. It's inevitable now. Pat's on the enemy side. Whether or not that's the losing side, we'll see. I think Karpov's going to be nailed first. Take out the top man, scare the rest of them. Then pick them off one at a time. If they get Karpov, Pat's dead. If your husband gets killed instead, Pat's on the winning side. Either way, I'm giving him the DVD.'

'You can't lose,' she said, smiling now. Better.

'I reckon so. Unless Pat decides to kill me.'

'Would he? He's your friend, isn't he?'

'True. That's what I always thought. Until all this shit happened. Until he threatened me. No more friendship. I'll just have to convince him that my professionalism means I'll keep my trap shut. I think he'll take that. I've genuinely never spilt the beans on any client.'

'Well,' she said, 'If he knows that, you'll be grand. Won't you feel like you're settin him up?'

'No way, Jean. This is all his doing. I'm not going to feel guilty about anything that happens tonight. Fuck no! I just hope to fuck you're not on his hitlist. I'll mind you, don't worry.'

She gave me a hug for that. She knew where I was coming from and left it there. There was a chance that myself or her husband would die before the night was out. And under it all, she knew that there might well be a Russian bullet waiting patiently somewhere with her own name on it.

We dressed, last meal over.

CHAPTER 64. HIDEAWAY, GETAWAY

Time was 9.10. We got in the car and decided to head for a hotel on the Dublin Road, past the University. Ideal for a fast getaway to Dublin.

On the way, Jean sent texts, gave orders for her BMW to be brought out for her. I wasn't sure about it, but she insisted it would be okay.

'This piece of shit won't get us very far, will it?'

'No.'

We stopped at a petrol station to get her some John Player Blue, magazines and chocolate. To help pass the time.

At the hotel, we checked in as Mr and Mrs O'Donoghue. Guy behind the desk insisted on a credit card, but I insisted I didn't have one. Too easy to trace us. Sorry, sir, hotel policy. I said I'd pay for a night in advance, ninety quid, and gave the twat a fifty into his blazer pocket. Then he said No problem with the card, sir. Fine.

There was a gang of kids playing in the reception area, looked like the remnants of a wedding party. Passing the function room, my worst fears were realised: a travellers' wedding. The singing was fucking woeful and everyone was shitfaced and itching for a fight. I winced to Jean and she laughed, keeping her eyes straight ahead in case she knew someone.

We found our room, one-one-nine, and opened the door with the swipe card.

The room was okay, nothing too special. I put Jean's bag on the bed and looked out the window. Good view of the front car park. Nice and busy. I closed the curtains and advised her to keep them closed and stay away from the window.

'Can I go to the bar?,' she asked, 'If I get bored.'

'I suppose,' I replied. 'Just keep your phone on you. If you see anything suspicious, get clear.'

'Okay. Thanks. What about my husband?'

'What?'

'You going to tell him where I am? Should I?'

'No. Everything's gone operational now. Now we stay quiet. I'm calling nobody until this is all over. You should try and do the same.'

'How will we know?'

'Know what?'

'How will we know when it's all over?'

CHAPTER 65. SHITSTORM

At first, O'Doherty's plan went smoothly. As I drove back into town, admiring the silhouetted city skyline against a deepening azure sky, a newsflash came on the radio.

Holy Christ! There had been an explosion at a Chamber of Commerce dinner in town. Only minutes before. No word on casualties. May have been a bomb. Then they played a Radiohead song, *High and Dry.* Apt. I scanned the skyline for palls of smoke as I crossed the Groody River in light traffic, heading for the office and my meeting with Pat. All I saw was a dense flock of starlings crossing the swollen, rising moon.

I passed the bright lights of the dog track and heard a roar go up.

'And that was the Ace of Spades winning his race, you dope.'

I was in town by 9.50, so figured I had time to check out the explosion before I went to the office. I parked handily enough and strolled up towards the hotel where the Chamber always had their dos. A large crowd had gathered. Fire engines, police cars and ambulances filled the street. A cordon was put up at either end, so I could only get to within about a hundred metres of the action. An ambulance siren roared to life and it sped up the far end of the street, off to the Regional.

Two fat jeeps were parked near my position. They were unmarked, but guys in blue fatigues, carrying machine guns - MP5s, as I now knew - stood around them with purpose. The Emergency Response Unit, must have been escorting Karpov. Yeah, off behind them, the dull gleam of a BMW 7-series. Armoured, you could tell from the extra bulges and folds. Custom job. Could take anything up to a well-placed RPG warhead or a hefty roadside bomb. Not worth hitting, especially with ERU footsoldiers swarming around it. It made sense to hit Karpov in a neutral venue, someplace with easy enough access, an event that was well-flagged. I listened to the talk in the crowd, plenty of old ladies and youngfellas.

'I heard there's two dead,' said one, a woman with a little mongrel.

'Look at their guns,' said a kid, 'They tink they're hard. Fuckin gowls.'

'There's the chopper,' said another, as the police helicopter arrived, circling low, its powerful searchlight on.

Then I spotted the forensics Oompa-Loompas in their white van. As they pulled up to try and get a fix on the explosives used, Pat left the hotel, pushing through a swarm of uniforms, leading Dr Fox. Pat's partner was with them.

They looked uninjured, just a bit shook. The three went over to a parked black Merc and got in. Pat drove. They left the scene and the rest of the guests started to come out for air. They were kept within the cordon, but a few came over to us and told about what had happened inside. They were in shock, desperate to share it all.

Karpov had taken the podium to make his big speech about investing in the dynamic local economy. In front of all the wankjobs that pass for local dignitaries, the podium exploded. He was killed instantly, his head in bits. The bomb had been fierce but measured. Nobody else was badly injured, some scratches, some bleeding ears. Just everyone freaked out.

Medics arrived within minutes, but Karpov was clearly dead. I mean, where's his head, dude? He was pronounced dead at the scene and brought to the hospital, along with the injured, plus another few who lost the plot about the whole thing. The attack was clean, efficient, and made for perfect TV. A clear warning to the world. Round one to O'Doherty, I figured, as I walked to the office, my head beating as loudly as my heart. Now for round two.

CHAPTER 66. THUNDER

Heavy black clouds rolled in and it got darker again, like the summer is nearly over when it's barely fucking begun. I heard a distant rumbling.

Plenty of squad cars and all sorts around, sometimes squawking, sometimes not. Dangerous for an armed confrontation now. What was planned for Fox, I had no clue. But surely it wouldn't be easy. Pat must be taking him somewhere pretty safe, for sure. Had he forgotten about meeting me? Maybe. I'd be waiting anyway. I worried about Jean and hoped she was safe. Christ, so many cops around.

My stomach was screaming, hurting. A problem with Class As, like coke. The crash is as intense as the high. But only when you run out. This explains the desperation of heroin junkies. How far was I from that shit?

Streets weren't too quiet. The explosion had electrified the place, brought a kind of buzz. Couples were going out drinking, a good few students and Spanish kids hanging about. I grabbed a bag of chips in the Golden Grill. I turned off a busy Patrick Street and on to a much quieter Ellen Street.

Around the corner, past the library and the Trinity Rooms nightclub and the office was ahead. The approach was clear, nobody hanging around.

The entrance was clean, no lurkers. I couldn't make any of O'Doherty's goons anywhere.

I opened up and gave the alarm the numbers it demanded. It went back to sleep. I closed the door gently behind me and trudged upstairs.

I decided to play everything in the open, so I switched the lights on and left the blinds open. I stood there, drinking water and watching the street, making myself obvious. Scenarios raced through my mind. Maybe O'Doherty has a sniper across the street, waiting for Pat to stand exactly where I am? Maybe they're sitting in a car around the corner, waiting for his car? Maybe they'll hit him and Fox and he won't even get here? All maybes.

I left the office door wide open, so I'd hear the buzzer downstairs. Plus, it helped conceal the assault rifle, which was exactly where I'd left it. I fitted a magazine, cocked it and put it in position. I sat at my desk, head spinning.

My mobile rang, startling me. Christ, I'd been zoning out. I looked at the display.

'Christ, not now. Hello Deirdre.'

'Where did it all go wrong, Charlie?'

What?

'What?'

'With us. Weren't we happy?'

'I can't really talk now.'

'I want to know. I want you to tell me,' she said, some kind of childish tone in her voice. Odd.

'Okay. When we first met, we fell in love, had a laugh, had sex a lot and lived for the moment. Then we got kids, loans, no sex, boredom. We tried swinging. Then I had an affair with Sara. You had an affair with your guru. You went home to your mammy and daddy. Now I live alone like a saddo. Plus I'm in deep shit at the moment. It's all my fault. Everything is my fault.'

'Mummy and daddy have asked me to speak to you. They cashed some stocks. They say if we can make a fresh start, they'll give us some money. A lot. To spend together on whatever.'

'Better late than never.'

'We could afford an au pair to help with the kids.'

'A cute French girl?'

'We'll see.'

'Okay, this is a bit *Stepford Wives*. Why the change of heart? Why now?'

I wasn't going to mention the guru's little accident. Let her do that.

'Lots of things. And nothing.'

'Look Deirdre, I'm intrigued and thanks for calling. But I'm literally in the middle of something big. People might be trying to get through to me.'

'Always the same excuse with you Charlie, never a good time to talk,' she said, sounded hurt, but just putting on the hurt.

'Well this time I'm serious. I know I exaggerate and fantasise my life away, but this is genuine. Can I call you?'

She said nothing for a long second.

'One more thing.'

'Yeah?'

Silence. Spit it out, for fuck's sake!

'Charlie, I feel really bad, but I have to tell you.'

'Just bloody tell me.'

'You don't remember our talk the other night?'

'Not a word of it.'

'I was afraid of that. Well, I'll tell you again. I slept with Dave a few weeks back. Just once.'

'You what?'

'I did it to hurt you. I'm sorry, Charlie.'

And she hung up.

Jesus fucking Christ. Just once! Dave?

The buzzer went down below. Fuck, Pat. I went to the window and looked down. The angle was bad and it was clouded over, much darker. Just a shadow waiting. 10.24. Shit, I'd completely lost track of time. Drugs do that. And panic. And hearing terrible, stinking news.

I went downstairs quickly and opened up. Not Pat. Mickey fucking Flynn, I recognised him from Pat's poop sheets. Jesus, Mary and Joseph.

'Yeah?'

'Doyle?'

He glanced behind him, worried. He was clearly concerned about all the cop activity. He pushed forward, I stepped back and opened the door wide for him. In he came. I looked around outside, nobody on the street. Nobody I could see.

I shut the door and turned to face him, puzzled. I figured I'd have to get him upstairs, maybe pretend I had wads of cash, get to my AK.

'Pat sent me,' he said, hands tight in the pockets of his leather jacket. 'He said you have somethin for him.'

'I do. Come on up,' I said, leading the way to my office.

'How much of what's going on do you know about?' I asked as I opened the top drawer of the filing cabinet. The disk was there. I handed it over. The rifle was within reach.

'Just doin my job, that's all.'

He stood there for another second. I waited for him to make his move. Then he turned and walked out. I followed him down the stairs and opened the front door. He glanced at me with one eye. The lazy one looked over my shoulder. Then he was gone.

As I made to close the door, two shots cracked off. Close by.

I ran out on to the steps, searching. Flynn was on the ground only a few car lengths away, a pool of blackness spreading. I saw a car speed off, squealing around the corner.

'In like fuckin Flynn.'

I ran to him. He was dead as fuck, his chest all blood, just blood. I grabbed the DVD from the dead man's grip and tore back into the office, upstairs, switched off the lights. I took the assault rifle and, moving good and fast, locked the front door just as a siren wailed in the distance.

The police Eurocopter whined overhead as I drove through town, a target-rich environment tonight. I thought about going to Jean but decided it was too early. It would put her at risk. A showdown with Pat still loomed. I aimed for home, figuring to have a smoke, a drink, watch Sky News, listen to the local radio, put together a picture. Be prepared. Hoped I wouldn't have to fire a shot.

I was lucky to avoid all checkpoints. My business tonight was all city centre, the police would be concentrating on the gang strongholds and the outer ring roads and protection. I got home easily and went into the house, trying to act *normal*. Harder than it sounds. Left the rifle in the boot. The street was dead.

I left the lights off in the front room and made do with a little lamp in the kitchen. I put my phone on the counter, charging, and sat at the back doorstep, smoking cigarettes, thinking What the fuck is going on?

TV babbled in the background. Time pushed on. The eleven o'clock headlines had footage of the blast, bored TV cameras got more than they expected.

It was unreal. One second, Karpov was stood there, talking shite to tossers. Then *Bang!* and he was gone in a puff of smoke. Maddest fucking thing I've ever seen on TV. After 9/11, of course.

O'Doherty rang. He sounded jubilant.

'Well Charlie. All set?' he laughed.

'Yeah. But that wasn't Pat.'

'What?'

'At the office. It was Mickey Flynn.'

'You sure?' He wasn't laughing anymore.

'Yeah. I'm sure.'

'Fuck. Okay. That fucker had it comin soon enough anyway.'

And he hung up. Not one for pleasantries, the old bastard. He was worried now. Pat was a loose cannon for O'Doherty.

'Where the fuck are you Pat?' I asked the sky. I was a little relieved when he didn't step up out of the shadows and answer.

On TV, it started to become obvious that Karpov's death was linked to the gang murders. O'Doherty was mentioned as a local boss. Then a report from Moscow said that Karpov was under investigation back in the Motherland. Tax evasion. Even a dim cop would make this for what it was. O'Doherty would be starting to feel some intense heat about now.

I guessed he was away from home, holed up somewhere with his men, waiting to hear where Pat was. Pat would be protecting Fox until O'Doherty was arrested or dead. Either Fox or O'Doherty would have to go before anything could settle. Whichever was left would make peace with whoever took over from Karpov, probably whoever runs the club. No more ego clashes. Back to business.

News coverage switched to Paris, and the miraculous appearance of the face of Jesus Christ on a croque-monsieur ham and cheese sandwich. Hundreds kneeled in adoration of the sandwich, like an insane Weightwatchers' club meeting. Jesus Christ is right.

The sight of the Divine and Godly Snack caused my stomach to scream at me again, so I called in some Indian, a Vindaloo. Ate and decided to take a holiday. Straight away. Get the fuck out and let the dust settle on everybody else. Fucking right. Just return Jean in one piece and go. I wished I could've called in an airstrike, but who to hit?

I packed a bag and put my passport on top. I stuck the bag in the boot, behind the AK-47. Then I figured the gun would be more useful in the house if the phantom house-shooter turned up again. That must've been Pat. What a prick.

I took the gun in, wondering about the neighbours. Was anyone watching me now? So many goings-on for the oldies to natter about. I whistled as I carried the bagged assault rifle into the house, checking the street, seeing nothing.

Back at my post by the back door, I got the AK out and admired it more.

A to the motherfucking K.

I sat there, against the doorframe, the gun in my lap, my trigger finger itchy. The sense of impending doom grew. I decided to call Jean, see how she was doing.

'Hi, can you put me through to Mrs O'Donoghue in one-nineteen, please?' I asked the receptionist.

'Certainly, sir. Just a moment.'

She put me on hold. No music, just a vague hiss.

'Sorry sir, she checked out?'

'Checked out?'

This wasn't supposed to happen.

'Yes, just an hour ago. With her husband.'

'But I'm her husband,' I roared, realising how weird I felt, just saying that.

'Sorry?'

Shit.

'No. No. It's just a misunderstanding. Thanks for your help.'

I hung up on a confused and panicked receptionist, cursing myself for being so dumb. I tried Jean's mobile. After six rings, she answered.

'Hi Charlie,' she said, sounding sleepy, distant.

I was now very alarmed.

'Hi Jean, what's going on? Why did you check out?'

There was a bump and a rustling sound.

'Hi buddy,' said Pat.

I said nothing. I literally couldn't speak.

'I said, *Hi buddy*,' he repeated.

'Hi Pat,' I said. That was all.

'Okay listen bud, I need you to get on to Jean's little man and tell him to get some money together. Two million. Cash. Only if he wants his lovely wife back. Got that?'

'You're holding her for ransom? Is that what this is all about?' I asked, my heart racing once again towards an early heart attack.

'It is now,' he said. 'Just do it, okay? I'll call you back in an hour.'

Then he hung up. I called O'Doherty straight away.

Told him everything.

'What the fuck?' he screamed. 'Where were you?'

'I had to come to meet Pat, didn't I?' I roared back. He wasn't going to pin this on me. I was shouting for my life.

'Well how the fuck did he find her?' he shouted, not caring who was listening now.

'All I can think of,' I said, working fast, 'is that she called a friend to take her car out to her.'

'You're not fuckin serious? Ah, Jesus Christ, the fuckin stupid cunt. Where?'

'The Plassey Hotel. Would Jean's car have been at your house?'

His place was now being watched twentyfourseven.

'Yeah,' said O'Doherty, quieter now.

'They must have tailed the car, told Pat and he went and had her identified from a photo or something. I hear they're planting bugs and tracking devices in cars now, tailing by chopper.'

'Yeah.'

'So let's get her back,' I said, wanting to save her. Not to cover my own arse, just to save her.

'Right. Shoot.'

'Okay,' I said, 'I reckon it's just a ploy to kill you.'

'Go on,' he said, agreeing with me.

'So the best plan might be to just follow instructions and have some firepower in reserve.'

'Won't he have the same?' asked O'Doherty.

'I'm not sure. Maybe he's out on his own now. The thing earlier must've really shattered all his illusions. Now he's just stuck in Limerick again with Dr Fox for company. Speaking of which, how is he?'

'I'll tell you later,' said O'Doherty. 'We need to meet up. I want to hear the prick when he calls.'

'Where?' I asked. Where the fuck was there for me to meet a hunted gangster at midnight?

'I'll send one of the lads for you,' he replied. 'He'll take you to me. If you're stopped, play dumb.'

'Okay,' I said. 'I'm at home.'

He hung up. Then I had time to think. Fucking Pat. What's he on? Maybe it was just about the money, I mused. His big payday had exploded before his eyes and, if he could make a couple of million as a consolation prize, why not? Ideally, he could kill the man who fucked things up for him as well. So he'd want O'Doherty to deliver the cash. Nail him. War over. Loaded, nice promotion, the main man. Their past business was simply forgotten. This was gangster morality.

And my strings kept twitching.

CHAPTER 67. NIGHT DRIVE

My head was pounding so hard. Truly painful. I looked for the Solpadeine and found only the empty box, which I crushed with anger. I rooted around in the kitchen drawer and found organic aspirin. Praised the Lord for ecologically-sustainable drugs. I swallowed three, washed them down with beer. I gathered my thoughts and put the AK-47 back in its bag. It was coming with me. I watched the street through a gap in the curtains, lights off.

A car stopped outside, engine running, lights still on. It was a new black Mercedes, nondescript. The driver got out and waved at the house. There was nobody else in the car. I slipped out of the house, closing the door gently behind me.

I reached the car fully expecting some new twist, like I was about to be abducted by fucking aliens or something. But it was just one of O'Doherty's goons. I'd met him a couple of times. Well, if not met, been in the same room as.

He smiled and opened the passenger door for me. I got in, put the gun between my knees and belted up.

'What's that?' he said.

'AK-47. Insurance policy.'

'Nice,' he said, smiling broadly. 'I'm Mick.'

'Good man Mick. You know who I am, I suppose. Where we headed?'

'A safe house. Up in Southill.'

'Jesus Christ. What's he doing up there?'

'We've done business up there for a long time. It's like our test market,' he smirked. 'We're safer there than on the Island, even. They'd need to get the army out to find us.'

I nodded and looked straight ahead as we sped through town and up past the railway station. The city was pure dead, just a few drunks staggering to the late chipper and bored taxi drivers talking shite at the rank. Mick was about forty. He looked hard, like the kind of guy you simply wouldn't start with if he accidentally knocked your pint. But he was getting fat, like so many whose means exceed their needs. He was bald-shaven and had a gold earring in his left ear. He wore a black leather jacket and black jeans. Uniform.

'And what about Fox?' I asked, eager to find out more.

'We lost him,' he answered. 'Prick was taken away by your buddy. They have him at home now, surrounded by the fuckin ERU. We can't get near him.'

'Shit. Pat must have got him home and come back to finish things off. He knows there's no way he can get your boss in Southill, so he's using Jean to flush him out.'

'Fuckin tool's goin to get more'n he bargained for. Stupid gowl.'

'Yeah.'

'Nice one with Flynn earlier, wasn't it?'

'You do it?'

'I was there, yeah. We made him, the mullet gave him away.'

'And you killed him anyway?'

He shrugged his shoulders and smiled.

He relaxed a bit and turned up the stereo - The Doors, sweet - as we passed the Roxboro shopping centre and saw Southill looming before us. We veered left off the roundabout, heading towards the Dublin Road.

'Which way we going?' I asked.

The time to hesitate is through.

'Main road in's got a checkpoint,' he said, using his phone as we coasted down the wide, deserted streets.

'Yeah, me,' he said when the call was answered. 'Okay?'

He turned to me.

'We're clear. The boys have torched a car at the top, our way in is empty.'

Come on baby light my fire.

We turned right, off the main road, passed under a railway bridge and up the hill. Swinging left, passing vacant industrial units, tinkers' caravans, bonfires and car wrecks. Then right and into the darkest depths of Southill, which was like another planet entirely.

CHAPTER 68. THE GANG'S ALL HERE

Half a dozen tough-looking shaven-headed teenagers stood at the first corner, watching us like hawks. They recognised Mick and waved us through. After a few sharp twists and turns, we arrived at a tiny cul-de-sac. The police helicopter buzzed nearby and more cornerboys lurked in the shadows. Otherwise, all was quiet. Mick expertly reversed the big car in, positioning it both to block access and to make a quick getaway if required.

We got out and I followed him to the door of an unassuming house, carrying my gun in its bag.

Mick knocked twice on the steel door. A small hatch slid aside, revealing a tiny glass pane. Dark glass. Then the hatch closed again and the door opened, the lock sounding heavy and well-oiled. The door was opened by a really young guy, just a kid. He nodded to Mick and eyed me suspiciously. He had an automatic pistol in his hand.

Mick led the way through a hallway like any other, flecked wallpaper painted beige, dark red carpet, painted woodwork on the stairs. The proportions were narrow and the air smelt sick and heavy, stale cigarette smoke and urine. The door into the front room was open and I saw a really old lady sitting with a cup of tea, watching *Will & Grace* with the volume up really high. O'Doherty's mother.

Fucking bizarre, but nothing spooked me any more. She smiled at me and nodded.

At the end of the hallway, Mick knocked on a door. A lock was opened and O'Doherty was there. He smiled when he saw me and asked Mick if we'd been tailed. He said No, no sign. O'Doherty nodded and invited us in with a twitch of his head.

The kitchen was warm and bright. O'Doherty had been seated at the table, drinking a cup of tea. He nodded to a chair and I sat down. He was listening to a police radio scanner, crackling with coded conversation.

He poked the scanner and said 'ERU.'

This made him smile.

'How did you get their frequency? Wouldn't they be using scramblers?'

'There's tea in the pot,' he said to Mick.

Mick filled two mugs and gave one to me. I put some milk in it. The tea was good, hot and strong. I put my mobile on the table.

'What's that?' he asked, pointing at my gun.

'An AK-47,' I said.

'Okay,' he said, smiling.

I must have seemed a right mystery: a drug-addled gangster wannabe, carrying an assault rifle around in the middle of the biggest shitstorm to ever hit Limerick.

'That was some attack,' I said. 'Fair play to you. A surgical strike, that's what it was.'

'Yeah, it was good, wasn't it?' said O'Doherty, looking delighted with himself.

'How come they didn't spot it?' I asked. It had been bugging me.

'It was a shaped charge, straight up,' he explained, making an inverted V with his hands, 'but made out of some new kind of explosive. No dog can pick it up. One of my pals put in the sound system and the podium and all. He gets all those kinds of contracts. We just put the bomb in the podium, mobile phone detonator. The phone was called by someone in the room. Bada-bing, end of story.'

'Fuck's sake,' I said.

'They swept the place twice before he got there,' continued O'Doherty, relishing his story. 'They didn't suss a fuckin thing.'

'Who made it for you?' I asked. There was no way he'd done it himself. That was a military-style device.

'Where'd you get your gun?' he asked, rhetorically.

'I see,' I said.

'Cost me a hundred grand. Money well spent, I'd say.'

'What about Karpov's men?' I asked. 'Surely they're gunning for revenge?'

'Ah, they only think they're hard nuts, most of um,' he said, dismissing the threat. 'Half of um are gone already. Scared shitless.'

'They could be dangerous, though,' I said.

'Well now they have to play ball with me. If they don't, there'll be more killins yet.'

Leila flashed into my mind. I hoped she wasn't involved in any of this shit and that she wouldn't get caught in any crossfire.

'What about the cops?' I asked.

'They know it was me,' he said. 'That's what I hear. But they've no way to pin it on me. Your mad friend Pat's thrown everyone. Made it easier for me to get stuff done.'

'He's fucking nuts, alright,' I said.

Of course the phone rang right then. And it was Pat. I answered it and put it on speaker so O'Doherty and Mick could hear it too.

'Hi Pat,' I said.

'Hi Charlie,' he said, the sound crackly. 'O'Doherty there with you, yeah? Good.'

O'Doherty glanced at me then, taking his eyes off the phone. He took over.

'I have your money, pig,' he said. 'Put on my wife.'

Jean's fractured voice filled the kitchen.

'I'm okay,' she said. 'Just pay him and get me home.'

The muffled sound of a phone being taken from someone.

'Where and when?' said O'Doherty.

'Thirty minutes,' said Pat. 'You and you alone. Poor Man's Kilkee. Stand in the middle and leave the cash in one bag on the bollard nearest the road. Got that?'

'Got it,' said O'Doherty.

'I'll stop, check the cash, then let Jean out. Then I'm gone, okay? We never talk again, okay?'

'Okay.'

'Don't try anything or she's dead. Got that?'

'Okay.'

'Okay so,' said Pat.

The phone clicked and the line was dead.

O'Doherty was angry now, his face red. He pounded the table in disgust.

'Right,' he said then, 'Let's make a plan.'

He called together his three best men. Mick, plus the young guy Robert who'd answered the door and a guy I hadn't seen before. O'Doherty drew a rough sketch of ground zero on a piece of paper. Poor Man's Kilkee jutted out into the river from a one-way road that passed along beside a strip of riverside pubs and offices and under Sarsfield Bridge. You could get down from the bridge on stone steps. Behind Poor Man's Kilkee was a rowing club building. There were plenty of spots for snipers, which made Pat's choice of drop-off spot more understandable.

'He must have a sniper there waiting,' I said. 'He figures you'll try the same. Maybe he'll try and get you before he even gets out of the car.'

'Could be,' said O'Doherty. 'I want ye here and here,' he said to his men, indicating the rowing club and the area under the bridge. Both locations offered concealment and would give good crossfire to where Pat would stop his car. 'Charlie, you stay up top on the bridge. He has to come towards you to escape.'

'With this thing?' I asked, lifting my gun.

'Yeah, with that ting. If anyone looks like they're about to collar you, run and drop it into the river. Otherwise you might need it. Okay, let's lock and load and go.'

The goon I hadn't seen before left the kitchen and came back a few seconds later, carrying three guns. Two were Heckler & Koch MP5s. Each weapon had a flashlight below the barrel and a second magazine taped to the one that was ready to fire. There was also an AK-47. Each man took a gun and they checked, loaded and cocked them. Mick got the AK and he winked at me. O'Doherty took a Beretta pistol from a kitchen drawer, cocked it and tucked it into the back of his jeans. I checked my gun too, just to join in with the lads. All set, so.

As we walked out the front door, the old woman hugged O'Doherty.

'Now you be a good boy, won't you son? There's all sorts of lunatics out at this hour.'

We drove in two cars. I went with O'Doherty, the three lads took the scanner and sped on ahead to get into position. O'Doherty drove, slowly. He was quiet, his attention focused on the job ahead. He knew he was the prime target. He knew he'd be lucky to get through this scenario alive. I had to respect him, risking his life for Jean. Or maybe he just knew that this would be his best chance to finish Pat off, wipe out the Russians' main inside man. Win the battle, finish Fox off at his leisure, win the war.

'How do you think the cops'll react if you kill Pat?' I asked.

'Hopefully they'll just do another cover-up,' he answered. 'They're good at that shit.'

We drove back towards the river, through deserted city streets. O'Doherty got a call from Mick, telling him about a checkpoint at the top of William Street. We went through King's Island and around by the castle. Into town on Sarsfield Bridge, he stopped halfway across, hazard lights blinking. We got out of the car and crossed over the road. Poor Man's Kilkee was below, to our left. There was nobody around at all. Suspiciously quiet, except for distant sirens and the thudding of the pork chopper, sounding like it was out over Moyross. I wished him luck. He nodded and sped off over the bridge, to take a left to Arthur's Quay, where he'd park.

I continued across the bridge, the gun bag under my arm, trying to look uninvolved to any hidden eyes. When I got near my designated position, I crossed the road and got a good view of Poor Man's Kilkee down below. A couple of lads sat there, eating chips. I could actually smell the vinegar.

O'Doherty soon appeared, walking straight out to the guys eating the chips. They immediately got up and walked away quickly, under me and towards Arthur's Quay Park. O'Doherty walked back and put his bag of cash on the only bollard near the road. Then he went and stood in the middle of the grass, nervously looking around, trying to make eye contact with his men. He glanced towards me. He saw me, but didn't give my position away.

So we waited. I checked my watch. Pat was due any minute. Then the roar of a powerful car. There, coming towards me, down the riverside drive, was Jean's BMW. It screeched to a stop beside

O'Doherty. I could make out Jean's dark hair in the passenger seat. Pat got out the driver's side, the engine still running. Leaving his door open, he went to the money bag. He had his gun in his hand and used it to gesture to O'Doherty to open the bag. Clever after the Karpov episode. O'Doherty went and opened the bag. Pat ordered him back and looked inside. Happy, he picked up the bag, frisked O'Doherty quickly and went back to the car. He got in and O'Doherty started forward, calling Jean. I got my gun out and held it at my waist, resting on the parapet.

The passenger door opened and Jean got out. She looked shaky but okay. The door closed behind her and the car roared and sped off. Jean stood in the middle of the road while O'Doherty reached for his arse and grabbed his gun.

'Lads!' he screamed, looking under the bridge to where his men should be.

No reply.

He raised his gun, taking aim at Pat. There was only one shot, one chance. As he squeezed the trigger, a volley of fire ripped into him. It came from directly under me. O'Doherty managed to get his shot off, but the guns kept firing and he collapsed in a heap. The noise was low enough, muffled by the bridge. Jean dropped to the ground as I raised my gun, waiting for whoever was under the bridge to show themselves. She rolled behind a parked car as bullets sparked off the ground all around her, slamming into cars and walls and windows.

CHAPTER 69. BANG, BANG

Two figures appeared from the shadows, each clad in black, wearing a balaclava with some kind of night vision goggles. They slowly moved towards Jean, firing their big pistols every few paces. Professionals. I knew that they would kill her. She screamed as a fat black jeep screeched around the corner sand came to a stop just behind her. It waited, the gunmen's getaway car.

I leaned against the parapet, raised my rifle and got one of the men in the sights. That would be enough. I squeezed the trigger, my heart racing. Nothing.

'Safety catch, you fucking eejit,' I said quietly to myself.

I flicked the catch on to full auto with my thumb and took aim again. They were only a few paces from Jean now, maybe she was dead already. I squeezed the trigger again. This time the gun jumped in my hands, shaking my bones and overpowering my grip. The harsh smell of the smoke made me retch. Through the smoke, I saw that I'd missed, my rounds hitting the ground ten metres beyond them. Watch out for Jean, you useless twat.

If they were surprised to face a machine gun unexpectedly, they never showed it. They turned to face me. They brought their guns to bear and I shot again. Four bullets left my AK and pulverised a chest. I riddled him. It only took one second. The other guy dropped to the ground and I fired again as his bullets whistled over my head or blew chunks of masonry from the bridge. I hit him, maybe in the shoulder, and he dropped his gun and ran to the jeep. I raced down the cold stone steps and to Jean.

She was crying, her mascara running, her face old-looking. She hugged me, delirious at her close escape. The shot guy got into the jeep and I saw a flash of blond hair. Fucking Leila. She reversed away with a squeal and a hiss and was gone.

'Hang on,' I said, gently pushing Jean away from me and over to the wall.

I went to the gunman. He was dead, his chest mush.

Then I turned to Jean's car. It was partially under the bridge, crashed, burning. A few people stood on the bridge overhead, staring down at the carnage. I took Jean's hand and we hurried to the car as a distant siren wailed.

Pat was there, sitting right back in his seat. He'd hit a pillar. The car was a write-off, its engine smashed and smoking. His face was covered in blood. Looked like O'Doherty had managed to hit him. Beyond the car, in the deep shadows under the bridge, I saw three bodies, laid out. Mick and the lads hadn't stood a chance. A goon massacre.

'It almost worked, Pat,' I said.

I held my gun to his face, sick of the fucker at that stage.

'Get me out Charlie,' he said, his voice feeble.

I could smell petrol. I walked around to the other side, watching that he didn't draw his gun. He didn't even move. He was fucked. The bag of money was on the passenger seat. I reached in through the shattered window and took the bag. I went back to Jean's side and he asked again to be left out.

Jean was crying, in shock at it all. He was finished, she could see that.

'Aw, come on lads,' he said, fading fast.

'I'm opening your door Pat,' I said. 'Just for old times' sake.'

He smiled at me as I opened the door. His legs looked trapped in the mangled car. No way he was getting out. Not my problem. As I put my arm around Jean and turned towards the steps, he called me back.

'By the way, Charlie. One thing,' he said to me.

'Yeah?' I said, hoping he'd say Sorry.

'You killed Dave, Charlie. Just never forget that.'

He smiled, then he passed out.

'Prick,' I said, pushing Jean to the steps.

The sirens were much louder as we reached the top of the steps and got on to the bridge. We walked over it, away from town. Half way across, I dropped the rifle into the river which swallowed it quietly.

Jean kept looking back.

'Save him,' she said finally.

'What?'

'Please.'

I put her in a taxi at the far side of the bridge, told the driver to hang on, made my way back to Pat. I saw two squad cars from Henry Street, screaming, rushing down to Poor Man's Kilkee, blue lights flashing across the black river. So I ran.

Suddenly a flash of orange under Sarsfield Bridge. Jean's car exploded with an angry roar. Too late.

We got back to my place. I remembered the revolver was in my car, so I set Jean up with a vodka and an ashtray and strolled down towards the office for it. The streets buzzing with police.

When I got back, she was crying. Jean sobbed for ages about how she thought Pat was going to kill her, no matter what. I agreed that her death must've been part of his plan.

'What a prick,' I said.

'Money. That's what it does to people,' Jean said. 'Money and power.'

'Fuck's sake,' I said.

So we counted our cash. Two million in fifties and hundreds.

'Not bad,' she said. 'It's still only a fraction, though.'

'I suppose you must be a very wealthy widow, so?'

'I suppose I must be,' she said, yawning. 'Christ, I'm wrecked.'

'It's been a manic few hours,' I said, putting my arms around her, my head spinning at the wealth that was sitting right there on my kitchen counter. 'Manic few days.'

So we went to bed, my revolver beside me. We didn't have sex. She was distant, in mourning for the loss of her husband, I guessed. I wondered if it really was all over. She took two sleeping tablets and conked out. I stared at the ceiling, thinking only of Dave.

CHAPTER 70. NICE AND TIDY

Half an hour later and the doorbell went. I held the revolver O'Doherty'd given me behind my back. I opened the door - wearing only underpants - to find Pat's cop partner standing there with his hands in his pockets. He looked glum as well.

'You here to arrest me?' I asked.

I wouldn't really have cared if he'd said *Yes*.

'No. No, I'm not,' he said, a bit surprised.

'Well would you like to come in so?'

Fuck, and me with a gun in my hand.

'No thanks.' Thank fuck! 'This is grand. I just wanted to tell you I know what Pat was up to.'

This was a bit of a shocker.

'He was dirty,' continued the cop, 'but that's not going to come out, okay?'

'Okay.'

'Keep everything to yourself, and I mean everything, and you won't have any trouble from me. Got it?'

'Got it.'

'And you can tell O'Doherty's wife that she should be okay as well.'

He smiled and glanced up the stairs.

'As long as she keeps her nose clean,' he went on. 'The Russians, what's left of them, are happy they nailed O'Doherty and his muscle. They'll leave it at that. It's a draw.'

'That's good to know,' I said, surprised at the cop's openness.

'The bodies won't be released for a while. Pat's funeral is in a couple of days. Full honours. Poor guy was burnt to a crisp.'

'How did he die, exactly?' I asked.

'O'Doherty shot him and he crashed. Bang. End of story.'

'Shit.'

'Yeah. Shit.'

He turned to walk away, stopped himself.

'Ever been to Sicily, Charlie?'

'Nah. Apparently it's full of gangsters.'

He smiled.

So the cop left, without mentioning the awkward facts that Pat was in Jean's car and had met Limerick's top gangster in the middle of the night without backup. These little details would be glossed over. Forensics would see to that, piece together a credible story based on scientific evidence. Who could argue with science?

Pat actually did me a favour, with his twisting of the law, his madness. The cops would now pin every possible unsolved murder on O'Doherty and everyone would be happy. Hero Pat saved the day. Fucking typical.

CHAPTER 71. RED MIST

It wasn't working and time was running away. If she didn't have an Irishman propose to her, she was on a chartered flight to Lagos. Home to her nightmares and - much worse - the gang she had betrayed. It was unthinkable that her final escape from Africa could be the cause of her death.

And now it was all too late. The way he'd looked at that stripper. She saw his eyes, saw that he had slipped away. She went to Precious's house at three in the morning, endured the namecalling, the threats, the sick graffiti.

'Oh child, I see your heart is broken.'

'They're sending me back, Precious.'

'No my child, they can't do that. My magic is too strong. Perhaps we have not been clever. Here. Sit. Let me make some tea.'

Etoile sat in the spell room, let its colours and smells overtake her feelings of despair.

Precious served a potion tea. That helped. Then she got the ultimate talisman.

'Take this and seduce him. Do everything. Promise everything. Then he will propose to you.'

'Will that be enough?'

'That will be enough. And if not, I will kill him for you.'

CHAPTER 72. CORN AND EGGS

The morning after the shitstorm, Jean took the two million home in a taxi, stashed it somewhere safe and packed a bag. Then we went straight out to Shannon and grabbed a Ryanair flight to Girona, hired a car, got to one of Jean's properties. She was now sole owner of half a dozen houses in Limerick and Dublin, two villas in Spain and one on a tiny island in Croatia.

Spain was hot. Kind of a dry dead heat that scorched your skin and sucked the will to live from your bones. Out on the plains of Catalonia, in the tiny village of Monells, we were surrounded by about a hundred million maize plants and sunflowers, flocks of swallows and just a few elusive Spaniards. We had a secluded villa with six beds, a cool pool, a maid and a well-stocked bar. An hour to Barcelona, twenty minutes to the turquoise Med, two hours to France. Sweet as a nut and nothing to do.

The first twenty-four hours consisted of Jean alone in her room, sobbing. I was surprised she was so cut up about her prick of a husband. She was full of surprises.

Then, days were passed by the pool, sleeping, getting slowly plastered on fancy rum and vodka cocktails. We were surrounded by an abundance of exotic fruits, vegetables and wines. The air was pure, the sun a constant. I was quickly intoxicated, approaching a state of near calm.

We took a drive north to Figueres, the Dali Museum. Huge eggs perched on the outer battlements of the palace of surrealism. Inside were so many pieces of art, pop culture classics I'd half-seen a million times, ephemeral trademarks of modern culture. But to see them in all their surreality brought on an acid flashback. The glasses of absinthe enjoyed in the shady sidewalk cafes didn't help. Then, in a black marble room, under a slab, Dali himself. I understood art, finally got it, cried. Outside, I looked at my watch and it melted before my eyes. I babbled about wanting to live in Spain as Jean drove us home.

She kept in touch with home, took ten private calls a day. Family, I guessed. Nobody called me.

After four days in sweaty heaven, Jean got a call from home. Greg's body was being released and we had to get back. I was about to tell her that I wanted to stay in Spain with her forever, but her mind was already in Limerick.

She held my hand the whole way home. At the airport arrivals area, she changed.

'We'd better get home separate,' she said coolly.

'I suppose,' I replied, comfortable now with loss and failure.

'I'll talk to you soon about the money, okay?'
'When?'
'Probably a couple of weeks, okay?'
'Jesus.'

'We need to be really careful or we'll blow it.'

'Okay so.'

'See you around.'

So she kissed me lightly on the cheek and walked alone to the taxi rank.

I'd been dumped!

CHAPTER 73. HEART OF DARKNESS

Into my still boarded-up house which, after Spain, was a smelly cave, a tomb, someplace I didn't want to be. No sunlight in ages, the place was regressing to a more primitive time, becoming an unwelcoming, dark feeling. The electricity had been cut, that depressed me even more.

A great pile of mail threw up two gems. A cheque for twelve grand from the Sunday paper for those pictures of Luke and Jean. Sweet enough to keep me going until we could have a go at the ransom cash. This reminded me of the DVD, so I called my pal at the paper. He got excited, said Okay, send it in so, could be worth another ton of cash. Sound as a bell.

And there was a little packet, postmarked Dublin, addressed to the office.

'Thanks, Fiona.'

It was a Wordsworth edition: *Selected Stories* by Anton Chekhov. A handwritten note on the first page.

DON'T FORGET YOUR QUEST!

I got a beer, found the story *Champagne* and sat down to read it, smiling at the memory of Karpov's party.

After two paragraphs, an insistent knocking on the front window.

'Who the fuck?'

It was Etoile, the uninvited guest. She was wild-eyed, very jumpy. She pushed past me, went in and sat on the couch where we'd kissed.

I followed her intoxicating scent trail. She'd opened her raincoat, showing a red bra and knickers and glistening skin.

'Sit here, Charlie.'

I sat. I was firm, had to be when she put her hands on my head, put her tongue in my mouth, rubbed my shoulders. But no.

'Sorry, Etoile. I can't. It's not you.'

She stood up and let her coat drop to the dusty floorboards. She posed. Dear God. But no.

'I can't. I think I'm in love.'

'Why did you do this to me Charlie? They want to send me home,' she wailed.

I swallowed hard, but my throat was dry.

'What do you mean? I thought you had citizenship.'

'No. I don't. I hate you. I hate you, Charlie Doyle.'

'Calm down, will you? What are you getting all uppity with me for?'

'You were the one. She told me you would be mine!' she screamed, rage in her eyes. 'I helped you get rid of your bitch wife and this is how you reward me.'

'What?'

'They're going to send me back to Nigeria, Charlie Doyle. Have you any idea what that means? I'll never get into Europe again. Never!'

'What's this about my wife?'

'They'll kill me.'

'That's not my fault, is it?'

'You should have married me, Charlie. I would have loved you, done everything for you. Now it's all no good.'

She was screaming like a demon, even worse than the worst argument I'd ever had with Deirdre.

'Get the fuck out!' I shouted back. I'd had enough. This was my breaking point.

'You bastard! You're like every other man I've ever met! Now go to hell!'

She pulled a little bundle from her coat pocket and thrust it at me. I took it and unwrapped the black fabric as she turned and ran. Inside was a hard lump of dry flesh, covered with congealed blood, red ribbon and human hair - my hair - tied around it. Though I'd never seen one before, I knew it was a human heart. A child's heart. It fell from my hand as a piercing pain shot through my guts, my body collapsed and my brain shut down, having had enough of me and my twisted reality.

CHAPTER 74. PURE MAD

So I accept now that all life is chemical. Physics explains the cosmic background, the Universe. Biology is chemistry. DNA is chemistry, is life.

And sex drives the evolution of homo sapien DNA to higher levels. For hundreds of thousands of years, we were but chimpanzee. The hair became less and the brain capacity increased. We were all born in Africa. Then we hit the bottle and evolved.

The Egyptians, the Mesopotamians, the Greeks: they discovered alcohol, built cities and society was created. They thrived on the stuff. Sexual urges were unleashed by the considered fermentation of grapes or oats. Social connection and casual sex improved the genetic mix and Darwin's theories came true much faster.

I found an old book - a kid's book - in the day room. *The Usborne Illustrated Handbook of Invention and Discovery.* 1986. Tattered, stained, torn. But at the back, proof. Inventions and discoveries through the ages. For starters: hundreds of thousands of years of cave art, spears and oil lamps.

Then, in six thousand BC, beer was invented. Writing, cities, agriculture, pottery, ploughs and wheels follow. By the year dot, there wasn't too much left to invent. Things progressed nicely. Then Rome fell. After a millennium of darkness, whiskey was sussed by the Irish in the late-fifteenth century. *Uisce beatha*, water of life. This led to vodka, gin and all the rest of my little friends. As well as the Copernican theory of the Universe, pencils, Da Vinci, the Renaissance, and - the ultimate civilizing invention of humans - plumbed toilets.

The modern age, with its quarks and electrons, software and DNA is as chemical as ever. What's the driver of this frantic phase of human evolution? Class A narcotics, weed and a whole world of lovely booze, opium driving the Industrial Revolution and cocaine in Coca Cola helping to give us planes and cars.

So I have reached some sort of understanding of life. I have time to think. But still I search for meaning. For the very first time, in desperate circumstances, I realise that I don't want do die until I find the meaning. I tell this to those around me, but they ignore me, they're worried about things that I know don't matter a fuck.

Because, when I came to in my hallway, I dragged myself to the hospital for the pain in my side. Turned out to be a kidney stone but the doctor, some bastard of a kid, became concerned about my general physical and mental condition. He asked me a few subtle questions during the checkup, mentioned the toxicology results on my bloods - cocaine, LSD, alcohol, cannabis, opiates. You're lucky to be alive, Mr Doyle, and we hope you don't have permanent damage. I exploded, *What about Etoile and the heart? Have you ever seen a child's heart?* He called security and the social worker. I had a flashback, lost control again.

Section 5B in the Regional for psychological assessment. A good few in, wanting to be classified as slightly mad. Just for the lifetime pension and free bus pass. Plus one or two genuine nutters, shouting and being restrained by the screws. And Poor Charlie.

I cooperated, asking *Are you taking the piss?* and *Who is truly sane anyway?* But I failed all their tests, their stupid questions, their awkward probing of my traumatised psyche.

They couldn't get hold of anyone, not my dad, not Jean, not even Deirdre. I gave them Dave's number, Pat's number. So I was sent along to St Joseph's after two long days, diagnosed bipolar manic depressive with suicidal tendencies, multiple addictions and unidentified underlying disorders. Cognitive therapies and medical intervention urgently required. *Charming.* Then I was truly fucked. They gave me lithium and fried my brain. Do they still do that? Do they fuck.

Can you picture the *Live 8* concert in a mental hospital? Half the wing in a room with a big TV, a sheet of scratched, heavy-duty Perspex bolted in front of the screen. Can you credit so many Pink Floyd fans in a mental hospital? Can you picture the hands in the air for U2? Can you hear the orderlies laughing? Can you smell the piss and sweat? Help these people. Can you see me in the middle of it all, mad as the rest? *Help these poor, poor people.*

So I stopped being aggressive, the old drugs all gone, the new ones working. They put me in a room of my own, someplace to think. I read. I write. I vomit. I scream. I think a lot about the heart in my hallway and the child in pieces.

I try to catch meaning, but it wriggles from my hands like a snake. So I look at the clouds outside my high, barred window, thinking again of the heart lying in my hallway, wondering what it means, what any of this damned life means.

CHAPTER 75. DECENCY

After a time, the doctor said I was okay. The neurological drugs had helped and the psychological cocaine dependency had weakened. I was straighter and cleaner than any time since childhood. They asked if I would keep taking the tablets. I said Yes, I promise. So they gave back my clothes, my money, my keys, my life.

Back home, I found the heart where I'd dropped it, by now covered in wriggling maggots, white things with tiny black eyes. Hundreds of them and flies buzzing around and the stink of death. I didn't even gag, just found a plastic bag, put my hand in, picked up the heart, closed the bag around it. Into another bag, tied that, into the bin. Put the bin out for collection. Washed and dried my hands eight times.

I looked in the fridge. A Pavlovian response to a bottle of lager made me open it, taste it. The taste didn't appeal, but I drank it anyway, flinching after each little sip.

I sat on the back door step, which felt comfortable, and began to write on a piece of paper. At the top, in capitals, I wrote FIND ETOILE, FIND THE KILLER.

Then a wave of lethargy washed over me. I dropped the pen and paper and leaned back against the frame, looked at the sky for a long while.

Then I got in my car, parked in town and read books - *Catch-22, Tropic of Cancer*, some true crime stuff about paedophiles - while scanning every black face that passed by. I did this for three days, watching the shops by day and the bars and clubs by night. It was how she'd found me.

I spotted her on Thursday afternoon. Adrenalin surging, I tailed her on foot. She went to Henry Street Station, which I didn't get until I drove after her bus to the immigrants' camp. Then it made some sort of twisted sense.

She wanted a husband, an Irish husband. Plenty of Africans believe in black magic, so she got the heart from a witch doctor, who'd kidnapped and chopped up the girl. I knew, just knew in my gut, this was how it all happened. But could I nail the bastard?

CHAPTER 76. PRECIOUS

The bus emptied. Its occupants went through a security check and trudged up the drive to the billets, all bulging Aldi bags and tired kids. I parked on the grass verge and, after the crowd had passed through, walked up to the security man.

'How's it going?'

'How we doin?'

'Grand. I don't know if you can help me. I'm a private detective.'

'Go on.'

'I'm looking for an African, maybe South African or Nigerian, big into witchcraft.'

'Man or a woman?'

'I don't know.'

'What's it about?'

'That I can't say.'

'You should probably go through normal channels so. I'm only the security.'

'There's two hundred quid in it.'

'Yeah?'

'If it's who I'm looking for. I'll give you half now.'

The guard looked around and edged in front of his hut, so he couldn't be seen from the camp. I moved with him, happy at the break.

'There was one headcase here a while back. South African. She said she was a healer and had all the Africans into her billet every day. She made a fortune from it. Alright lookin.'

'Did she ever use the word muti?'

'No, but others did. She spooked the Romanians and the Ukrainians big time. They were always givin out yards about her. I'm glad she's gone.'

'Gone? Where?'

'She got a green card, the bitch. She must know someone or maybe she used her fuckin magic. Although, she claimed to be part-Irish. I don't know. She's up in Moyross, I think.'

Moyross! This is her!

'Can you get a name and address?'

The guard looked at me and folded his thick arms across his thick chest.

'Okay look. I think this is who I'm after, so I'll give you all the cash right now.'

'Serious?'

'Serious.'

The guard found a number in his mobile phone and called it.

'How we doin Paddy. Listen, I need a favour. Are you on the computer? Can you look up someone for me so? Okay, she was from South Africa and moved to Moyross. I'd say it was back in June, but I'm not a hundred percent. Yeah, the witch doctor.'

He turned to me.

'Does he know who you mean?'

'He does. This one is a piece of work, I'll tell you.'

'Was she ever in trouble?'

'Nothing like that. But if looks could kill, you know?'

'Yeah.'

'Hang on. Paddy? Go ahead so.'

The guard wrote in a pad, slowly, like the words were being spelt out for him.

'Thanks Paddy. So we're goin for a pint after the shift, yeah? My treat. Good luck so.'

He tore the page from the pad and handed it over.

PRECIOUS O'REILLY, 47 CAPPANTY ROAD, MOYROSS.

'O'Reilly?'

'I'm not jokin you.'

I gave the man two crisp hundred euro notes and thanked him. I had the killer's scent now, so I said Fuck it, and then drove to her house in Moyross.

CHAPTER 77. THE FRIDGE

I parked around the corner from 47 Cappanty Road. I checked my revolver and put it in the inside left pocket of my new denim jacket. A small gang of kids, average age five, watched me closely from across the road. An emaciated pony was tied to a pole. The blackened skeletons of two cars lay rusting on an open scorched-grass area, lush countryside just beyond.

I walked around to the house, in the gate and up to the door. There was a wreath hanging off the brass-effect knocker, weird leaves and twigs. It was hot. I was sweating. I knocked: three sharp clacks.

Movement through the small patterned yellow glass panels in the door. A bolt slid back, the door clicked, opened enough for most of her head to look out.

It was Etoile's aunt, Emily. In all my analysis of the operation and its variables, this one hadn't occurred to me.

'Hello. Emily, isn't it?'

'Yes.' She paused. 'Do I know you?'

Without make-up and in daylight, she looked different, but the eyes were there. Her skin was light and clear, her hair loose over her shoulders, dead straight, shiny.

'I'm Charlie, Charlie Doyle. I went to a club with you and Etoile, your niece.'

'Ah yes. I remember you. What do you want?'

'I'm looking for a lady and I thought she was living here.'

'Who?' she asked, her body still behind the door.

'She's a South African lady. I was hired by the embassy to track her down. Apparently she's been left a fortune back home and if she doesn't claim it soon, it's gone.'

'What's this?' she asked, opening the door a little more, her eyes fixed on me now.

'Yeah, it's a good one. Her name's Precious. Precious O'Reilly.'

Emily smiled for the first time and opened the door fully.

'Come in, Charlie. I'll make you some tea. I'll see if I can help you.'

'Lovely. Thanks.'

She led me through a dark hallway, filled with powerful, alien smells, pungent odours that lodged in my brain, instant memory. She led me into the living room, which was simply decorated with natural wood furniture and red walls. The most unusual feature was the single carved mask over the fireplace. Its features were contorted into a demon's leer, teeth that would bite you and eyes that would burn your soul. She lit an incense stick and excused herself.

I stood while Emily made the tea. I was fearful of the mask, concerned that it had spirit powers. On the plus side, it maybe offered evidence that Precious had been in the house recently.

Emily came back into the room, closing the door after her.

'The kettle is on,' she said, sitting then.

'So where's Precious?' I asked.

'Precious lived here for a short time. What do you really want her for?'

'Like I say, it's the embassy. They'll give her the details.'

'Who do you know in the embassy?'

'I'm only the help. I was contacted by a secretary. Do you know where she is?'

'Have you been seeing Etoile?'

'I haven't seen her for a few weeks, no.'

The memory of the dead heart flashed at me. I swayed, vertigo, then sat opposite Emily.

'A pity. That girl really loved you.'

'She wasn't just after a husband then?'

She said nothing, but her manner changed. She'd been lured by my story. But she hadn't taken the bait. Still the threat remained. Etoile must have betrayed her, she imagined, told me about the killing.

'How did you get this address,' she asked.

'Etoile. She said Precious helped her with some love potions or something.'

'The tea,' she said, getting up.

I sat with the mask, wondering how I'd salvage something, anything. She returned, handing me a mug of steaming red tea.

'It's African tea. Try it. It's really good for you, your mojo, yes?'

'Mojo tea. Smells potent. I'll just give it a sec to cool down.'

She sipped from her own mug, watching me intently.

'Listen Emily. I wasn't totally truthful with you.'

'Really?'

'I don't want Precious for what I said.'

'The fortune?'

'There is none.'

'The truth shall set you free, child.'

'It's all complicated. My wife's left me, my job stinks, I tried to kill myself. I need help. Muti.'

'Muti? What do you know of muti, Irishman?'

'I know that it works for a lot of people. I don't believe in god or prayers or any of that shit. I want something that's chemical, tangible.'

'Magic potions and talismans?'

'Exactly. And Etoile told me that Precious is the best in the country.'

'Yes. She is.'

I picked up my tea, willing to drink it to make the woman feel more at ease with me. She jumped up and grabbed my cup.

'No, please. Let me make you a cup of Irish tea. I wasn't being fair.'

'It's okay.'

'No. I insist.'

So I let her take the cup. She left the room, poured its poisonous contents down the kitchen sink and put the cup to one side. As she made a fresh brew, she was thankful to her gods for yet another luckless customer.

'Your tea, Charlie. Now tell me what it is that you need.'

'I really need to see Precious, don't I?'

'You're talking to her.'

I nodded dumbly and drank some tea, so hot it burnt the roof of my mouth. I was in her lair, caught off guard, but maybe she was fooled.

'Mind if I smoke?' I asked.

'Not at all. I'll get the ashtray.'

I lit a cigarette with a shaking match as she, the killer of children, went back to the kitchen. I thought I heard voices, but decided they were in my head. I stood up and went to the mask.

'You don't scare me,' I said to it.

The mask said nothing, just looked at me.

'Your ashtray.'

'Thanks, Precious.'

'You're welcome. Now sit. Tell me how I can help you.'

'I'm just a mess, Precious. I need you to tell me what I need so I can get some fire back. You know? Fire in my belly. I don't care what it takes or what it costs.'

She took my hand and examined it in detail, looking at the lines, following their tracks with her finger. Then she looked into my eyes, so close I was startled. She squeezed my bicep hard, then my thigh. Finally she got closer still and inhaled deeply, smelling my essence.

'I could give you some potions, but - '

'But what?'

'They wouldn't be powerful enough. You need the full treatment.'

'What's that?'

'It'll cost you.'

'How much?'

'Five thousand.'

'Jesus Christ!'

'Nothing to do with him. For that sum, I can guarantee you a life of success, wealth and virility.'

'Jesus. I like the sound of it, but I don't know if I can afford it.'

I looked at her, all sad eyes and shaking lips, like I was going to cry. No act.

'There is another way,' she said.

'Tell me.'

'You could assist me with the ceremony. I need something special, something common and cheap, but which attains great value when muti takes it.'

I smiled. Go on, I thought.

'What is it. Tell me and I'll get it.'

'I need a virgin.'

I stood up slowly, turned to her, smiled again.

'So you're saying you want me to get a virgin for you to cut up?'

'Yes. That doesn't disgust you, does it?'

'No. Life is cheap. Did you do that other kid before? Have you done many more?'

'Yes. She was impure, as it turned out. This time I need to be sure. Can you help me, Charlie?'

'Have you done many more?'

'Dozens.'

Her eyes narrowed, suspicion returning. I thought for a moment.

'Yes. I'll help you.'

I took out my gun, flicked the safety catch off, pointed it at her head. Suddenly, two sharp cracks from another room.

'What's that?' I asked, alarmed.

'Just my fly killer in the kitchen, sir' her face pale, unguarded shock in her eyes.

It was the *sir* that did it. 'Show me.'

So I followed her to the kitchen. It looked more catering than domestic, all stainless steel work surfaces, huge fridges, a heavy duty bug zapper with an evil, blue glow, long knives, cleavers. There were jars lined up on the counter, full of liquids and anonymous globs. Lots of red globs. The sunlight was kept out by sheets of red plastic over the windows. Place was like a slaughterhouse or something.

She kept glancing at a fridge, one of those big American-style jobs.

'Open it.'

'Open it yourself, honky bastard.'

'Fucking bitch.'

'White trash,' and she spat on me.

Keeping the gun trained on her, I walked the three steps to the fridge and pulled the curved, chrome handle. The door popped open. There was no light in there and it took a second to make out the heads among all the rancid food and cider pint bottles. Two of them. One was Luke O'Doherty, the other was the murdered child. Just sitting there, each on a Delft dinner plate. Every hair on my body stood on end. I shuddered as I took it all in. They looked at me, their stench sending my guts into spasm. I retched and puked dark liquid onto my shoes.

Precious grabbed a knife and lunged for me, screaming like a banshee. I shot her in the side and she roared and fell to the ground. She writhed there like an eel, cursing me in a dozen tongues. The fridge light at last blinked on. Too much, way too much.

She sat on the lino, screamed at me.

'Stop it! Stop! You shot me! I'm bleeding to death.'

'Shut the *fuck* up,' I grunted, vomit coming up my throat, burning my tongue. 'Just shut it.'

There was a nice bit of blood alright. She was writhing.

While I swayed, trying to work out what the fuck to do, a shock to my lower back, like a hot poker pierced me. An odd smell, the blur of movement. An arm around my neck and a gun stuck hard into my spine.

'Drop it you cunt,' came the slurred words, loudly into my ear, spit and stench as well.

I dropped my gun.

The arm was pulled away and the pain in my back pushed me onto my knees. I turned, *Who is he?*, almost died then.

Mickey Flynn!

He wore just a pair of boxer shorts, had a bandage rolled round his chest, blood all over it.

Another big, filthy dressing on his left thigh. He looked gaunt, like he'd been doing coke for a few days straight, no need for food, but his eyes shone into mine.

There was a tiny connection between us, just an instant's empathy. Then he was gone, back to hell.

'You see?' she screamed, 'I told you my magic was real. It's keeping my man alive.'

Voodoo zombie magic. *But Jesus, he should be dead.*

Mickey's arm was outstretched, gun pointed at my head. Shaking now. I had the sense of being in a cruel trap.

Mickey fucking Flynn.

Precious made a move for my gun. She'd finish me. I knew that. Go. Now.

I leapt for the weapon, real low, slid over the lino for the last couple of feet. I'd gambled that Mickey was so fucked-up and drugged-up that I'd be hard for him to get a bearing on. I was right. He managed to squeeze off a shot but it hit the floor just in front of Precious, freaked her enough to give me a clean grab.

I had the gun. In one flowing movement, I rolled on, over towards the door. Bang, a bullet ripped a panel off the door. I was on my side, the gun moving up, up and finding Mickey's freakish face.

Pulling the trigger was easy.

His brain sprayed the inside of the fridge. No fucking way he was getting up and I don't care if

Jesus fucking Christ himself was doing the party tricks.

Precious was pale, had the shakes. She started crying.

I got to my feet, grunting, pushed the door shut with my back, then sent four bullets into her bitter face. I put the gun to my own head and put a little pressure on the trigger. I paused, puked some more. *No bullets left anyway.*

I put the revolver back in my pocket, walked calmly out the front door, thinking Enough. To tell you the truth, the very last thing I expected was for Tony Flynn to be waiting for me outside, complete with pistol and one-testicled younger brother.

CHAPTER 78. REQUIEM FOR MICKEY

I was dragged to a burnt-out house two streets away. The kids that had snitched on me followed close behind as the Flynns pushed and pulled me, their gun bruising my ribs, their whispered threats sapping my will.

Sam walked ahead - still a bit of a limp - and pushed open the blackened door. The front of the house had only recently been torched. The Chinese immigrants - who had no clue about where the Council was housing them - only lasted a week. I knew because it was all over the news. Plus, there were burnt newspapers in Mandarin and melted ornaments on the floor. The back of the house was fine and they sat me in the hastily-deserted kitchen, the place frozen at a bad moment in time.

'Who did you just shoot?' asked Tony.

He pointed his automatic pistol in my face. I was expecting a kicking from young Sam at any moment. My gun was in reach. But I'd no bullets. Four would've done the bitch.

'I shot a black woman. She killed that kid from around here.'

'The witch doctor?' he asked, very interested.

'Yeah.'

'They're tryin to pin the murder of that young one on our brother, the bastards.'

'Well I can prove he didn't do it?'

'How?'

A siren screamed somewhere in the middle distance. Tony looked at Sam and the kid went off to investigate.

'You should be okay. Nobody'd have reported the shots. Now prove it about Mickey.'

'Why did you grab me?'

'We've been watchin that bitch since Mickey disappeared. He was up to some sort of shit with her, I just didn't know what. He'd keep goin on about all the young ones he was gettin, thanks to that black cunt. Now prove what you're sayin or I'll put a fuckin hole in you right this minute.'

'I shot her because the kid's head is in her fridge.'

He winced. He was different to Mickey, the finally-dead *bastard*.

'That's it?'

'That's it. She used to cut up kids to make magic potions and charms. Would you credit it?'

'I'd fuckin believe antin now.'

He lit a cigarette, offered me one, let the gun drop to his side. I could've - maybe - used my weapon to bluff him then, but gambled to wait. Soon Sam came back, said all was *cool*. As I'd suspected, he hadn't made me. *Ballboy hadn't made me!*

His brother explained the deal to Sam, explained how he was going to let me go. What could Sam do but swallow hard, say Grand.

Tony told him to get home pronto, get the camera. They'd take photos of the scene before they tipped off the cops. Then they'd leak to the media, clear Mickey's name.

Well, they'd have another little surprise or two first.

They pointed me to my car and I drove towards the river to ditch the gun. On the way, I stopped at a phone booth and called 999, told them Precious's address, that there had been a lot of shooting. Checking my mirrors every other second, I sang a song from the eighties that had lodged in my frontal lobe.

Oh Mickey, what a pity, you don't understand -

And I vowed to never set foot in Moyross again.

CHAPTER 79. CONFETTI

Awake and restless all night, Fiona played on my mind. I felt guilty about holding on to her dirty pictures, so I slipped out of the bed before six and rummaged under it, to find and destroy them all. Got a few, but there was one beyond my fingertips, I couldn't get a grip. So I got down on my knees and peered under the bed. A golden gleam caught my eye. I lifted the bed with one hand - she didn't stir - and stuck the other under. Out came the glossy photos of Fiona's fantastic body. And a bullet.

It was a thirty-eight. The missing bullet from my first gun. It had fallen out of the chamber the night of my drug-induced *Apocalypse Now* fantasies.

'I didn't kill you, Dave. I didn't kill you!' I muttered, looking to the ceiling.

This was the best news. I put the bullet in my pocket, along with the photos. Fiona stirred, slept on.

Dressed and left quietly and down to the bridge. I stood in the rain - it'd been pissing for three days solid - and threw the bullet into the river. Then I ripped up the photos. They fell on the flood-swollen water like perverted confetti. This made me happier. At last. Sustainably, justifiably happier.

But I just couldn't get the image of the heads in the fridge out of my mind. More than anything else, they stuck. Isn't that mad?

And Jean. Always inside my head, even when I was with Fiona. I'd finished it with Sara and Deirdre so I could have a fresh start with Fiona. But Jean, Jean.

I admitted to myself that I had to see her, snuck away towards town, called her. She said to come out to the house for nine.

CHAPTER 80. MORNING, NOON AND NIGHT

The castle loomed, mist hovering over the river, a hot sun finally driving away the rain and messing with my head as I drove to Jean's. A distant impulse to take a picture of the scene was suppressed by my calculating mind. The odds on my getting murdered were not healthy. Maybe five to one. Maybe three.

But I figured it was worth the risk. A million quid and the memories of Jean in my garden added up. I wanted it all. Right or wrong, I wanted it all.

If she took me to her bed, I would've betrayed Fiona. Still I was calm. I was more comfortable with my emotions, my insane thoughts, my crazy brain. The hospital and the whole fucked-up experience of recent life had taught me a lot about myself, about human nature. To be honest, I felt like Superman.

The street was quiet, just a couple of puffy-eyed stragglers on their way to school. Nobody outside the house, her cars in the driveway, so I parked on the street and knocked at Jean's door.

'Come in,' she said, dragging on her fag.

'I hoped you'd be still in your bathrobe.'

'Fuck off, sure I've been to the gym and everytin.'

She went to the kitchen, switched on the kettle, a nervous me behind her.

'Sorry Jean, but I'm thinking about you morning, noon and night.'

She turned towards me. I reached for her waist. When I made contact, she moved away.

'I can't. You've changed Charlie. Anyways, there's someone else.'

'Wasn't there always?'

'You don't know the half of it.'

'What do you mean?'

'Remember the photos? Me and Luke?'

'Obviously.'

'I knew you were taking them. I made sure we went into that park.'

'What? The only person who knew about it was your husband. And Pat.'

'Exactly.'

'Jesus.'

The kettle boiled but she made no move.

'When you wanted me to go back for Pat - '

'Well, I had been ridin him for nearly a year. And we were partners, weren't we?'

'You go through partners, don't you?'

'I won't say no more. You can see yourself out.'

'What about the money?'

'Still too hot. Anyway, I haven't decided what to do with it yet. It was meant to be our retirement fund. Australia.' She looked straight at me then. She was sad. 'Looks like I'm stuck here now. I'm needed.'

'What about my cottage by the sea? I've no chance of it, like, now?'

She gave me a look that almost cut me in two.

'What? Don't you be lissnin to me at all at all, you gowl? Fuck off out of my sight, will you?'

Jesus. I had to go before I cried, begged or did something stupider. I stumbled towards the front door.

'Come here I want you,' she called, a roughness in her voice.

I stopped, turned to her, a stupid grin on my face. Call it hope.

'Yeah?'

'Don't open your mouth about any of this, yeah? Jah know what I mean?'

I was being threatened by Limerick's new Godfather - Godmother? - and decided to not show my fear. I swallowed.

'Give us a shout when the cash is cool so. See you later.'

Confidence faked, I left the house, slammed the door behind me. There was a deep scratch down the whole length of my car. Three youngfellas on the corner opposite.

So I forced a smile as I drove off the Island and in towards town, hated myself again.

Everything went dark, night falling way too fast. I don't remember getting home.

EPILOGUE

So I write it all down. In a bright, high room without a view - just the tops of yellowing horse chestnut trees, heavy cloud - I tap away at the keys and pour my story out. Everyone says it's good for me and how good I am to be doing it and all. They even joke that I might have a bestseller on my hands.

'How is my writer?' chirps the doctor, a happy young woman from Karachi.

'Nearly finished. Just working on the Epilogue.'

'Very good, Charlie. I am very happy for you.'

'Thanks, doc. How's my mother?'

'She is good. She would like to speak with you. Is this okay?'

'Of course. Yeah. Now?' *I just want to get this damned book finished.*

'She is outside.'

'Cool.'

In walks mam, looking even skinnier, but a kind of peaceful look to her. The doctor left and mam sat on the edge of my bed.

'Charlie, son, there's something I want to talk to you about.'

'Oh, okay. You don't want to skirt around the issue, suppress it? Sorry. I'm sorry. Go on.'

'It's been burning me up inside for so long. Oh, since you were about one, I suppose.'

She went quiet then, staring at the clouds through my high window. Big, juicy black ones.

'Just tell me, mam. It's fine.'

'You were not an only child, Charlie. You had a twin brother.'

Jesus.

'We called him Michael,' she continued. 'Everything was alright at first but, once the fuss died down and with your father out galavanting morning, noon and night, I couldn't cope with ye. I started to go a bit, you know - '

Fucking.

'So we decided to put one of ye up for adoption. It was common in those days. Anyone who wasn't married or had what they call post-natal depression now. Common.'

Christ.

'Yourself and Michael were so alike, so cute together, it broke my heart to give one of ye away. In the end, I chose Michael. I picked him because he had a lazy eye. A local family took him. But you were my perfect little boy, Charlie.'

Almighty.

'I feel so bad, Charlie. Am I an awful mother?'

'No mam. You're - ,' I was so stunned, I couldn't finish a sentence. I had my longed-for brother. And I killed him.

'I feel much better now I've told you,' she said, standing. 'The doctor was right,' she glanced out the window again, 'I think it's going to lash.'

'Yeah.'

'Oh well, I'll see you later, son.'

She was out the door, her step a little lighter. Maybe the truth would set her free. Whereas it might crush me. But I couldn't lose the plot. Not just yet. One more breakdown and I could be in this fucking nuthouse for the rest of my life. Back to the story.

The doctor came in.

'So tell me, how you are feeling?'

I push my chair back from the laptop table, turn to face her.

'I feel at peace with myself. Like it's time to go.'

I know it's what she wants to hear. And I do so desperately want to leave. The room is too small to share with so many spirits. Now one more.

'Good, good. Will you print me out a copy when you are done, please? If it is okay, I think you can go back to your home sweet home. Maybe tonight. This time, will you take your medicine every day?'

'I promise. I'll get a watch with an alarm on it.'

Life on a promise.

'Very good.'

So I hit the print key. There's a long wait as the file processes. Then, as the little inkjet slowly spits out *Pure Mad*, the doctor smiles, takes a seat, starts reading. She judges me by my words. I gather books, pack my few things in a plastic bag and sit on the edge of the bed.

Alone again.

THE END

CHARLIE DOYLE RETURNS IN

PURE HATE

A rich couple hires Charlie to rescue their daughter from an arranged marriage, so he leaves Limerick for Dublin. The missing person trail crosses a terrorist cell, becomes a hunt for Stinger missiles stolen from an IRA bunker. The police, foreign intelligence agencies and criminal gangs are all after the missiles, but Charlie must find them first, or the girl will be killed. Is President Obama the target, or the Queen?

And he's got to stick to his medication, attend group counselling and cope with Ireland's downfall. His brush with pure madness still resonates. Has he progressed enough to keep it together and crack the case?

www.GaryJByrnes.com

APPENDIX 1

GLOSSARY OF LIMERICK SLANG

Bollick/bollock: Testicle.

Crater: Creature.

Droot: Drought, thirst. "I've the droot on me."

Fanny: Vagina.

Flute: Idiot. Also: champagne glass.

Galavanting: To be out and about in search of pleasure. "He's off galavanting. Again."

Gap: Female crotch.

Gobshite: Fool.

Gombeen: Chancer.

Gowl (origin: ghoul): Term of abuse, similar to idiot, asshole etc. Also: vagina.

Half-cut: Partially drunk.

Half-langers: Partially drunk.

IRA: Irish Republican Army: now defunct terrorist organisation.

Jamrag: Sanitary towel.

Jeekist: Jesus, exclamation

Manky: Dirty

Noggin: Head.

Pure: Totally.

RA: Slang for IRA

Rapid: Great.

Real IRA: Splinter group which is against peace with Britain or weapons decommissioning.

Continuity IRA: Another splinter group.

Langer: Penis. Also: idiot.

Langers: Drunk.

Sham/shom: Buddy/pal.

Shift: Kiss. "I shifted your man last night. I swear."

Sláinte: Irish drinking toast, literally 'health'.

Steamer: Homosexual.

Tackies: Runners/sneakers.

Tinker: Traveller; itinerant. Caravan-dwelling nomads, recognized as an ethnic minority in the UK, but not so in Ireland.

Tiocfaidh ár lá: 'Our day will come' (Irish). Republican slogan.

Tool: Idiot. Also: penis.

Wanker: Masturbator/idiot/waster.

Withered: Deeply bored.

Well-cut: Very drunk.

For a constantly-updated Irish Slang Dictionary, please visit www.GaryJByrnes.com.

APPENDIX 2

CHARLIE'S PROUST QUESTIONNAIRE

Favourite virtue: Courage.

Favourite qualities in a man: Respect for women and children.

Favourite qualities in a woman: Interest in me.

Biggest flaw: Self-delusion, selfishness, laziness.

Favourite occupation: Private investigator, writer.

Chief characteristic: Egocentric.

Idea of happiness: Rich, stoned, screwed.

Idea of misery: Being alone.

Favourite colour and flower: Azure. Sunflower.

If not me, who would I be?: Bill Clinton.

Where would I like to live?: Someplace quiet, by a warm sea.

Favourite writers: Elmore Leonard, Brendan Behan.

Favourite poets: Patrick Kavanagh, WB Yeats.

Favourite painters and composers: Dali, U2, Bob Marley.

Favourite heroes in real life: 9/11 firemen, Bill Hicks.

Favourite heroines in real life: My mother.

Favourite heroes in fiction: Indiana Jones.

Favourite heroines in fiction: Bridget Jones.

Favourite food and drink: Vodka, tonic, lemon.

Favourite names: Steven, Sebastian, Kathy.

Pet aversion: Bad manners, racism, litter, ignorance, illiteracy, Nazis.

Characters in history I most dislike: Hitler, Margaret Thatcher.

Present state of mind: Fucked up, nauseous, suicidal, lonely.

Fault for which I have most toleration: Nymphomania.

Favourite motto: Live and let live.

How I would like to die: Loved.

APPENDIX 3

THE DOCTOR

By Gary J Byrnes

There came a knock at the window.

'Christ,' he said. 'Not again. Not now.'

He'd reached the critical point in his story, the turning point. The bottle of champagne had fallen to the floor.

He left his stiff typewriter and went to the door.

'Yes?' he said.

'Doctor Chekhov. I hate to disturb you, but my daughter is very sick. She has difficulty breathing,' came the reply. A woman's voice.

He didn't want to open the door but, of course, he had to. It was Mrs Putin, the coalman's wife. Her face was flustered, cheeks red, beads of sweat on her brow. She'd run to his house.

'Mrs Putin.'

'Doctor Chekhov, I hate to disturb your writing, I heard your typewriter.'

'Not relevant. How is your daughter?'

'She can't catch her breath. Coughing always.'

'Is she coughing blood at all?'

'Not yet.'

'Good. Let me get my case.'

He put on his heavy coat against the bitter night, found his medical case and followed Mrs Putin into the snowy streets.

'My husband is doing deliveries, so my neighbours have stayed with her. I'm so worried, Doctor. She is our only child.'

'I understand, Mrs Putin. Your husband must be quite busy this weather. I can smell the results.'

He suppressed a chesty cough, tasting the telltale saltiness of blood.

'Yes Doctor. It's the new year in just a few days. Everyone needs to have a hot fire at this time. What will 1878 hold for you?'

'More writing, I suppose.'

'My husband and I love your comedies.'

'Yes, they are popular. But I feel that my work is becoming more serious.'

'Oh yes?'

She looked at him for an instant, just long enough for him to see the disappointment on her face.

'Yes. When you knocked, I was working on a story called Champagne.'

'How joyous! I love champagne. I tasted it twice, you know,' proudly.

'Well my story isn't very joyous, I'm afraid.'

'Doctor, isn't there enough misery in the world?'

'Yes. That's why I must write about it. It will be easier to improve our miserable lives that way, knowing the truth.'

They walked on in silence, the snow starting to freeze his toes. She stopped at a gate, just wide enough for a horse and cart, fumbled in her apron pocket for the key.

'Once you're happy, Doctor. You're still so young. Here we are.'

They entered a long yard, piles of coal against the walls, everything blanketed with dirty snow. A candle burned in a window and Mrs Putin led the Doctor through her back door and into the kitchen of her home.

A fire roared in an iron grate. The child lay on a makeshift bed, pale, coughing. Two elderly women sat beside her. One rubbed the girl's cheek gently, the other prayed with rosary beads.

Chekhov took off his coat, sweating now, and opened his medical bag, rummaging for his stethoscope.

The girl's mother helped her to sit up so the Doctor could listen to her lungs as they laboured on each breath.

'What's your name, child?'

'Petra.'

'What a lovely name. How do you feel?'

'It hurts inside my chest when I breathe. Sometimes I am so hot, sometimes so cold.'

He listened to her for a long time as the women looked on, dreading the prognosis. Finally, he took the stethoscope from his ears and held the girl's hand.

'I fear she has consumption. Tuberculosis.'

The mother cried with anguish and all three women blessed themselves. Chekhov stood with his hands by his side, feeling impotent, sorry to have been - yet again - the harbinger of sorrow. Then the woman fetched a bottle of vodka from the parlour, along with four small glasses.

'I'm afraid we have no champagne tonight, Doctor. Will you have some vodka?'

'Thank you.'

'What caused her consumption? The coal dust?' asked the woman as she carefully poured the clear liquid.

'No. That's what was thought. Recently a German doctor discovered that it is caused by a bacterium.'

'Bacterium?'

'A tiny living thing that takes over the host body so that it may reproduce. It seems that most diseases may operate in a similar manner.'

'Oh, I don't like the sound of that. How did she catch the disease, Doctor?'

'Does she drink cow's milk much?'

'No. She doesn't like it.'

'In that case, she caught it from somebody. If an infected person coughed near her, that may have been enough. It's quite easy to catch in a cold and crowded city such as our Moscow.'

The woman gave the Doctor his glass of vodka and they toasted the new year and the little girl's health.

'What you must do,' said the Doctor, 'is make her comfortable. Try to keep her away from the dust, if possible. If she begins to cough blood, come for me again. Unfortunately, there is no medication that I can give her now. And only pain-relieving morphine if she gets worse. The only possible treatment is to take her to a drier, warmer climate. Perhaps the Crimea.'

'You know so much about this, Doctor. I am thankful.'

'I was diagnosed with it myself, Mrs Putin. Just a few months ago.'

The women blessed themselves again, imperceptibly stepping back from him. But he saw it. He put his stethoscope into his bag and found his coat. He accepted a rouble from Mrs Putin, for his family relied on his income and writing didn't yet pay enough.

As he left the warm kitchen and stepped back into the frigid night, Chekhov felt old before his time. On his way home, he worried about whether he would be remembered at all, if his writing would continue to develop as he wanted.

The moon hung low in the black sky, accompanied by two motionless white clouds. Chekhov smiled to himself.

THE END

APPENDIX 4

CHAMPAGNE by Anton Chekvov

A WAYFARER'S STORY

IN the year in which my story begins I had a job at
a little station on one of our southwestern railways.
Whether I had a gay or a dull life at the station you
can judge from the fact that for fifteen miles round
there was not one human habitation, not one
woman, not one decent tavern; and in those days I
was young, strong, hot-headed, giddy, and foolish.
The only distraction I could possibly find was in the
windows of the passenger trains, and in the vile
vodka which the Jews drugged with thorn-apple.
Sometimes there would be a glimpse of a woman's
head at a carriage window, and one would stand like
a statue without breathing and stare at it until the
train turned into an almost invisible speck; or one
would drink all one could of the loathsome vodka
till one was stupefied and did not feel the passing of
the long hours and days. Upon me, a native of the
north, the steppe produced the effect of a deserted
Tatar cemetery. In the summer the steppe with its
solemn calm, the monotonous chur of the
grasshoppers, the transparent moonlight from which
one could not hide, reduced me to listless

melancholy; and in the winter the irreproachable whiteness of the steppe, its cold distance, long nights, and howling wolves oppressed me like a heavy nightmare. There were several people living at the station: my wife and I, a deaf and scrofulous telegraph clerk, and three watchmen. My assistant, a young man who was in consumption, used to go for treatment to the town, where he stayed for months at a time, leaving his duties to me together with the right of pocketing his salary. I had no children, no cake would have tempted visitors to come and see me, and I could only visit other officials on the line, and that no oftener than once a month.

I remember my wife and I saw the New Year in. We sat at table, chewed lazily, and heard the deaf telegraph clerk monotonously tapping on his apparatus in the next room. I had already drunk five glasses of drugged vodka, and, propping my heavy head on my fist, thought of my overpowering boredom from which there was no escape, while my wife sat beside me and did not take her eyes off me. She looked at me as no one can look but a woman who has nothing in this world but a handsome husband. She loved me madly, slavishly, and not merely my good looks, or my soul, but my sins, my ill-humour and boredom, and even my cruelty when, in drunken fury, not knowing how to vent my ill-humour, I tormented her with reproaches.

In spite of the boredom which was consuming me, we were preparing to see the New Year in with exceptional festiveness, and were awaiting midnight with some impatience. The fact is, we had in reserve two bottles of champagne, the real thing, with the label of Veuve Clicquot; this treasure I had won the previous autumn in a bet with the station-master of D. when I was drinking with him at a christening. It sometimes happens during a lesson in mathematics, when the very air is still with boredom, a butterfly flutters into the class-room; the boys toss their heads and begin watching its flight with interest, as though they saw before them not a butterfly but something new and strange; in the same way ordinary champagne, chancing to come into our dreary station, roused us. We sat in silence looking alternately at the clock and at the bottles.

When the hands pointed to five minutes to twelve I slowly began uncorking a bottle. I don't know whether I was affected by the vodka, or whether the bottle was wet, but all I remember is that when the cork flew up to the ceiling with a bang, my bottle slipped out of my hands and fell on the floor. Not more than a glass of the wine was spilt, as I managed to catch the bottle and put my thumb over the foaming neck.

"Well, may the New Year bring you happiness!" I said, filling two glasses. "Drink!"

My wife took her glass and fixed her frightened eyes on me. Her face was pale and wore a look of horror.

"Did you drop the bottle?" she asked.

"Yes. But what of that?"

"It's unlucky," she said, putting down her glass and turning paler still. "It's a bad omen. It means that some misfortune will happen to us this year."

"What a silly thing you are," I sighed. "You are a clever woman, and yet you talk as much nonsense as an old nurse. Drink."

"God grant it is nonsense, but... something is sure to happen! You'll see."

She did not even sip her glass, she moved away and sank into thought. I uttered a few stale commonplaces about superstition, drank half a bottle, paced up and down, and then went out of the room.

Outside there was the still frosty night in all its cold, inhospitable beauty. The moon and two white fluffy clouds beside it hung just over the station, motionless as though glued to the spot, and looked as though waiting for something. A faint transparent light came from them and touched the white earth softly, as though afraid of wounding her modesty, and lighted up everything--the snowdrifts, the embankment.... It was still.

I walked along the railway embankment.

"Silly woman," I thought, looking at the sky spangled with brilliant stars. "Even if one admits that omens sometimes tell the truth, what evil can happen to us? The misfortunes we have endured already, and which are facing us now, are so great that it is difficult to imagine anything worse. What further harm can you do a fish which has been caught and fried and served up with sauce?"

A poplar covered with hoar frost looked in the bluish darkness like a giant wrapt in a shroud. It looked at me sullenly and dejectedly, as though like me it realized its loneliness. I stood a long while looking at it.

"My youth is thrown away for nothing, like a useless cigarette end," I went on musing. "My parents died when I was a little child; I was expelled from the high school, I was born of a noble family, but I have received neither education nor breeding, and I have no more knowledge than the humblest mechanic. I have no refuge, no relations, no friends, no work I like. I am not fitted for anything, and in the prime of my powers I am good for nothing but to be stuffed into this little station; I have known nothing but trouble and failure all my life. What can happen worse?"

Red lights came into sight in the distance. A train was moving towards me. The slumbering steppe listened to the sound of it. My thoughts were so bitter that it seemed to me that I was thinking aloud and that the moan of the telegraph wire and the rumble of the train were expressing my thoughts.

"What can happen worse? The loss of my wife?" I wondered. "Even that is not terrible. It's no good hiding it from my conscience: I don't love my wife. I married her when I was only a wretched boy; now I am young and vigorous, and she has gone off and grown older and sillier, stuffed from her head to her heels with conventional ideas. What charm is there in her maudlin love, in her hollow chest, in her lustreless eyes? I put up with her, but I don't love her. What can happen? My youth is being wasted, as the saying is, for a pinch of snuff. Women flit before my eyes only in the carriage windows, like falling stars. Love I never had and have not. My manhood, my courage, my power of feeling are going to ruin.... Everything is being thrown away like dirt, and all my wealth here in the steppe is not worth a farthing."

The train rushed past me with a roar and indifferently cast the glow of its red lights upon me. I saw it stop by the green lights of the station, stop for a minute and rumble off again. After walking a mile and a half I went back. Melancholy thoughts haunted me still. Painful as it was to me, yet I remember I tried as it were to make my thoughts still gloomier and more melancholy. You know people who are vain and not very clever have moments when the consciousness that they are miserable affords them positive satisfaction, and they even coquet with their misery for their own entertainment. There was a great deal of truth in what I thought, but there was also a great deal that was absurd and conceited, and there was something boyishly defiant in my question: "What could happen worse?"

"And what is there to happen?" I asked myself. "I think I have endured everything. I've been ill, I've lost money, I get reprimanded by my superiors every day, and I go hungry, and a mad wolf has run into the station yard. What more is there? I have been insulted, humiliated,... and I have insulted others in my time. I have not been a criminal, it is true, but I don't think I am capable of crime--I am not afraid of being hauled up for it."

The two little clouds had moved away from the moon and stood at a little distance, looking as though they were whispering about something which the moon must not know. A light breeze was racing across the steppe, bringing the faint rumble of the retreating train.

My wife met me at the doorway. Her eyes were laughing gaily and her whole face was beaming with good-humour.

"There is news for you!" she whispered. "Make haste, go to your room and put on your new coat; we have a visitor."

"What visitor?"

"Aunt Natalya Petrovna has just come by the train."

"What Natalya Petrovna?"

"The wife of my uncle Semyon Fyodoritch. You don't know her. She is a very nice, good woman."

Probably I frowned, for my wife looked grave and whispered rapidly:

"Of course it is queer her having come, but don't be cross, Nikolay, and don't be hard on her. She is unhappy, you know; Uncle Semyon Fyodoritch really is ill-natured and tyrannical, it is difficult to live with him. She says she will only stay three days with us, only till she gets a letter from her brother."

My wife whispered a great deal more nonsense to me about her despotic uncle; about the weakness of mankind in general and of young wives in particular; about its being our duty to give shelter to all, even great sinners, and so on. Unable to make head or tail of it, I put on my new coat and went to make acquaintance with my "aunt."

A little woman with large black eyes was sitting at the table. My table, the grey walls, my roughly-made sofa, everything to the tiniest grain of dust seemed to have grown younger and more cheerful in the presence of this new, young, beautiful, and dissolute creature, who had a most subtle perfume about her. And that our visitor was a lady of easy virtue I could see from her smile, from her scent, from the peculiar way in which she glanced and made play with her eyelashes, from the tone in which she talked with my wife--a respectable woman. There was no need to tell me she had run away from her husband, that her husband was old and despotic, that she was good-natured and lively; I took it all in at the first glance. Indeed, it is doubtful whether there is a man in all Europe who cannot spot at the first glance a woman of a certain temperament.

"I did not know I had such a big nephew!" said my aunt, holding out her hand to me and smiling.

"And I did not know I had such a pretty aunt," I answered.

Supper began over again. The cork flew with a bang out of the second bottle, and my aunt swallowed half a glassful at a gulp, and when my wife went out of the room for a moment my aunt did not scruple to drain a full glass. I was drunk both with the wine and with the presence of a woman. Do you remember the song?

> "Eyes black as pitch, eyes full of passion,
> Eyes burning bright and beautiful,
> How I love you,
> How I fear you!"

I don't remember what happened next. Anyone who wants to know how love begins may read novels and long stories; I will put it shortly and in the words of the same silly song:

> "It was an evil hour
> When first I met you."

Everything went head over heels to the devil. I remember a fearful, frantic whirlwind which sent me flying round like a feather. It lasted a long while, and swept from the face of the earth my wife and my aunt herself and my strength. From the little station in the steppe it has flung me, as you see, into this dark street.

Now tell me what further evil can happen to me?

THE END

www.GaryJByrnes.com

Printed in Poland
by Amazon Fulfillment
Poland Sp. z o.o., Wrocław